Kill

Kill

█████

ANTHONY GOOD

atlantic · *fiction*

First published in Great Britain in 2019 by Atlantic Books,
an imprint of Atlantic Books Ltd.

1 2 3 4 5 6 7 8 9

A CIP catalogue record for this book is available from the British Library.

Hardback ISBN: 978 1 78649 567 9
Trade paperback ISBN: 978 1 78649 685 0
EBook ISBN: 978 1 78649 568 6

Printed in Great Britain by TJ International, Padstow, Cornwall

Atlantic Books
An Imprint of Atlantic Books Ltd
Ormond House
26–27 Boswell Street
London
WC1N 3JZ

www.atlantic-books.co.uk

For my father, who wanted to see this in print, and didn't.

For Hayley, always.

Publisher's Note

After taking legal advice, the publisher has obscured all references to or descriptions of actual living persons in the novel. Several characters' names have also been changed, in order to distance the fiction from the real events and personalities it was inspired by.

Kill

How settle that account? I am entitled to
exact payment, of course. Every Debit
must have its Credit, the First Golden Rule.
But payment in what form?

B. S. Johnson, *Christie Malry's Own Double-Entry*

Every tyrant shall another know.

The Thousand and One Nights

The last words I said to my wife: "Please don't leave."

It was an argument. She left. Those were the last words.

Angela wants to know more. She always wants to know more. Now she asks me to write about it – not just talk. She thinks I'll be more forthcoming, perhaps.

I said to my wife, "Please don't leave," while we were arguing, and she said she was going to be late and so she had to leave, and she did, and on her journey she was killed by an explosion on the Underground.

Apparently my last entry wasn't enough. So I'm tasked again with writing another entry on the same subject.

Clearly, I don't have a talent for confession.

Dear Angela,

This is my fourth attempt at writing this letter. It is NOT a "Self-Expression".

There is a man I hate and I want to talk about him. But you have to know my reasoning first. I can't skip straight to the end, though I think about it every day. Because I want you to hate him, too. I want you to understand my reasons, and agree. I'd like you to try to refute my reasons, and fail. I'd like you to try very hard. I want you to admit that I'm right. But you wouldn't let yourself – would you?

This letter isn't going well.

I missed last week's appointment with Angela – to my surprise, she rang me. In truth, the phone ringing was surprise enough in itself.

I don't find Angela attractive. Is that the truth or am I writing it to hurt her?

The truth is I haven't had a sexual thought in years. I look forward to discussing these points on Wednesday.

And again, the old topic:

Angela asks for the details, for the content of the argument, the time of day, how the morning had started, the first sign of disagreement, was it me or my wife that started it – is that my guilt, for starting the argument, for being angry the last time I saw her? – or is it that she was angry with me, she started it and was angry with me and that's my guilt, that I can never re-live the last part and have her not-angry with me, that we were denied any reconciliation? –

The explosion nearly split the train carriage in half. It put a hole in the top and bottom. If I'd wanted to, I could have gone to court and listened to their explanation of precisely where my wife had been sitting, or standing, when the explosion occurred. I could have listened to them describe the injuries she incurred, in the long list of injuries that day. Well, I didn't.

Will you try to get rid of this anger? I ask.

(She doesn't respond. Her silence is greater than mine.)

I'm not sure I want it gone, I say.

Perhaps I'm free-associating, now, I tell her. Can you be free-associating while talking about it?

(I keep pausing like this, as if she'll answer.)

I'm trying to work out my anger. I know it has an object. An objective, maybe.

I look at her directly, which she doesn't like, I don't think.

There's a real person that I'm angry at. I can tell you his name, what he looks like.

Then I stare at her, just to measure her curiosity. To measure her technique. There are silent ones and chatty ones, and Angela seems like something else. Like both, or neither. It can't be *productive* to be comparing her like this, so much, in my mind.

"Who is it?" she asks, and I wonder whether it's curiosity or technique guiding the question – my neurosis or hers?

███████, I say. It's the first time I've said it aloud in many years. ████████, I say again (though I don't know whether that's neurosis or technique either).

I wait to see if she'll ask a question. I practically will a *Why?* from her lips, which never comes. I scratch my face, cover my open mouth.

I don't think it's fair, I say. What happened to my wife.

Not just my wife.

My daughter.

Myself.

My father.

Paul, of course. And his family.

If you were to ask me, I say, that's where this sickness has come from. You probably think of it like that, as a sickness. An acting out of something or other.

She writes something down. If it was one of the other ones – one of the other therapists – I'd guess it would involve the word *transference*. That's the catch-all. But who knows what Angela's writing? It could well be the necessary ingredients for her dinner.

Are you even listening? I ask.

She looks at me.

"To every single word," she says.

She told me to stop endlessly referring to the process of my therapy. She banned me from using her name, which seems an ineffective prohibition. I won't stoop to giving her an alias. She told me I'm frightened (she may have used the word *scared* at some point, as well) of *engaging* with the tasks she sets.

I pretend to believe in Good and Bad, Right and Wrong – but what have I really done? I've been subject to the most heinous injustice, and what do I do? – I mope, watch daytime television, attend endless therapy, sit at home, break things, act like an adolescent.

The fact is, someone caused it. Someone did this to me. It was wrong.

Is my anger at myself? At my unhappy victimhood?

This is what I have to do:

Delineate the Causes.
Identify the Principal Actors.
And then?

The People Who Matter to Me

My wife
My daughter Amy
Paul, a former pupil and family-friend
Paul's family
Frank (aka Frankie), a close friend of mine
Angela, my therapist, for whom I'm writing this list

My wife played the piano. She earned money, sometimes quite a lot, writing jingles for advertisements, mostly. She had a deep respect for her clients, who would often make very odd requests. Sometimes she'd be paid as an arranger. She would take a melody and make it fit a variety of timespans – five seconds, fifteen seconds, thirty, forty-five, etc. Often, this work came to her after it was abandoned by the original composer, who no doubt felt such a procedure denigrated their work. Sometimes she'd have to make an old jingle sound more modern. In these cases, I remember, she had learned to do very little: the client, for whom she had great tolerance, would never want to deviate from the original work, but nevertheless would want to get their money's worth. She'd usually change the key or the time signature or remove some extraneous notes or make a particular chord louder (or softer). She would complete her changes in an afternoon, but deliver the manuscript many weeks later. These briefs were the most handsomely paid.

She'd sit and play into the evening. If I was lucky, I'd arrive home to her playing and I'd soften my entrance. I'd defer our usual kiss – instead I'd go to my study and put away my bag, whatever folders I was carrying. Only once did I indulge myself by going to the bedroom and lying down, listening with my eyes closed.

If she was playing haltingly, repeating chords or phrases, I'd know she was closing in on her goal. But if I was lucky, she'd be very far from it – utterly lost, even. When she had no idea what to put into her thirty or forty-five seconds, I might sit in my study, above her, and listen as she invented whatever pleased her. It's difficult for me to imagine those times.

The old piano still stands there – the upright she intended to replace with a baby grand (a full grand was too immodest for her liking) were she ever to become a millionaire. Sometimes I go to that old piano and lift the fallboard, and poke a key, with no intention except to hear a note. It sounds bright; I can't tell if it needs tuning or not, but of course it must. I imagine I can play a single chord. I imagine my hand in the right shape.

If I'm in a particularly self-pitying mood, I'll open the lid of the stool and stand one of her manuscripts on the music tray. I sit, and pull the stool closer, as if I might play. Then I look at her handwriting, at the dots and lines and numbers and crossings-out.

On my blackest day, I turn to her last manuscript – it is unfinished. I look at where the pencil marks stop.

Paul

He was one of my students. He was a Year Seven and I barely had cause to ask his name, being that he appeared a quite solemn and well-meaning boy, except that his shoes were not correct.

Regarding the school uniform I was always to-the-letter. In my brief career as a policeman I had the same attitude – enforce the small things, was my motto. The small things make a character. What I mean is that it's the everyday details that accumulate and begin to shape us. They are the life-changing things we can control. The life-changing things we cannot control come in the form of tragedy (a car crash) or fortune (winning the lottery) and both tend to destroy rather than build character.

On average I stopped half a dozen boys on account of improper uniform every day. Mostly it was the shoes. Young men have a thing about shoes just as strong as young ladies, and for very much the same reason. Shoes were the main way these boys compared themselves with each other. Apart from the usual acts of intimidation, of course.

And so it was one day I came across a young, solemn Year Seven whom I addressed for his non-regulation shoes. They were black AstroTurf football boots with defiant white trim.

His excuse was first-rate: they didn't have the right shoes yet. *They* being his family, of course. I liked, and was intrigued by, that "yet". He said it very meaningfully. I asked him why not – he said his mum hadn't got round to it.

This excuse, or similar, was fairly old even two decades ago. When confronted by Authority, boys will seek to hide behind Propriety – this often manifests itself in raising Ethnic boundaries, or, failing that (in young Paul's case), luring authority into the sensitive area of Family, where it must tread very carefully and usually make a hasty retreat.

I said I expected him to have proper shoes next week, and he nodded.

I asked him if that would be a problem, and he said, No, sir.

Then I told him to fix his tie, and he looked down at his chest in crooked appraisal. So I adjusted his tie for him and dismissed him with a pat on the shoulder.

When I discuss my retirement, it's in guarded language. I speak about it defensively, as if about a mistake.

Angela tells me – reassures me? – one of the reasons for the long course of my therapy is the need to *disentangle* two kinds of loss. This is Angela's scheme: that the root of my emotional malfunction is the double-whammy of losing my job and losing my wife in fairly close succession.

She asks me how I'd planned to spend my retirement, and I believe it's just a way to underline her point.

Dear Angela,

This is my fifth attempt at writing this letter. It is NOT a "Self-Expression".

There is a man I hate. You have to understand my reasoning. I can't skip straight to the end, though I want to. Because I want you to hate him t

Dear Angela,

This is my sixth attempt at writing this letter. <u>It is NOT a "Self-Expression"</u>.

I thought I was above hate all my life, and now look at me.

One teacher – at wits' end, shortly before his resignation – asked me:

"I'm paid to teach them, am I to police them as well?"

Of course! Police them foremost! How else will we teach them? We flatter ourselves when we talk of our roles as Teacher and Headteacher – better call ourselves Constable and Superintendent instead.

He told me he respectfully disagreed. To which I said no he didn't, he disagreed and saying the word *respectfully* was neither here nor there, respect wasn't something you issued from your mouth.

And then I said, You don't know the first thing about Respect.

It was an ugly moment.

She told me to "zone in" on the "big points" and "expand" upon them. She said I was too "deliberately oblique", which I thought was presumptuous.

I'm sure she'll dock me more points for prefacing this passage with her critique. Every Wednesday for fifty minutes I sit with her and talk – she asks her questions, I am deliberately oblique – and at some point she reads over what I've written, my journal, if that's what it is – except it's always a loose sheet of paper or two.

She doesn't wear glasses, except to read. She swallows quite often, when glancing down the page. When finished, she gently lays the page back on her desk, like a living thing being put to rest. And, gallingly, when the time is up, she asks me whether I want to keep it. And – more galling, even – I say I do.

I've not kept hidden my opinion that her vocation can be boiled down to a matter of guesswork and answering questions with questions. Or worse – *silence*. But all the same, I come. Because it has occurred to me that, apart from fifty minutes every Wednesday, I hardly utter a word to anyone.

She's told me to address everything I write – from now on – to my daughter Amy. I told her this wouldn't be conducive to my *self-expression*, as she calls it.

"You're not the Headmaster of the World." That was one of Amy's sayings to me.

And then, much later, with a touch less venom: "You're not the Headmaster any more."

Amy is distant. She doesn't like me. I believe she blames me for what happened to her mother, in a way. It's not always easy for me to be frank with her. I believe she interprets this as coldness.

When we meet, there is a politeness about our conversations. There is an awkward formality, like we've been appointed to these roles of father and daughter when, really, we have nothing in common.

When she was small, her mother called her "Daddy's Little Girl", but I think it was hopefulness on her part. Amy was a very adoring child and perhaps she did focus her affections slightly in my favour. But when she reached adolescence she grew to hate me – because, of course, I was the disciplinarian. She felt I treated her as just another pupil. I can appreciate how it might have been, how it might have seemed I was indifferent to her.

She was utterly, utterly wrong, of course. Yes, to an extent I treated her as my pupil. But I have no capacity to decode a girl's psychology – I barely made progress with the woman I lived with for nearly thirty years. So when I was stern with her, and she cried, I floundered. Even the tenor of her crying was different from a young boy's – fuller, less ashamed.

When a young boy cries – and tries not to – he may appreciate a hand on the shoulder, encouragement such as "keep your chin up", and – importantly – nothing more. Anything more is to further emasculate him, to heighten his shame.

When Amy cried and I didn't know how to respond, she would storm away – often to her mother. This wasn't an option any of my boys had, of course. I was, in this way, critically undermined.

I remember this conversation I had with her, when she was perhaps fourteen. We were sitting sullenly at the dining table. To my mind, I must have been enforcing some prohibition, perhaps I was preventing her from seeing her friends, or punishing her for coming home late or a bad mark. A kind of detention. I had my books open in front of me, which I normally kept to my study. I could feel her glaring at me as I wrote. She had her Science exercise book and textbook in front of her, and was meant to be doing her homework, but she'd made a performance of closing both – I remember it was this, above all, that irked me: the petulant drama, which made her wretched to me. I had made the mistake of standing, walking around to her, and opening her books, one after the other, and then sitting down again, and turning to my own materials and reviling myself, in my mind, for entering into her performance.

She, of course, closed her books again, this time with a casual flick of the wrist. I admit I looked at her then as a problem. I was, at that moment, trying to solve her. She was defiant, but without a sense of what she actually intended to do – apart from, that is, disobey me. I stared at her a while, and she said,

"Why are you looking at me?"

I held my pen slightly above the page, poised. I stopped myself from capping it, laying it down meaningfully – stopped myself from entering further into histrionics. I said,

"Which, of the two of us, do you think has the greater determination?"

"I don't care," she said without a pause, and looked away. I went back to my page, with my pen still poised above it, but was at a complete loss as to what I'd intended to write. It was only a second later, perhaps, that Amy threw her exercise book across the room.

I didn't follow the trajectory of the book, but kept my gaze on the child. Then she reached for her textbook. She must have felt my stiffening – must have sensed the stakes were raised, now. Looking back, I should have stopped her then – with her hand on the textbook, with the book still on the table, with the picture frame still hanging on the wall. Of course, to her mind there was no way she was going to stop, not without some kind of intervention, perhaps even physical. She was, perhaps, looking to be stopped. But that was never my style. So she threw the book and it flapped heavily against the wall – hit the edge of a framed picture, some dreary watercolour my mother had given me, I think. It fell, the glass cracked.

I grabbed her by the wrist and raised her out of her chair. I hit the back of her thighs, six or seven times – still with one of her arms held above her. She wailed even before the first strike. I let her sink, crying, back down on to the table, then I went and picked up the book, unruffled its pages and laid it down in front of her heaving, small body, and asked her,

"Why don't you throw it again?"

She tried to run out of the room, but I caught her again by the wrist. She flailed and kicked at me with her free limbs. I felt rotten, at how puny she was, at how unfairly matched we were. I held her, dangling from one arm again, until she couldn't cry and scream any more.

Her mother stood in the doorway, asking what on earth was going on. I told her our daughter had taken to throwing books. She frowned, came forward, and Amy reached for her, but she held back. When she left the room, Amy screamed all the harder, still with her one arm held high above her, not even struggling any more.

Angela said,

"In introducing the scene of your abuse of Amy, you referred to it as a conversation."

I admit I felt angry at that word, *abuse*. I thought it over, trying to find the most compact and forceful rebuttal.

She said, "A grown man hitting a child repeatedly – how is it not abuse?"

The difference, of course, is this: on the rare occasion I hit my daughter, it was to discipline her. It wasn't out of sadism or mere meanness. The violence (as Angela is so fond of describing it) is a consequence of her action.

"She asked for it, is that what you think?"

I had to hold down my indignation at this. Asking for something and causing something are two different things. Asking implies understanding. I can cause someone's death without asking for it.

She waited, as usual, for me to carry on. She held her silence for over a minute, as did I. I pushed my glasses against the bridge of my nose, and held them there firmly against the bone.

"And so, as you see it, she caused the beatings."

"How many do you suppose there were?" I asked.

She looked up at me, tried to subdue her surprise, as far as I could tell – she had her reading glasses on, was holding my confession in front of her. She looked at me over her glasses.

"Do you think the number is important?"

"Guess," I said.

She shook her head. "I'm not going to guess at such things."

"You said *beatings*."

She put down the page.

"Guess how many, then. You have already."

"I haven't."

"I wrote about a single instance, but how many times did I beat my daughter? What was the extent of my abuse?"

She looked at me evenly, like I was acting out.

"I'm not going to play games," she said. "I'm not going to guess. It's not productive."

"Because you'd be wrong," I said. I leaned back. "Your whole job is not being wrong," I said. "And still you are."

"All right, then," she said. "I'll be wrong for you." She took off her glasses, swallowed. "Given your character, given your – " she paused, as if to stop herself, but carried on " – inability to express your emotional state, combined with your fear of vulnerability, and above all your controlling, domineering behaviour, all in all I'd say the beatings would be consistent. You believe, as a headmaster at the time, that you were, by definition, fair, a stickler for rules, even. The child throws two books and you punish her for the published textbook, not for her exercise book. Her exercise book is of no value. In an act of defiance, but, ultimately, an act of comparison, she throws the textbook, to see what the difference is. Well, the difference is enormous." She pauses, to take a breath. "So, really, I'd guess you'd beat her every time she failed to uphold some high moral standard of yours, utterly opaque to her. I don't know much about your daughter, but I'd guess a child would fall far from your standards quite often. You're shaking your head."

I was.

"So how wrong was I?" she said.

"Dead wrong," I said, still shaking my head. I cleared my throat, half in victory. "Dead wrong."

"So tell me, then," she said.

"Twice," I said. "It happened twice."

If she was surprised, she didn't show it.

"Twice in twenty-five years. That is the extent of my abuse."

She won't read my Self-Expressions (her awful phrase, not mine) any more. There's no point, she says, if they always circle back around to the manner of my therapy. They are, in that case, *counter-productive*.

Counter-productive is not a phrase I would ever use.

Angela (I can use her name now, if she won't read it anyway) often uses words and phrases I'd never use myself.

I asked her, in that case, whether she felt she'd failed, with regard to my Self-Expressions. She said there were many *strategies* for *coming to terms* with trauma.

"Perhaps we'll come back to them," she said, "later."

When I'm *willing to engage*.

This notion of *engagement* would come up at the school sometimes. It was a favourite of the younger teachers. Not engaging meant you were generally misbehaving. Whenever a teacher was sat in front of me, across my desk, with the boy sitting next to them, and the teacher used that phrase "refusing to engage", or "not engaging", or "he really must engage more", I secretly sided with the boy.

In my attempt to slip the word, I might address the boy, "Now, why aren't you paying attention in English, or History or whatever their class was?"

And the boy might eye me, with lowered chin, while the teacher piped up, saying, "It's not just a matter of his attentiveness…" and I would feel the strength of my failure.

I appointed some bad teachers in my time. Sometimes, you

just need the numbers – the bodies to attend the classrooms, just hired presences, whether they can teach is really less important. A Presence, to keep Order.

So if a good teacher left, it wasn't always possible to replace them sufficiently. So I settled with a Presence rather than a Teacher. How many, in my time? A dozen? Two dozen? The best would always leave too soon. I never ranked a teacher by my personal attachment to them or by how likeable they were, but I could see a few of those teachers were loved by the boys. Actually loved. I wondered at that – imagined how it must feel. I didn't envy them it; I was just grateful such a thing were possible. Imagine going to your workplace and being actually loved there?

When they left – when I read their brief letter of resignation, full of goodwill and sentiment – sometimes I admit I struggled not to despair. I thought of the boys' disappointment. But the worst of all would be the wretchedness I felt, when I filled the hollow space they'd left with a Presence.

One time it was Paul sitting across from me at my desk, with a Presence sitting sternly by his side. He was a Year Nine by then. It was only the second time we'd met, but I remembered his face, his manner. He had a kind of bemused innocence about him, not really disputing the teacher's charges. He'd grown a little in the interval between our meetings.

"So, Paul, do you understand why whatever the teacher's name was has kept you with us today?"

"Yes, sir."

"Why do you think it is?"

He looked up at his accuser and made a good guess:

"I wasn't paying attention in class."

"And why's that?"

And he shrugged, looking away.

"You were talking to your friends throughout whatever their name was's lesson? Look at me when I'm speaking to you."

He turned to me, quite despondent.

"Is that right?"

He shrugged again.

"Well?" – a little irritated.

"Yes, sir."

"And what were you talking about?"

He paused, as if the question were merely rhetorical.

"Tell me what you were talking about."

He shrugged again.

Quite softly: "If you shrug once more you'll be in Saturday Detention."

The look of horror was quite golden.

"Why?"

I shrugged.

He looked at his teacher – for help, perhaps. The teacher began, "You mustn't shrug, it's bad manners –" but I raised my hand to shush them.

"If you don't know something, Paul, you must say, 'I don't know, sir.' Or 'I'm not sure.' Or, if you prefer the idea of coming to school at nine o'clock on a Saturday morning for two hours, you should sit there slouched in the chair and shrug your shoulders at the next question I ask. Do you understand?"

"Yes, sir."

I sat back, inhaled deeply.

"So what were you and your friends talking about in whatever their name was's class?"

"I don't know, sir."

"You don't remember?"

"No, sir."

"Good!" I said. "And presumably you don't remember the content of the lesson either?"

Hesitatingly, in case it was a test, "Not all of it, sir."

I nodded. "Very good." I turned to the referral slip which was lying next to my ring binder on the desk. It had the teacher's comments about why Paul had to attend a detention with the Headmaster – something like, "Paul once again refused to engage with lesson. Persistently talking, disrupting class again." "Again" was underlined. I scratched my brow, realigned my glasses.

"Do you remember anything from today?"

Paul frowned, unsure.

"What do you mean?" he said.

"Is there one thing that you can remember from your lessons today?" I asked. "Anything at all," I said.

The boy's eyes widened. His mouth opened slightly. He looked at his teacher again, who appeared trance-like – who now took non-engagement to an art form.

"What lessons did you have today?" I said.

He falteringly recited the procession of lessons that day, with one or two corrections.

I nodded. "And what do you remember of them?"

He pursed his lips, his gaze shifted madly – I could see he was mentally emptying the rucksack and picking through the contents. As it were.

"It can be anything at all from the lesson. A fact, a personality. A rule of grammar, if you must."

He settled back in his chair and a small smile broke across his face. He shook his head – then stopped himself, in case it might be interpreted as shrugging's brother, and said, "I can't, sir."

"Not a thing?"

He shook his head again, not stopping himself any more. "My mind's gone blank."

I thought to say something like, "Its native state." I was inclined to meanness at that moment, because, I knew, I was being confronted with failure. It was about the only thing we three in that room shared in common – Paul's failure.

Those first nights, trying to sleep without her next to me – they were nearly the worst.

Those very first mornings, when I awoke to her absence, and had to remember what had happened – *they* were the worst.

Small things would crush me quite easily. With regularity. It took me an age to finally throw away a discarded drink bottle she'd drunk from. And you can imagine how I treated the mug still half-full with her tea – from our last morning together. Still warm, I imagined, from the touch of her lips, days later, though of course it was dead cold when I finally tipped it away.

Why my daughter hates me:
1) (She doesn't hate me)
2) Because I treated her not as a daughter but as a pupil
3) Because I was emotionally closed to her
4) Because I was fastidious (she thought) which she doesn't like in people
5) I was terrible at buying presents
6) I was terrible at receiving presents
7) I was terrible at enthusing about things children are wont to enthuse about
8) I met her distance with my own
9) I never tried to overcome her distance, in fact was vaguely pleased by it, it settling the issue of my emotional closed-ness, etc.
10) Because, in contrast, I loved her mother so utterly, and that was unfair (she thought)
11) Because, in contrast, I was so attentive, absorbed, enchanted + delighted by her mother, + tolerant and forgiving and sympathetic and in love with her rule-defying, even though I was so stringent with everyone else
12) Because she misunderstands the difference between loving and being in love, which is a treachery worse than emotional closed-ness (for her boyfriends)
13) Because she suspects I'd prefer what happened to her mother to have happened to her instead – NOT true

14) Because even though I wouldn't want that ever to have happened to her especially, I probably, even so, would have coped

15) Because she thought my treatment of two family members – wife and daughter – to be irrationally different and unfair and completely on a separate scale, because she didn't understand that I simply held one woman, in particular, above all the standards I held everyone else to

16) Because she's female and so she compared herself to her mother, and probably needed me to demonstrate prototypical male qualities that she would take forward with her for the rest of her life – I was to be the standard-bearer of maleness, if you believe all that, and my aforementioned distance, etc., distorted her attitude + outlook, etc., forever. (She + Angela in agreement there no doubt.)

17) Because if she'd been a boy I would've preferred it (SHE thinks) – NOT true, but my behaviour, emotional closed-ness, etc., would have been more compatible with a boy + (s)he wouldn't have compared him/herself with his/her mother AND

18) None of the business with Paul would have happened.

I will admit I hate him. Even though I prided myself long enough on being above hate, since hate was ignorance, as I saw it, before. But now it's the only certain thing I feel.

And when I see his face on the television, I imagine what I'd do. I fixate on it so that the news ends long before the vivid images in my mind, particularly when I strangle him, with the force I exert on his Adam's apple with my thumbs, left thumb high, right thumb low, so I can press on his throat to shut it tight.

And I'm actually clenching my jaw, staring at the television screen, and sometimes my arms are raised as if I might grab him from the screen, though he's long gone from it, though the news isn't even on it any more, just my arms slightly raised and my jaw clenched and my thumbs, especially, feeling for his windpipe and Adam's apple, and a tingling sensation that runs down the back of my neck, or the side of my face, that comes in waves, or not at all.

So, that is hate.

And that is the part I won't tell Angela.

For the past week I've not kept up my notes/journal. Last Monday morning my computer failed to switch on.

I generally use the radio as my connection to the outside world, day-to-day, but my notes/journal have become an important ritual. Without them/it I felt cut-off from something necessary.

I think I tried to switch the computer on ten to fifteen times. Perhaps more. I nearly swore. I made fists, tensed my bowels. I half-considered putting my fist through the screen.

It was a bad week for my relations with electronic appliances. Just the day before, the washing machine paused mid-wash and beeped loudly, and the panel that usually shows a timer instead showed ERROR-14. I felt very lonely, then.

On the same day, on my way to the hospital, my Oyster card wasn't recognized by the ticket barrier. It was just a momentary glitch – it happens now and again, that I have to present my Oyster card a second time before the barriers open. I'm sure it must happen on thousands of occasions every day. But it seemed at the time like a correlation. That the world of electronics – or perhaps just the world – had taken against me.

I wrote some notes by hand. They were filled with crossings-out. I suppose this is why Angela wanted me to write these notes by hand in the first place: so that the process was visible. No doubt the printed pages of A4 are less interesting to her.

But in any case those handwritten scraps felt like a different thing altogether. I actually burned them. I can't remember what they said.

I have a new computer now, and barely any idea how it works.

There was a little ritual, where I showed the old computer the new. I practically told it that it was being replaced. I made some tea, listening to the World Service – this was all just a few minutes ago. I took the old computer outside to the street and smashed it against the ground. I picked it up and smashed it again. I think I did it a third time.

A person saw me and pretended not to see. Then I picked up the largest pieces and chucked them in the bin. I was sweating. I kicked a few bits to the road, but still there was plenty of glass and plastic remains.

Then I sat back down, where I sit now. I had to stop – it took me a few moments to realize I'd got some blood on the keyboard. It's from my hands. I half-thought it was from the old machine.

Me: Do you remember how she used to play?

Her: Of course.

Me: It was lovely, wasn't it?

Her: It was.

Me: And do you remember she'd sit you on her lap, sometimes, while she played?

Her: Really? I don't remember that.

Me: You don't? You were quite small.

Her: How old was I?

Me: Quite small. Possibly only a year or two. Perhaps you don't remember.

Her: Tell me.

Me: She'd sit you on her lap and play with her arms around you.

Her: Really?

Me: You'd throw in a note sometimes – or sometimes a whole fist of notes – and she'd try to accommodate it. Play around it, do you know what I mean? You really don't remember?

Her: Oh, *Dad*.

Me: It was really lovely.

Her: Come here, Dad.

Me: And have I told you, sometimes I'd come home and she'd be playing? She'd be composing one of her commissions.

Her: It's OK.

Me: It was funny, one time – I fell asleep listening, and when I woke up she'd completed the whole piece.

Her: It's OK. It's *OK*.

Me: And, you know, I had the strangest dream. It's funny.

Her: What's that?

Me: I had the strangest dream.

Her: (*quietly*) Say it again?

Me: The dream I had, it was so strange, with her music through it.

Her: A dream? Was it nice?

Me: It was.

████████████ I want to strangle you and feel your pulse fade beneath my fingers.

I want you to know why I'm strangling you, and, before you lose consciousness, for you to agree with my reasoning.

I want to commemorate your death with songs and happy proclamations. The children will light a fire, the TV channels will run specials, and the artists will all compete for public commissions to mark this day. The day I stood over you with your neck in my hands and your weakening pulse fluttering against my thumbs.

There are the notes I share with Angela, and there are the notes I keep to myself. Perhaps this is what she means by my being *opaque*.

In the night I sensed something in my lower back. I turned on to my side and grimaced – not quite painful: more the feeling of being marked, like the brush of a nettle before the sting enters your blood.

By morning I could barely move. The pain in my back was quite extreme. Deep breaths were treacherous.

Even peripheral movements, like extending my arm, seem to tug against that plane of my back. Not the spine, but the muscular base, distinctly the left side – not muscular enough.

I've reviewed, in my mind, the shenanigans with the computer, tried to replay each wild movement – to identify, if I may, the precise moment of trauma. The possibility of such movements, now, seems a crazy fantasy. I'd struggle, now, to even give the computer a stern look.

Most galling, obviously, is how, in the longer view, the computer won.

I telephoned the hospital, asking them to tell my father I wouldn't be visiting. Having reached the front room, I didn't have the will to get back to bed, and so sat there until evening, trying to doze.

My new computer is a sleek abomination. The old machine, as much as I hated it by the end for its infirmity, was at least familiar.

This thing, by contrast, is impenetrable. All my old applications, my familiar routines and shortcuts – all gone. Now I have this glossy fortress instead. The text is as sharp as print, and each window is accorded a soft shadow. But where the hell is everything?

In my current crippled state, there's little else I'm capable of except sitting in front of a computer, and so I've been studying it. I've discovered that underneath the shiny, drop-shadowed exterior, the operating system is UNIX-based. As soon as I opened a new terminal session, forsaking the lush desktop in favour of plain text, I was taken back to a similar moment, decades ago: hunched (less painfully then, it should be said) over a black terminal screen in my office in the dead of night, entering commands with slow fingers, with two large text-books whose names I forget (one of them was something plain like *Computer Networks Vol. 3*) and a notepad where I'd try to describe which commands did what.

My night-time tutorials at the computer were my desperate effort to understand a new threat: the internet.

A few years after the school had been connected to the internet, I experienced my first IT crisis. One of the boys at the school, a cunning and over-achieving Year Nine boy, had deployed a computer virus that had spread to every host on the network, rendering them inoperable. Every machine had to be laboriously reformatted. Our email server was effectively destroyed, as well as those of several other schools (though in those days it hardly mattered, since no one really used email).

It was easy enough to find the culprit – he'd achieved legendary status in the schoolyard, an unlikely feat for such a bookish lad (which only further gilded his fame). He didn't even deny his crime, such was his honesty. Initially I was too amazed by the enormity of his achievement to discipline him. I wanted answers – *how?* How had he wiped out the school's network? Had he physically tampered with the machines? Did he have any accomplices? You have to understand my ignorance of computer systems was total in those days.

He was a smart boy but too daunted, or just too inarticulate, to explain the mechanism of his IT blitzkrieg. So I arranged to speak with his parents to discuss his crime (which I couldn't myself describe), and his father explained that he was the one to blame: he worked with computers and his son took an avid interest, and like a father teaching his boy how to light a fire and hunt, he'd been showing him how to network two machines, how one could speak to another, what port scanning was and where the danger lay.

So it was the boy's father who counselled me on our IT systems and recommended a consultant to perform a full audit of our networks. This was in the days when information security was only considered by financial corporations and the military – so I accepted his excuse that he couldn't provide me with any references because of the nature of his work. He (the consultant) wrote a ten-point wish list to improve the school's *cyber security posture*. At the time, his every bullet point was gibberish to me. Slightly worse was that our IT teacher understood him almost as little.

Top of his list was switching (*migrating* in his parlance) every machine to a different operating system. A monumental change, it turned out – and one I had no understanding of whatsoever. But I could see well enough that my ignorance was preventing me from reasoning about the threat I faced, like a village elder trying to describe a thunderstorm. I had no choice but to begin that laborious job of understanding, a job that began with the soul-destroying sentence: *TCP (Transmission Control Protocol) was specifically designed to provide a reliable end-to-end byte stream over an unreliable internetwork.*

I first met her at the school. She was a music teacher. She came to my office shortly after joining, so we could discuss how she was settling in. I was struck by her, of course, even if I refused to admit I thought she was beautiful.

I can never know what she really felt, on that first occasion we met. We never really revisited it. We weren't quite old enough, I don't think, to consider such nostalgia essential, yet. So I can never be sure whether she thought me handsome, or precisely how her feelings towards me – though I hate the immodesty of saying it – developed.

That first time, I'd been distracted by my apprehensions of a different meeting that night. I was at war with the governors. I was new at the school, and I was crass and young(er) I suppose, and I explained to them that, despite whatever impressions I may have given them in the interviews leading to my appointment, actually my opinion was that parents had essentially no role in the running of a school, and in particular no role in the exercise of necessary discipline regarding expulsions, etc., and that if they were dissatisfied with my actions they could perhaps write me a letter, and not to phone or try to intercept me in person, and of course they could always seek, in the very worst case, my dismissal, through the official channels. I was rather confrontational about it. Well, they had written me a letter. More than a letter.

And in the midst of these hostilities, she came into my office and sat down, and looked at me for only a moment, and said – as if she weren't my subordinate – "You look haunted."

I was somewhat taken aback.

"I've had a busy day," I said, I think, or something like it. I was intensely distracted, by the interaction of so many contra emotions, topped with her unexpected remark.

We talked a little aimlessly at first, from what I remember. She sensed my distraction, my inability to quite look her in the eye. I asked how her first week had gone. She said the boys were a bit undisciplined, that in truth she was spending a lot of class time getting them to shut up (as she put it), that she'd spoken to some of the other teachers for advice and they'd all told her something different.

I inhaled deeply – gradually my war with the governors was receding to mere background noise in my mind. I didn't realize, then, quite what a rough time she'd been having, since she seemed at that moment so unperturbed, even light-hearted.

"Your last school was all girls," I said. I took my glasses off, momentarily, before putting them back on. "I suppose it was a different dynamic."

"A bit, yes."

"The problem, in regard to the boys, is that you're a woman."

She was impassive as I broke this to her.

"It's very difficult, for a woman, to command their respect. You have the advantage of not being overweight, with no visible deformities or the like, so you're not a target in that way – though actually being attractive can be equally problematic, or more so – " I began to blush at my error " – by which, I mean – " I tried to look at her evenly, and then looked away "– it's not simply a matter of physical appearance." I regretted that word *physical*. I took a breath, as if to start again.

"The fact is, your gender will work against you. That's not to say it's the only factor, of course. I think, in general, a woman can less afford to be kind in the classroom, with boys . . . You seem a kind person, at least."

She shrugged. "Not especially. I've tried not to shout at them, since – " she gave it some thought, appeared to imagine herself screaming at the class, and I got a glimpse of the difficulties she was facing, which I only really learned about much later " – since I think I'm not much good at shouting. I already know it's no good to do something half-baked."

"What have you been trying?"

"Well, I've been putting them in detention like mad. But even that's a struggle. I tell them they have detention and they don't turn up. I have to chase them through their form tutors. It's a bit thankless, I suppose."

"It's early days, yet. Every teacher has to bed in." I closed my eyes, in a kind of resigned fury, at myself. *Bed in.* I'd stumbled upon every euphemism and innuendo, it felt like, and surely the next inevitable step was to mention fornication outright.

"Is that so?" she said, a little coquettishly – a little tiredly. "I hope that's the case. I just can't see myself lasting very long, at this rate."

"Well, I'm very sorry to hear that," I said. I chewed on my lower lip. "Perhaps I should sit in on a few lessons. That'll help, in the short term."

She appeared unconvinced. "In the short term," she echoed.

"That'll help get you over this slump, I hope – and I may be able to offer some insight to the boys' personalities. Often it's a matter of identifying the chief actors. If you can pacify them, the whole group comes under control."

She tilted her head. I believe she found my strategizing appealing.

"I think that'd be helpful," she said.

I smiled at her, was able, finally, to look her in the eyes a little, before saying, "Give me your teaching timetable, and I'll let you know what lessons I can sit in on. Give the little bastards a surprise."

Her momentary shock, I remember. Her feigned horror at my words, her excitement (I like to think). Perhaps that was the moment I really fell for her.

My back is relenting. But when I try to touch my toes it feels like the brace of my pelvis is about to crack.

It's laughable, how little I can fold towards the ground. I thought the pain was muscular before, but this other pain feels like a misalignment of bone, or as if my lower skeleton is dense with cancer.

I can barely even gesture at my toes. And when I straighten up, the old pain, the one that seems to reside in the muscles, surges back, redoubled. From the kitchen I can hear the kettle boil, and the sound of a news announcer just above it. I imagine him – the news announcer – young and fit, and I envy him. The kettle switches off, and I dig my fingers into my back, as if I might excavate the rotten abscess, or the rampant cancer, or the outgrowth of bone.

Angela inspired me today.

I was still wincing in pain from my back, and I had plasters on my fingers from where I'd cut myself on the computer casing. I must have looked a wreck. She showed concern and asked me about my injuries. I told the story – offered to bring her the notes, but she declined – but I told it in a way so that she laughed. Then she stopped herself and pointed to her temple and asked where I'd got the bruise from, and I said it was nothing to worry about, that the back was killing me most.

I think it was on account of my appearance that she took a softer tone with me. In fact, the whole thing was less formal. She even discussed her own stresses, from her colleagues and her boyfriend (he believes she is always analysing him; she is, most of the time). And she came back always to My Case – or Your Case, as it is from her perspective. She was circumspect, advisory – I did hardly any talking.

I told her she was acting unusually (I avoided the word *unprofessionally*). She told me that many in her profession would agree. She smiled almost sinisterly at this. Many of her colleagues, the older ones especially, she said, would berate her for her *unanalytic* behaviour.

I was beginning to suspect Angela was something of a dark horse, not the staid mediocrity I'd presumed her to be. I was slightly overwhelmed when she turned her gaze back upon My Case.

"I think you're suffering because of your relationship with

people. You relied on your wife to socialize you. In a way, she was your main connection to the rest of the world, to how other people think and feel. Then, this awful event happened, and anyone would struggle to come to terms with it. But it's doubly traumatic because it takes away the companion who has helped you every day for the past twenty-odd years. Tell me if what I'm saying upsets you.

"The loss of that companionship, and the manner of that loss, has caused you to retreat into yourself – but rather than feeling sadness or depression, as is more usual, you've rejected grief. To a great extent you've refused to grieve."

I admit I laughed at this.

"You've even shut yourself off from your daughter's grief. Instead, the hurt expresses itself in these damaging patterns of behaviour. Physically damaging, even – " she gestured at me, at my miserable, hunched figure.

"Instead of being sad, you're angry. But you won't even admit that much. The world doesn't touch you. You're aloof and superior, you consider therapy beneath you, but secretly you crave it. You undermine all the exercises I give you, you mock them and chide me about them, but you do them all, without fail.

"And it's because your whole life you've been able to live by the illusion that you've been in control. You're the Head-master – what you say, goes. Even the bad teachers are your fault, you think. Then you retire and suddenly your world falls apart. And now in the most difficult way you have to accept that you're not in control.

"And you have to cede some of that control. Let your daughter back into your life. But, most importantly, you have to accept this: that there was nothing you could've done. That what happened to your wife was beyond anyone's control. It wasn't your fault."

She's wrong, of course. But so nearly right. When the terrorists killed my wife I didn't think about it enough. I didn't reason about it. But Angela is right – I have to accept I'm not in control. I have to take stock. I've been sitting on this grief, as she calls it, for ten years now. It's still brand new.

"I want to hurt him," I said.

She nodded. She let my declaration hang awhile in the air. Did it shock her? Did it shock me, to say it?

"You mean ███████?" she said.

"I blame him," I said. "And I think he should suffer," I said. "I want him to suffer."

She waits, lets me listen to the effect of my own words.

"In what way?" she asks.

"I don't know," I say. "Every way. Any way that would make him regret. I want him to know what he did. What he caused. The suffering he caused me. *Is* causing me."

"It's natural to be angry," she said. "Completely understandable. And it's OK to think anything. It's good to think these thoughts, and to speak them. It's very good. Think of it like a breakthrough," she said. "You can say, 'I want to hurt ███ ███.' You can say it and nobody gets hurt. And maybe it even feels good to say. But I want us to find out why you feel that way. When you understand why you feel that way, you're no longer controlled by it."

I nod at that. This is her faith: that my anger is unreasonable. It is soluble. That it can be rooted out – that it will die when exposed to the light.

There is a prevailing wisdom that it's never wrong to forgive.

Whenever their students fought, Forgiveness was every teacher's watchword. All disputes were to be resolved with mutual forgiveness and perhaps a handshake – a resolution to put any wrongs behind them. Water under the bridge, as they say.

If the teacher in question didn't espouse forgiveness they suggested something worse – that the boy should *ignore*. Ignore the insult, forgive the blow. All because a classroom of stoics would make their own lives easier. It is, I begin to realize, a despicable edict.

We're brought up on this crude teaching. Ignore and Forgive.

So, I am to argue the cause for Revenge. That it can be Justifiable and even Right, though it may be Bad.

I will argue that it is a patent truth that killing can be moral, and therefore that *not-killing* can be immoral.

Then, I will describe how we may determine the moral necessity of Conventionally Wrong Actions.

I will conclude that Inaction is compatible with concepts of Negligence and Recklessness, and that between the choices of Inaction and Revenge, Revenge can be the so-called *lesser evil*.

Finally, if the argument can be validated in theory, it must accordingly be validated in deed (or else what use is theory?).

Angela: may we begin *A Treatise on the Justified Murder of* ██████? Or, for short: *Kill* ████████.

I touched my toes. I have to fight through the bone-pain and then the muscle-pain. Plus, the cords of my legs feel like the rusted cables of a Victorian bridge. My eyes are watering by the time I've finished.

On my right side I manage to prod my big toe with my middle finger a few times. On my left (the pain side) I nearly reach my ankle.

To celebrate my recuperation I played a C major scale on the piano with my right hand. Sitting with my back straight was challenge enough. My scant musical knowledge was sufficient for C major – otherwise referred to as "the white notes" by my wife.

There was a predictable stuttering to my playing. Eventually I could manage the simple scale with my right hand, though my left seemed incapable of any kind of traversal beyond the initial five notes.

As I played, I remembered the ease with which she'd play. It made me laugh, to think of the comparison. It made me proud of her, as I indulged myself in how incapable I was. Every fumble – and there were many – was a kind of tribute to her talent, a demonstration of the gulf between proficiency and – whatever I am. Rank amateur.

Then I became sad, and disgusted with my inability to command my fingers. I was dispirited especially about my left hand, and when I opened a book of sheet music – a collection of varied classical music for piano – I was overwhelmed by just how inscrutable the little black marks were, the lines and bars and scattered dots, most of them with tails, a few of them un-tailed and hollow, some of them with smaller dots or accents, most of them connected by their tails, some struck through – some of the pages were heavy with ink, so that it seemed impossible that anyone with a mere ten fingers might ever play them.

These were the pieces she'd play when she was upset or at a loss for inspiration. I became emotional just thinking of how she'd touched these pages, and touched the keys of the piano. I regretted my playing, felt distinctly that I'd rubbed away something of her that lingered still – and in the crassest way.

When I stood up my back and pelvis protested, and I grimaced. I stood there for a moment in a great deal of pain.

Angela has asked me about my relationship with my father. I believe she's concerned with filling out the mental flow chart of what she now considers my *de facto* abuse of Amy; so that she can illuminate some blindingly obvious cause (namely, my father's abuse of me) and draw an arrow from one to the other.

My father never abused me. He hardly touched me. I haven't told Angela this, because she'd interpret my protest in some insidious way. And what of my siblings? she asked, early on. I have none. I had a brother, for the briefest time, in my childhood.

This is the problem with Angela and her kind: she is so pleased to find an explanation. It never occurs to her that explanations are abundant. Was my father distant? Yes. Am I now distant to my child? Yes. That is the extent of psychoanalysis.

And my mother? Ours was a standard relationship. I loved her, but not overly, and she likewise me.

In any case, my relationship with my father was never an issue. We were both comfortable at our respectful distance. Visiting him in hospital has distorted what we'd believed were our official roles: Father and Son. Now it is more Son-Father and Father-Son. I take my seat beside his bed and, once or twice, will venture an encouraging word:

"I'm sure tomorrow will be better"

or

"You must let me know if there's anything I can do"

By now, our stilted conversations are disguised by the diffi-culty with which he talks. He speaks softly and slowly, feigns fatigue or else is genuinely exhausted. Our reticence has become more natural, more in keeping with the circumstance.

I told him about my injuries, about my back. He gestured with his eyebrows, mostly, to show concern. His mouth was incredibly dry and I kept offering him water, which he refused.

He was admitted to hospital just a few weeks after the bombings. Prior, he'd been a shrunken but indomitable old man. There wasn't a particular cause, medically speaking, to his sudden admission. He had dangerously low blood pressure and a "reduced immune response" to some typically non-threatening virus. There may have been some kind of lung infection in the periphery – mere embellishment to a more fundamental failure. It was, as I saw it, as if he had thrown himself between me and my wife's detonation in an attempt to shield me from harm. Indomitable as he was, the effort had fatally compromised his nervous system, though not entirely wiped him out.

Or perhaps it was some kind of stunt to save me from myself? A feat of distraction that stopped me at the precipice, caught my attention in the most dramatic fashion.

Or perhaps he is just old.

Out of pity, perhaps, Angela is reading my notes again. Or maybe there's some hidden intention to her change of heart. It seems she's intrigued by my office romance, so to speak. Her manner changed, I thought, as she read about my wife, and she was soft in her questions.

Well, I didn't manage to pacify the boys for her. We did succeed, though, in giving the little bastards a surprise.

It was probably a week or two after we'd had that first meeting – and I realized later what a long stretch that felt for her at the time – before I got round to sitting in on one of her lessons. I remember it was the last period of the day – early in the week, I think, perhaps a Tuesday. I thought the last period was a good option in terms of detentions, since there might be a good deal of them.

It was one of the first times I'd visited the new extension of the Music department. (I was, throughout my career, on a quest to increase the surface area of that school, because, by some outlandish oversight of some government bean counter, the acreage of the school was a key funding consideration. So the completion of each new annexe and extension marked a small ((index-linked)) bump in total budget.) The rooms there still smelled of paint, and the graffiti on the desks was startling for its scarcity.

I made a point of arriving five minutes into proceedings. This would allow her time to get the class naturally under her command, or else allow the boys to become comfortable in their havoc. And so it was.

She caught my eye as I appeared in the windowpane of the door – she looked unrelieved. One of the boys saw the direction of her gaze and glimpsed me. In the time between me opening the door and having entered, he'd gestured to the others to be quiet. He'd even, by the time I'd entered – just as I was about to clear my throat to formally declare my presence – raised his index finger to his lips.

Two of them weren't even in their chairs, but standing around, casually chatting. I remembered only one of their names at the time – a James/Steven – but not the other, so I pointed at them both and said, "You two." They froze.

She watched me, and them, tensely.

I asked for their names – knowing the James/Steven, but committing the other to memory: Sultan, an outlandish, Indianish name, I thought, though no more outlandish than the black Kings and Dukes, perhaps. I told them both they'd join me after school, and James/Steven looked relieved to be able to sit down, though Sultan, I remember even now, barely hid his smirk. The rest of the lesson went without incident. They got out the new keyboards – two boys to each keyboard, which meant they couldn't use the new headphones. The noise was horrific. The two troublemakers disappeared into the lesson. They all played, mostly, as if they were working at some very complex combination lock.

Occasionally she'd stop them all – waving down their inept playing – to give them some guidance or instruct them on the value of a note or rest. And then she'd start them up again. Occasionally I would stand near a pair of boys and click my fingers, pointing at the keyboard to get them back to their work, though it pained me to do so. Some of them, I could tell, could play the simple exercise easily – presumably they had private lessons – and these boys were the most bored of all.

There was some light relief when one of the boys discovered the button to play a garish demo track. Another discovered the sound effects – this set off a ripple of exploration, and soon a variety of laser and drum noises reverberated around the room, and I dutifully took the names of these boys – whom I believe had quite forgotten my presence in their glee – and promised them a substantial detention.

Once the boys had left for afternoon registration, she sat at the head of the class and closed her books and looked at the desk in front of her without saying a word. I didn't think it had gone so badly – but neither was I surprised by what she finally told me.

"There's no point in any of it."

I was still standing by the door, where I'd stood sentry while the boys filed out. I looked at the floor, at the new plasticky lino, laid in large sheets, with a vaguely cloudy chemical pattern to it. I understood what she meant.

"Is there?" She was looking at me.

"In struggling to teach them to play the keyboard?"

She waited.

"I suppose not, no."

She sat back, exhaled dismally. "Mrs Richter suggested a practical lesson." The *Mrs* was derisory.

"I see," I said.

She laughed, quite genuinely. I smiled.

"God, they were awful. I was awful. What a shit idea." She carried on her laughter and I felt inclined to join in.

"Is it so shit an idea?" I asked.

She smiled at me. Me, a few paces from the door by now, and her at the head of the class, with an exhausted, elated look, like someone who knows they've been through the worst.

"You heard it as well as me."

"Some of them enjoyed it," I said. I took a few steps closer and sat – unusually casual for me, excitingly so – on a desk near the back.

"They liked their sound effects, didn't they?" she said.

"They understand the sound effects."

She scraped her chair back, stood up, turned to face the whiteboard – her hopeful markings. A stave, a time signature, a treble clef (things I'm recently familiar with), some notes hanging at middle C, of different time values.

"But this," she said, gesturing at the whiteboard, "was ambitious."

"It's confusing, perhaps, how the C note sits a bit beneath the lines, rather than upon them. It seems a little *ad hoc*."

She considered it, momentarily, before taking the eraser to her lesson. "At least someone was paying attention." In a few strokes, the stave and its notes were gone.

"If this was a practical lesson, so to speak, how do the theoretical ones go?" I asked. I was still sitting on the desk near the back, side-on to her. I practically had my sleeves rolled up.

She shook her head, standing with one hand on her books. "They're worse, in a way. Things like: identify what part of the world this African-sounding music comes from."

She gathered up her books.

"It's pointless."

What do you do with the voice message of your loved one? After they're gone and the message remains?

If I dialled the number, I could listen to her voice again. I could listen to her speaking to me.

There is her magazine subscription I still haven't cancelled, though I dread its heavy arrival through the letter box each month.

Isn't it sad that a bus ticket or a bookmark can outlive her? That she can be survived by the contents of her pockets? That her clothes and accessories are still here, without her? The hat she wore on holiday, the book she didn't finish. There are some very old shoes in the cupboard, that she hadn't worn for years; I look at them and I don't have the heart to tell them she's gone.

she was perhaps fourteen

I wasn't entirely honest, in the retelling of my abuse of Amy. I feigned an incomplete memory. I used phrases like *she was perhaps fourteen*. In truth, I don't quite remember her precise age at the time. But I could calculate it.

In the same way, I always forgot Paul and Amy's relative ages. I always had to do the sums, whenever I thought about it.

Was I vague because I couldn't be bothered with the mental arithmetic? Or was it to save face? Sometimes, when you're in a social situation and you remember a person but they don't remember you, it's best all round to feign only a vague awareness of who they are. To feign a dawning remembrance, as it were. How many times have I squinted at someone as if in thought, and told them that, yes, I *did* in fact remember meeting them – when actually I remembered the whole occasion in great detail? When I remembered some intimate fact they'd previously shared with me, and which sometimes (often) I'd have to hear again, and raise my eyebrows in fake surprise, in fake congratulation or fake sorrow. Whom was I sparing, then – them or me?

Whom am I sparing now?

Perhaps it's conspicuous, to remember details too well. Or to have possibly calculated them. *She was fourteen.* And how did I remember? *She was fourteen – according to my calculations.* You'll want me to show my working.

And there was a lie, too. The framed picture, which was

struck by the heavy textbook she threw. I described it as *some dreary watercolour*. The sentence was: *So she threw the book and it flapped heavily against the wall – hit the edge of a framed picture, some dreary watercolour my mother had given me, I think.*

There is a dreary watercolour, *given me*, as it were, by my mother. I placed it there, in the retelling, on the wall, to be struck by Amy's textbook. So I did revise the facts. And I lied, outright, with that short clause, *I think*, even as my hesitation was intended to suggest the possibility of doubt.

she was perhaps fourteen – prevarication
some dreary watercolour my mother had given me, I think – lie

Perhaps (and I use the word in earnest now) I felt the truth would be too neatly set upon by Angela. Because, in truth, the picture was of myself and my wife, young and abroad somewhere (I know perfectly well where). Does that explain my reaction? Did my daughter intend such a shot, with her textbook?

It seems to me that Angela sees herself as some kind of exorcist. She considers me laden, or beset, by distress. Through discussion she thinks this distress – this black fog, as it were – will be lifted. That the sadness is a thing to be removed or dissipated.

But I wonder if she's wrong. This persistent, obstinate anger that fogs my existence these days – what if the reason for its persistence is that it's justified? Morally right, even? What if waiting for this anger to dissipate is like waiting for the contradiction of a patent truth?

What if this hate I feel is not a black fog at all but rather a burning light? Then the job isn't to dissipate it – not to wait for false to be true – but to be guided by it – to see what hidden surfaces it might illuminate.

Someone killed my wife, and what have I done about it?

Should I tell you, then, about the man I hate? Would it help me, to describe the colour of my feelings (black) when I imagine the things I imagine? Would it help you?

Christ invented Forgiveness in order for the victim to get on with his day, to enable him to carry on, to not be consumed by grief. Forgiveness, then, is an escape from Victimhood. Perhaps I can learn to forgive, and escape – but that's not the question. The question is, What is Right?

Some man blows up your wife, in an action co-ordinated with other men, blowing up other men's wives. Whom can I blame? Not the man, who's dead, or men, who're dead.

Besides, I don't hate those dead men – or at least, less than I hate the bombs they made. Blaming them is like blaming the soldier's gun for killing. It's true, in the most literal sense, in the shallowest logical sense, in the most worthless sense.

Because if you removed the man who blew himself up, there'd be another. Some other blameless mad person. They are like guns – less than guns. They are parts. The triggering mechanism for a bomb. A mode of transit, a light sensor and a sound sensor. They are less than the bombs they carry. They defer to the bomb.

Then there are the men who make the munitions, the bombs – and they, too, are more parts. Drones of a higher order, following instructions, committed to replication. They don't originate anything.

And then there is the man I hate. The man who, when I think

about it, actually did it. Who moved the parts – who moved the bomb-makers and the bomb-triggerers. Who set things in motion. Who is mad himself, in a way. Utterly loopy, in a way. But only in a way.

There is a line – at one end there is my wife being blown up. And at the other end – him.

And where do I fit in, on this line?

But there isn't just my wife, on that line, connected with that awful man.

(*Awful* is the wrong word.)

Poor Paul is connected, as well. Poor Paul, whose misfortune I'm even more culpable of, perhaps, than that terrible man.

(*Terrible*, too, isn't right.)

Paul, whom I came to look upon almost as a son. The only boy, I think, who ever looked to me for guidance, really. He who started life unjustly, confined and mistreated, or at least morally neglected, which is the same. He was often late because he needed to look after his infant brother while his parents ran some errands, and I came to understand that his parents accorded school a low priority in the boy's life. Over the months and years I built up an image of his father as someone who used violence for the gratification of his short temper, rather than a means of control.

At first I sought to reform Paul. But in fact there was nothing to reform – he was like a plant, just needing space and light to grow to the correct proportions.

Paul, who went to a foreign country to get destroyed, and did so, nearly. Whose letter I kept, though it wasn't for me – and whom was I sparing, then? I think I know.

I sent him away, in a sense. I sent him to that country. I moved the parts, set things in motion. I planted a seed in young Paul's mind. But I didn't tend it correctly – didn't take enough care.

So, who is to blame most? The man who makes the war, or the man who makes the soldier?

Can you imagine what I said to the boy's mother? They were braver than me, or more demented – they were endlessly strong, or seemed so.

They thanked me for visiting. They were kind, far kinder than I thought them capable. Kinder than they'd been to the lad his whole life.

It wasn't one hundred per cent my doing: I could see that although Poor Paul had accepted my preaching wholesale, perhaps in the end he'd still sought to be recognized by his mother and father.

And my preaching amounted to this: *You must make something of your life*. What shoddy, ill-defined terms. I spent so much effort encouraging noble thoughts in Paul's young mind that I never considered where, actually, I was leading him. I never reached a summary. I dealt only in the moment-to-moment bits and pieces. I put him off littering (a triumph), I made him attend (imperfectly) to his punctuality, I told him the value of honest labour, of applying one's intellect, which he slowly warmed to. These were the Basics, I thought. But I never taught him how to be wrong – how to understand it and make amends. How to identify a compromised position when one is in it.

The thing I spent so long cultivating in Amy – the capacity for being wrong, for accepting misjudgement as inevitable – I absolutely neglected in Paul. I had no time, of course. I never really understood my position with him, the role I'd unwittingly taken – until it was all too late. So I drew out in him a general *can do* attitude. It was, perhaps, the very opposite of what I'd (again unwittingly) done to Amy.

I felt Paul had an immense catching up to do. I had no patience. By the time I became aware of what I must do with him – by the time he'd sat in front of me, in detention again, for the fifth or sixth time, perhaps – though now with Amy, outrageously, in the classroom (did I intend it? I sometimes wonder, though I can't believe it) –

And can you imagine what I said to the mother? Though I hardly had to say anything, they treated me with such kindness. And can you imagine my private shame, when it was they (stalwart, resolute) who comforted me? I cried as if he'd died out there. I visited them before his abbreviated body – still alive – had even been returned. And wasn't that always to be, from then, how we must speak of him? He was, from then, always the object of any given clause – not the actor, but the acted upon. He *was taken* back to England by an RAF transport plane. He *was returned* to his home. He *was cared for* by his still not very old, still rugged parents, who seemed to finally love him wholly now.

He'd sacrificed himself in the most violent way. The son they'd never got along with became a pride to them.

And do you imagine what I said to the mother, after the news had broken, but before Poor Paul *was returned* home? In that small, quiet front room of theirs? And that I judged them and their home as less than Paul deserved – can you imagine? – even as I was comforted by them. They understood what their son meant to me. Almost perfectly. They understood – less so, surely less so – the extra effort I'd focused upon their son. I'm sure they had no idea about Amy (Paul was too private a soul). Above all, I'm sure they were in complete ignorance as to my role in his disfigurement – as to my role in sending Paul away to be destroyed. In inspiring him in such a way –

I said I was sorry. I told them I couldn't help but feel partly responsible.

They told me that was nonsense, of course.

I said I felt more than partly responsible.

They shook their heads, in that quiet little room, and it was only then that the mother had time enough – after my emotional entrance into their flat, insisting I wouldn't stay long, though finally entering that small front room and agreeing to sit down, but do so without anything to drink – it was only then she had time enough to turn the television set off.

I think of how bad it must have been, watching the recurring news segment – barely a minute long, because they had no video footage, and besides no one had died – briefly describing the events that had nearly destroyed their son.

The mother let the father speak for them both. He said that Paul had done a courageous thing. He said that he'd live – they'd told him that – that he could live well, that prosthetics these days were marvellous, that given enough time he'd be able to overcome his injuries, though they were so incredibly severe (the mother closed her eyes in imagining them). The important thing was this: he was alive. He was being returned to them. They'd stand by him, look after him, do whatever it took. He'd done a courageous thing.

It was as if they'd known such a thing was coming. Perhaps that was why they'd had no time for him, all the while, before – perhaps they'd been waiting for this catastrophe, waiting for their son to fulfil his dark promise. And now they loved him with full force.

The mother went to the kitchen, to make tea for the both of them, and wouldn't I join them? Of course I would, it was very kind of them, though I only meant to stay a few moments.

I looked around the little quiet room, breathed it in. I felt as if I were a boy, in the father's presence – in the presence of his stalwartness. I believe he judged me negatively (only a little) for crying openly in front of them both, though at the same time he was touched by it, honoured by it, in a way – in the same way that they'd forever be honoured, now, by the sanctified grief of others for their son, for what he'd sacrificed, and what I offered now pathetic as my tears were – was a foretaste of that everlasting honour they'd been bestowed by their son's detonation. In truth I judged myself more harshly.

I told him his son was a unique soul – I told him Paul had a remarkable character, had been quite unlike any other boy I'd taught. The father seemed to accept this as a matter of fact – he had none of the sensitivity of the mother, the sensitivity that I'd never at all suspected could exist in either of them.

I apologized for my tears – finally had resolved firmly enough against them – and he dismissed my apology, seemed to thank me for my grief.

I know how much time and effort you put into the boy. That's a great thing, what you did with him (the mother had returned with a tray of cups and saucers, teapot – *and some biscuits, even, at a time like this*, I'd thought at the time, not judgingly then but astoundedly, that she could muster such mute propriety, such faith in routine conventions), and we're both so grateful for all the help you gave him. He was such a tearaway, sometimes. We fought with him, sometimes. I physically fought him, he got so out of hand, sometimes, but you had a tremendous effect on him. You really chilled him out, if you know what I mean?

I nodded that I understood, a sided nod, to disregard the flattery at the same time.

So you should be proud, as proud as we are. And they beamed at me, as I lingered over my tea (not having the stomach for any kind of biscuit, not even being able to contemplate the things).

Both of Paul's legs had been removed from above the knee. Half of his right arm had been removed. Blown away. He'd lost the sight of his right eye. There were, of course, broken bones, a collapsed lung, punctured organs, splintering and fracturing and shearing, snapping – but of the irrevocable injuries, that was it: both legs (or most of them), an arm (or some of it), an eye. Some of his mind, I worried then, and still sometimes do.

I kept reciting, in my mind, those injuries – legs, arm, eye – and imagined myself similarly transformed. I tried very hard to imagine the shocking absence of a limb – of two limbs. I wanted to understand how it might feel, to have your body reduced – before you got used to it, I mean, as you surely must.

And I kept reciting, in my mind, the various short episodes which constituted, to my mind, Paul's decision to enlist. And I kept imagining what different things I might have said to avert Paul from that path, different arguments which might have appealed to him.

He toyed with the idea at first, or I assumed he was toying with it, the way he always picked up an idea but never followed through. The key difference being that the army was his idea, and not mine. I can see now that he must have been thinking about it long before he airily dropped it into the conversation that first time – the same way someone might explain they were considering a tuna sandwich for lunch. I dismissed the idea out of hand. It came back, now and then, more and more solid as an idea, and I kept batting it away, suggesting other ideas (other ideas which he picked up, but never followed through).

By the time he explained he was going to enlist, I'd already lost too much ground. I tried, finally, to muster my arguments against him, real arguments and not the "that'll never do" sort, but he was already gone from me. He listened to me explain the needless risk he was exposing himself to, and that, worst of all, he was relinquishing control over his fate – the control he'd only just begun to acquire in the first place. He nodded solemnly and told me that he had to go. *Had to*, like some kind of spiritual fanatic. Duty? I told him his only duty was to himself and those who loved him, that his real duty was not to do something so terrifically stupid. He swore at me and left. That was the last time I saw him standing on his own legs.

This is what happens when I tell people not to leave, and they do.

If I accidentally blind someone with a champagne cork, am I to blame?

If the cork flies directly into the eye of my unintended victim – am I guilty? If the cork ricochets off some surface and then strikes the eye of my unintended victim? If the cork ricochets not once but twice? Three times? How many rebounds will exculpate me?

What if the cork rebounds a thousand times? Ten thousand times? One hundred thousand times? Upon which rebound does my blame expire?

And how am I to answer if – after as many rebounds as will void my guilt – my victim says, "But had you never been here, I'd still have both eyes"?

Must we say, simply, "Bad luck"?

Or is it my duty to ensure the projectile never leaves the barrel of the bottle? By letting it fly am I taking responsibility for its whole course, rebounds and all?

After all, surely the man who shoots his gun into the ground acts more kindly than the man who shoots his into the air and says, "Let it land where it may. If it lands in a child's head, it wasn't my intention."

The interaction of physical forces may be amoral, but has moral consequences: the bookshelf cannot be blamed for falling on the family dog, but the death of the dog is a moral act. If we are to say, "The bookshelf fell purely by chance and there is no moral question about it," then we take a nihilistic view.

Someone put the bookshelf there. That is, someone is responsible for the physical fact of the bookshelf. Indeed, most moral dilemmas are predicated upon the physical realm, on the interaction of forces and structures we cannot control: illness, accident, chance. So-called *acts of God*. If a baby cuts itself on a knife, we blame the parent. We say the parent is responsible for the child's well-being, no matter where the child rebounds.

Murder and death, after all, are the moral expressions attributed to physical phenomena. Without morality, a death is the termination of a node: the cessation of a particular set of biological activities within a given node. It is our morality which groups these biological activities together as Life.

That is to say, morality is contingent upon our physical *being*.

At the very least we can say of physical bodies: when we emit a projectile, or increase a given body's velocity, that projectile becomes a moral proxy for ourselves. Likewise, when we effect an impulse or generate any force, that force belongs to us, insofar as it expresses our will.

We can understand this is true because shooting someone is a crime. It is understood that, though the shooter doesn't directly kill his victim, he intends death and effects it indirectly. That is, he applies the mechanism of gun and bullet in order to kill. So, while in the physical realm it is the bullet that kills and the gun that emits the bullet, in the moral realm we say simply the shooter has done it.

What do we say when the same physical events occur – the shooter kills the person, via the application of forces – but the shooter didn't intend the consequences? Do we just say, "Bad luck"?

In law, this concept is referred to as *mens rea* (guilty mind).

For the purposes of law, we stratify culpability according to exactly how guilty the perpetrator's mind is. In the cork example, someone blasting their victim directly in the eye would demonstrate *direct intention*. Our question, however, pertains more to the concepts of *recklessness* and *negligence*.

After all, can we not compare the flying cork with a reckless drunk's flailing limbs? The drunk, like the cork, can't control his actions. The drunk, therefore, isn't responsible – but the sober man who drinks the bottle is. The sober man who drinks himself senseless says, "Let me wander where I may." He is reckless. When he wakes the next morning he must account for the actions of his other self. He cannot say, "But I was someone else that night."

When the bullet falls from the sky and lands in the child's head, the shooter must say, "I shot that child, though it wasn't my aim."

When the cork strikes the person's eye, I must say, "Through my recklessness, I did that," and take responsibility.

When the bombs launched far away rebound on the Underground, the politician must say, "I admit I was reckless."

Yesterday, when I saw my father's mouth was covered by an oxygen mask, I was vaguely relieved. The awkwardness of our latter-day conversations immediately subsided – I was able to talk in fragments, to myself, almost. I could sense even my father preferred it – sensed the possibility that the breathing apparatus was his idea.

My father's doctor – a brilliant youth – recommended me plenty of exercise, especially walking. For my back.

"Get some audiobooks, and go out for a long walk in the evening," he told me. This is the kind of impression I must give people.

She says my interpretation of my own relationships is skewed.
She says my father isn't distant, but rather I enforce distance.
She has a skill for blaming me.

   She says I'm exhibiting *projection*. She delineated the ways.
   She said she was worried about how much weight I'd lost.

Remembering the early days with her provides sometimes a moment of real joy, then followed by a quite deep sadness. Other times it is only a sadness, less deep. But never only joy.

I was able to decode one of the songs in her manuscript – an early one, the scribblings of an abandoned jingle. It is titled "Themes for Touchstone". It is in F major (F). The time signature is 3/4 or waltz time. The B-flat (B♭) is prominent in each variation. It was quite easy to play, the left hand simply playing a bass chord (or note, in my case), allowing me to concentrate on the movement of the right hand. Sometimes, though, the left stumbled over the B♭.

Do I remember this music? Can I pick it out from a hazy memory? Perhaps it was after dinner. The child was in bed, asleep, or listening – like me. I tell myself I remember it, as I play. Perhaps the memory is what makes it easy to play – because I can hear, before I touch the next note, what the next note should be. Or perhaps that is the strength of her composition.

I should ask Amy.

My back is nearly better. I've been running, in defiance of the audiobooks and walking therapy recommended to me. I was fascinated to find I still own a pair of tracksuit trousers. And I have enough T-shirts, from various epochs.

I now pay over £50 per month for access to a private gymnasium. The sum is fairly astronomical. Maybe I was punishing myself, signing that direct debit order. When the instructor asked me whether I'd ever been "inducted" to a gym before, I told her I'd once been a policeman, as if policing were a superset of aerobics. In any case, she left me alone.

And I was surprised, above all, by how my lower back took the whole thing – without even a twinge or cramp. At least, after the first few disorienting steps on the treadmill. Of course, the rest of me soon ached – and I tasted blood after a few minutes – and by evening my calf muscles had set like concrete.

The two of them met in that detention – another Saturday morning detention for Paul, I forget what for – in the early days it was mainly his boisterousness, his tendency to shout and clown in lessons, or one time for spitting in a boy's hair.

Amy was struggling with her marks. Until Year Nine she'd been an almost straight-A student – or so I'd thought. In all the parents' evenings I'd attended (of course there'd been a professional awkwardness at such times, which I tried hard to ignore) her teachers had expressed delight in Amy, so that I believed she'd prosper with just a little encouragement, left to her own devices, more or less.

But it happened that when she entered Year Nine the reports that came back no longer reflected the child's delightfulness but rather her projected grades for GCSEs. Then the Bs and Cs came out (even a strident D in Maths). I waited until we'd finished eating dinner, the three of us, tried to avoid the issue that was utmost in my mind. Then I told her: "It would seem your teachers have a fairly low opinion of your academic abilities."

Her small face was shocked, enough that her mouth hung open. She looked at her mother, then emitted a lame, "No."

"They don't have very high hopes for your GCSE grades."

She looked at me in confusion, almost angrily.

"They're not for ages anyway."

"Your teachers are predicting you'll make something of a dunce of yourself."

My wife reprimanded me, then rose, gathering the plates from the table, evacuating.

Amy was frowning. I could see, even at the time, she was close to tears. Why was I so hard on her? Surely I knew it wouldn't do any good?

"What did you feel, when you saw those predicted grades?"

Did I ask my daughter that? Or have I pressed Angela's question into the memory?

She dropped her head, looked at the table, stared at the tabletop, must've been studying the grain for all the immobility of her stare.

"Nothing," she said.

"Nothing at all?" I didn't believe her.

She didn't answer.

"Your teachers have practically branded you an idiot and you don't even take offence?"

She kept her gaze on the table, dead still. I sensed tears.

What did I want from her? I think I wanted her to admit her true feelings, her true vulnerability. And then, I suppose, we could commiserate together – and plan a proper response.

The truth, of course, is that it was I who was offended by those grades. Not because Amy's academic performance reflected somehow on my own intelligence – but that those Bs and Cs (and that D) contradicted my own view of her chances. I judged her an A student, and those predicted grades were an affront to my judgement.

"You aren't angry?" I asked.

She didn't respond. Her gaze shifted, minutely – along the grain of the tabletop, as I imagine.

"Why aren't you angry?" I said.

She brought herself to – visibly shook herself out of her stupor, almost.

"What do you mean?"

"Do you believe you're a C student?" I asked.

Amy shrugged. Was it then that I unconsciously made the coupling between her and Paul? I had to stop myself.

"Have you really put no thought into this at all?"

"I don't care!"

My wife returned, didn't sit down but gripped the back of the chair she'd previously sat upon, and said, "Perhaps we should talk about this another time."

"I just want to say one thing," I said, and Amy gave a throaty sigh. "I think you're capable of attaining whatever grades you want."

She was looking, again, at the tabletop, but glancing all over its surface, now. She had her knees up to her chin, ungainly in the chair.

"So if you don't, it'll be because you *don't care*."

I paused, tried to subdue something.

"C isn't a fail." She peered up at me, over the crenellations of her knees.

I took my glasses off. I rubbed my right eye. There was still some residual tension I felt, from the discovery of the predicted grades, of the betrayal, of something being wrong.

"Listen to me. You're intelligent."

This immediately returned her gaze to the table.

"You have that much for free. The truth is, that isn't worth very much. Morally, it's worth nothing."

I saw, in profile, her eye dart my way, as if I'd said something queer. Which perhaps I had. My wife adjusted her grip on the chair, shifted her weight.

"When you have talent, you mustn't squander it. I mean morally. It would be my failing if I let you. So I want you to come to school with me this Saturday."

At this, her head rose quite clear from her knees as she cried, "What!"

And in the next breath: "Mum, that's not fair – why should I go to that school, anyway? And on a Saturday? I'm not going."

And I remember her mother said: "Love, you have to work hard at school."

"I'm not going to that school, and definitely not on a Saturday!"

"I appreciate you don't want to go," I said.

"I'm not going! End of."

"I appreciate you'd like to avoid going," I said.

"I'm not. I'm not going."

"And I appreciate it's frustrating for you, that your say in this counts for so little."

"I'm not *going!*" This time with a vague, disbelieving smile.

"All the while you don't put the effort in, I'll have to resort to these kinds of measures."

She kept shaking her head, so that I was sure she must be getting dizzy.

"I'm not going and that's that."

"You are."

"I'm not!"

"You are, primarily because I'm your father and have decided so."

"I don't care!"

"And secondarily because I'm bigger than you and can make you do what I want."

She gritted her teeth.

"Come Saturday, I'll drag you out of bed by your hair and deliver you to that school in your pyjamas if necessary."

She wanted, I could see, to appeal to her mother – who had let go of the chair and rocked back on her heels, as if to distance herself from the edict.

We discussed, of course, my threat. She kept referring to *your threats*, as if I'd made more than one.

Do you think it was healthy to physically threaten a child?

The hair-pulling, in particular, came in for scrutiny. There was, she felt, a tinge of misogyny about it. That I was *punishing her femininity*.

At one point, she went so far as to describe me as a "thug", and I told her I didn't think she'd ever seen a thug or had any idea at all about what that word meant or whom it described.

"I'm a thug, and you're a privately educated twit," I said, and she recoiled visibly, was momentarily cast adrift.

"I don't see what my education has to do with any of this," she muttered.

So I said, "Your costly American education. Are you the dual-citizenship type? I think you are."

She couldn't help replying, "What on earth is that supposed to mean?"

I tried to read from her response how near the mark I was. I suppose her endless criticism had affected me, made me tetchy.

"You have your assumptions and you're sticking to them fast," I said. "You're not capable of actually listening to me – instead you have some cartoon version of me in your head that you listen to. I talk and talk and you still have no idea about me, everything gets distorted by your assumptions about who I am, what my motivations are, which are always nefarious, of course. And then, on the other hand, you hardly talk at all except to berate me, and it seems I've gathered your character fairly well."

And she said, "Why are you trying to compete with me?" Then she rested her chin in her hand, locking her jaw shut in case she might answer her own question.

I considered a response, but before I could speak she did follow up –

"Do you feel you've been in a war against private education, in your career?" As if her last question were merely a jab to keep me at a distance, while she restored her stance and balance.

It took me a moment to realize the question wasn't humorous.

"I don't have anything against private schools."

"*Privately educated twit*," she said. "Just empty words?"

"Not empty, entirely."

She sat back in her chair, pretended to consult her notes, or actually did.

"It's only natural to form biases," she said.

"Biases?" I said.

She waited a moment. These are the moments she most relishes: the unfurling of her theses, the putting me in my place.

"You can't just disagree with a particular point of view. You've staked out a position and everything outside of it is the enemy. So it's natural that you're biased against private education. You've picked your side."

"Picked my side?" I chewed on the phrase a moment. "You believe they're comparable. You believe one against the other is like McDonald's versus Burger King, denominations of the same church, as it were."

She stared at me.

"Children have attempted to murder each other outside my

school premises. And do you know my first reaction? Relief. Because they didn't dare try it in the school grounds. Because of me. Well, at least I managed that much. They can stab each other outside, fight and kill each other outside, like dogs, if they have to. But not in my school. A private school teaches subjects like History and Art and English and Physics and Maths – but we have to teach these boys Decency, Respect, How to Sit Up Straight, How Not to Mumble, How to Spell and Add Up. Some of them can't read, *for Christ's sake.* And you think we'll teach them Shakespeare? Thirteen-year-old boys who can barely grasp *the back of a fucking cereal box.*"

She looked at me as if I might go on. As if there were anything to add.

Why didn't your wife intervene, when you fought with Amy?

And

I'm trying to square your wife as you describe her, and as she acted those times. What changed?

Isn't that Angela's style, always *trying to square* things. She thinks – but doesn't have the temerity to say it – that I gelded my wife, somehow, with my *controlling nature*.

So maybe Angela is drawing me out on this, baiting the truth from me. I can't tell any more. But if I smooth over those details, if I omit the parts where we might have fought, husband and wife, where she accused me or told me to be reasonable, said she wouldn't stand for this or that – well, I'm entitled to that much, aren't I? It makes no difference if I skip the sadder parts, which are mere flavourings to you anyway. What good do such details do? Except to make the telling more plausible?

Well I didn't have to drag my daughter to that Saturday detention, by the hair or otherwise. But Amy was frosty with me
for the rest of that week, frostier than usual. She answered
me in monosyllables or ignored me outright when I tried to be
pleasant. But her mother intervened – I heard the two of them
talking softly in her room one evening. I believe my wife was
negotiating on my behalf.

You mustn't be so hard on her.
    And, *She doesn't want to be your enemy, you know.*
    And, *You should trust her more.*
    These were some of the things she'd say to me.
    That I never followed her advice – that I could only some-
times try, and fail to – is a sadness to me now. That I troubled
her with my fights with our daughter, that I was the cause of
such conflict in our lives together, when, as it turned out, we
had so little time.
    Every memory of her now is measured by its distance to her
destruction. The closer to that day I venture in memory, the
more tragic her every word and gesture is to me, as if it were
all foretold.

So, thanks to my wife's negotiation, Amy was cooperative on
that Saturday morning, and we drove in silence to the school,
Amy in the passenger seat, her arm resting on the thin ledge
where the car door meets the window, her head resting in her

hand. Now and then her elbow would slip from the movement of the car, and she'd sigh and reposition her arm.

I think she was surprised by how busy the school was. Indeed, most of my Saturday detainees were surprised, the first time they saw the school's weekend life. Outside the term timetable we leased the rooms to a variety of organizations – the Saturday music school was particularly popular. In fact, it was this busyness that served as a kind of cover for Amy's presence – and indeed the slightly older, mixed-sex crowd of music students often cowed the detained boys who were so confident during school hours.

Paul, for whom there probably wasn't much novelty left in these detentions, was already waiting outside the Maths classroom that I made my home on these mornings. I bid him good morning and introduced him to Amy, explaining that she was my daughter. Paul nodded, glancing at her. I unlocked the door and gestured for them to go ahead.

Paul picked his usual spot, front row, at the middle desks, and Amy hesitated, finally picking the desk by the door, perhaps for a quick escape. I enquired after Paul's spirits this morning, taking my seat, and, as I predicted, his tone was moderated by Amy's presence. He said he was OK.

I asked him to remind me why he was there, though of course I knew, and by then I think he was aware of my ploys.

"Because I fought with Morgan in class," he said. The reference to the second combatant was pointed, being that Morgan wasn't there in detention.

"And what homework will you be doing for the next hour?" I asked.

"Maths," he said.

"Good. Get out your exercise books, please."

Amy was watching him intently. She was slightly younger in actual years but a little older in temperament. I turned to her. I was surprised by how exposed I felt by Amy's presence.

"Amy, are you working on your French this morning?"

And she hoisted her backpack to the desk and got her things out, and Paul watched her with the same intensity. But then he turned to look at me, astonished, perhaps, by the possibility that I could ever have reproduced.

Then I took out my own folders and, with my effects in place, I said, "Let's do some work, shall we?"

Amy and Paul shared a glance with each other – the very first connection, perhaps – and then they attended to their work.

Angela asks me when I was most fatherly towards Amy.

As with all questions dealing in superlatives, it takes me a great deal of time to consider the likely candidates.

Angela is sitting opposite me, moored just in front of her desk. Her chair is on wheels and the seat rotates, so that, when she wants to be, she is highly mobile in her chair. It looks expensive, not your typical Argos number.

When she reads my thoughts she'll be behind her desk. I find the desk and her sitting at it unusual. Perhaps this is more of the *unanalytic behaviour* she was talking about.

But as I say, for the time being she is on the fringe of her desk's protection, and I am to understand we are conducting an open, fair dialogue this way.

I am beginning to suspect that Angela is asking another trick question – a question she knows I can't answer – when she interrupts her carefully constructed silence by saying,

"For instance, there was that time when she came to you, in the night, having a panic attack."

It surprises me – though it shouldn't – that she remembers these things. That she is becoming fluent in these stories that perhaps constitute my life. I imagine it is gratifying to other types of personality: to have someone finally listen and recall their life, as hardly anyone will do (except true friends and lovers – and even then).

I look queryingly at her, though I know exactly what she's talking about – perhaps, just like her other clients, I want her to retell my life to me, as she understands it, and find some affirmation this way. And, of course, she obliges and says, "I think that was a very tender moment between you both."

"I don't think *panic attack* is fair," I say, in defence of my seven-year-old daughter. "The panic was caused by a frightening change in her perceptions. In a sense, the panic itself was well-founded."

"Yes," she says, "how did she express it? It was something quite succinct, I remember." Though I believe she remembers exactly.

"Everything is small," I said.

"Everything is small," Angela repeats. "Do you think you were disarmed, to some degree, due to the circumstances?"

I wait for her to elucidate.

"Amy comes to you, in the night, in a state of panic. Your wife is away that night, and so you have to contend with your daughter's fear on your own. And then your daughter tells you the cause of her fear – that everything is small."

"A visual hallucination," I said. I rather felt she was overly cherishing my daughter's naive phrase. "The first of a recurrent condition," I said. I was trying to counter Angela's spin on things, perhaps. To lay out some facts.

"What was your initial reaction? It must've been bewildering, before you understood that she was suffering from a hallucination."

I thought back. "I wanted to comfort her," I said. "She was frightened, so I held her. The cause of her fear, and trying to understand it – that came after."

"And she clung to you," she said. Again, her fluency in my story was strange to me. I didn't like her telling it.

"We went around the house," I said, "touching things, one after another, to see the size of them. The piano. A doorknob. The taps in the bathroom. Everything we touched was far away, she said. Even as we touched it."

"Did it alarm you?" she said.

"My main concern was how I'd explain it to my wife the next day. I could see it was hard enough for Amy to describe. I didn't fancy I could tell it quite so vividly, this business of things looking small and far away, or big and far away, or slow, or fast. I wondered about how I'd explain it, without making it sound worse."

"And how long was it before the episode passed?" she said.

"I'm not sure," I said, "I suppose it must've been about an hour. Something like that."

"And then she went back to bed?"

"I tried taking her back to her bed, after we'd done a lap of the house, in case lying down might help, but she didn't want to. I managed to get her to compromise and she lay on our bed, but she said closing her eyes was too frightening, that it was even worse, so I sat next to her and tried to distract her. I got the radio and put it nearby, on some late-night talk show, just as a kind of background noise. At first I tried her on her times tables, but she wasn't having that, so instead I resorted to telling her about how nice she'd feel when she woke up tomorrow morning and all the nice things she'd do, since tomorrow was Sunday and Mum would be home and we might all go to the park together or even go to the cinema, since she deserved a treat after all this scary business, and that all she needed was some sleep. And eventually I think it passed. Or she fell asleep, one way or another."

"And what did you do, then?" she asked.

I pictured it. "I sat next to her on the bed. I didn't want her waking up and me being asleep. So I turned the radio down a bit, but left it on, in case it helped, and I read for a while, until I was convinced she was sleeping quite soundly, then I went to sleep next to her."

"And how did you feel, while she was sleeping by your side?"

I hesitated. "I felt guilty."

She waits for me to explain.

I think back to that night. Angela's tender moment, which was my personal nightmare.

"Amy was born premature," I say. "About twenty-eight weeks along." I look at the palms of my hands. "I felt guilty then, too. I was very scared, then."

I hold my hands apart in front of me, so Angela could imagine it too.

"She was so tiny. It was frightening. I held my tiny daughter like this, cupped, like rainwater, and prayed she'd be OK."

I close my hands like a book.

"And that's how I felt, again, that night."

Angela's mistake is in trying to make me "get over" my wife's death. But that would mean consigning her to the past, finally. And, really, that would mean consigning myself to the past.

And I'm not quite ready for that.

Is it just pitiful self-indulgence to learn to play her old songs? She'd laugh at me, no doubt. She'd feel a twinge of embarrassment, too, as I played them, not just for me, but for herself, I'm sure. The better I get, the more embarrassed she'd be to hear me play them – to hear her music played to her.

Sometimes I do look over the pictures of us. The holiday snaps – sad that it's only the holidays that get recorded. But what about all the precious days between? I should've documented her every waking morning, her every breakfast, lunch and dinner. I should have asked Amy to take a nightly portrait of us two together, when we all lived together. Maybe an archive of every day we shared would be enough to sustain me. But instead it's the same holiday snaps, a bright beach in Portugal or a crumbling Sicilian backdrop, and mostly I'm imagining those days in between, all the time before and after the picture – the picture that hardly expresses anything, a single posed frame, but a totem all the same of the life immediately before and after. In some she has a silly face, and there is something true about those. Or in Amy's sullen grimace. Or in my own face – either too serious or grinning fakely. And then once again I'm imagining the flights back, the long tedious stretches together, and the arrival home, and the re-settling into normal life. I look at the holiday snaps as a portal to those other days, but I don't get far before my memory – and my imagination – fails me.

I remember when I proposed to her. Her teasing look, as if she were considering her options. But after she'd answered the mask slipped and she had to fight the tears. And her answer? "Obviously." With a laugh. Obviously.

Imagining what Amy might think about ███████:

Obviously I've spoken to Amy about the matter. Or perhaps not obviously. I basically trust Amy's judgement, not that it's right, but that it's essentially consistent. But Amy's real talent is for reserving judgement entirely.

I think this is her approach to the question of ████. Her favourite refrains: *Does it matter?* And, *It doesn't help me to think about it.*

So that would be where I start: It doesn't help me to think about ████. What benefit is there in blaming anyone?

I have to pause there, as I believe Amy might. When a person comes up with such a defence, a kind of protection against having to think about it, the whole purpose is to foster this kind of pause – a terminal pause.

Amy is pragmatic. Like her mother. In life she's usually determinedly in motion. She never relaxes in the true sense of the word – she constantly keeps her mind ticking over on whatever trivial distraction is in front of her (often her phone), and I see this is a kind of defence as well.

I know I'm becoming too much like Angela, now.

But surely there's something a little frantic in how Amy flits from purpose to purpose. In any case she's done the opposite of what I've done: she has decidedly *not wallowed*. She has steeled herself – or was already steeled.

So my problem with Amy's verdict, if she were ever to

be drawn on one, is this: that it's too slight by far. That she spends her life avoiding making such judgements. She might say, "Yes, ██████████ is partially to blame." Or, "Many people contributed to what happened to my mother." Or, "The blame is diffuse. Pinning it on one person is blockheaded and wrong. You cannot blame a single person for a whole string of different events. He wasn't a tyrant, we live in a democracy, his decisions could have been overturned. Therefore you cannot blame ██████████ without blaming every politician" (I admit this is a strong point) – "such is the diffuse nature of the events which led up to what happened with my mother."

At this point perhaps I (or someone else?) would have to interject, to avoid another of her terminal pauses. Or maybe not – as I imagine the workings of her mind, a completely different thought occurs to her, one that I admit I am powerless against:

"What would Mum want?"

I bet she'd let it sit there a few moments.

"Mum wouldn't be interested in blaming anyone. She'd want us to get on with things. To carry on with life. So isn't there a duty, to her?"

She has me there, nearly. Perhaps meekly I might say to her: "You can't defer such judgements to someone else. Of course, I don't doubt your mother wouldn't want blame and anger ruling our lives."

And this is where the discussion breaks down, I suppose: when I come out with it, that her mother's opinions and wishes are void. Because she's dead and her influence over us has drawn to a close, and that there is no honouring her memory, as there are no ghosts or spirits, and when anyone says they are honouring a memory they are helping themselves to something false and crass with phrases like *She's in a better place now*, or *She'll live on in our hearts*, or *What survives of us is love* – which is only to say we expire absolutely and completely. To honour a memory is to pretend death is something else, all for our own meagre comfort.

And, of course, Amy is shouting at me for what I'm saying about her mother, and perhaps decides at some point to storm out, to run away from my words and the possibility of their meaning and the possibility of their worming into her conscious and making her suffer with thought. And then I'm alone again, debating now only with myself.

"In your imagined debate with Amy, I found it interesting that you made Amy say this: – "

(She has her glasses on, has my notes raised in front of her like a theatre director squinting at the script.)

"You cannot blame ███████ without blaming every politician."

(She puts the script down, takes off her glasses.)

"But you don't counter her point. Which, of course, is really your point."

(She pauses – I'm ready.)

"Is this the stalemate you've reached, in this argument with yourself?"

I smile indulgently at her. I take my time now – now it's my turn to be the therapist. I have all the material, all the knowledge and the expertise. I'm ready to offer her an interpretation she can keep in her dossier, one for the archives.

"It's not an argument with myself. That should be clear. I wouldn't conduct an argument with myself in that manner at all. So for me there's no stalemate."

"So what's your rebuttal?"

"Simple: the buck has to stop somewhere. For instance, at the school – you might ask whose fault was it, all that litter in the playground?"

(She's surprisingly quick.)

"You mean you think it was your fault? The children's litter?"

"Not solely, of course," I say. "Not even mainly, maybe. But if a passer-by were to see the state of my playground – and see and hear the gulls that circled overhead – he might think to himself, 'That's not right, I should have a word with the headmaster about the state of the school playground, about how many crushed drinks cans are being kicked around by the boys like hockey pucks so that it's a game to them – about the swirling tornadoes of crisp packets and plastic wrapping.' Certainly, he wouldn't think, 'That's not right, I'll have a word with the children there, and tell them they must recycle.'"

"He might," she says. "That might be a perfectly sensible thought."

I shake my head. "Even if you find the culprits, they're only partaking in a culture And who's responsible for the culture?"

"And you say the headmaster is responsible? Top to bottom? From floor plans to paint chips?"

I stare at her, to let her know that she's the one who's said it.

"It's … a little exacting," she says, I believe humorously.

"Who else, then?" I say, not humorously at all.

She doesn't answer. Possibly she wants me to answer my own question.

"Exactly," I say. And if I'm saying it only to myself – fine.

"It's a little inhuman, even," she says. "Perhaps the more humane answer is that it's no one person's responsibility. The responsibility is collective. The whole school bears it."

I nod. I don't think even she believes these thoughts are worth the air they're spoken upon.

"An authority of convenience, then? Take charge here, pass the buck there. The one at the top will prosper, the ones at the bottom will take the blame. Well, I suppose that would suit me."

"And the children bear no responsibility at all? Even the ones dropping the litter?"

"Of course they do."

She laughs. I'm caught between anger and incredulity.

"Is there anyone not to blame?"

Angela commands me: "Write from the perspective of ███ ███. What does he think of your situation?"

I could try to fulfil the brief, except for that question. I believe Angela hasn't thought it through. How would ███ ever come to be aware of my predicament? Am I to assume some backstory has been developed to facilitate his frank contemplation of the matter? – perhaps with a letter outlining the situation (a brief recap of the wars, then summary of a particular node in the vast network of consequences, namely: my wife, Paul, myself). Well, who wrote the letter? Did I write the letter? Should I start first with the letter and then answer the case from his view? Or does he come to this knowledge by some other means? Is it a dialogue, perhaps? Should I simply imagine him in Angela's place, and the conversation we might have?

In any case, I think Angela underestimates the feat of characterization she is demanding.

Because, ███████████████████████████████
██
██
██
██
██
██
█████████████████████████████████
████████████████████████████████████

Over the years, I've doled out many cans, and though I've occasionally varied the recipe, the general flavour remains.

I am, as I've said, superficial.

Angela's right: I'm suffering because I'm not in control of anything. Certainly not this grief. Nor my sleep or moods or bowels, even – all of me is off-kilter. I'm unwell. I get headaches or coughs out of nowhere, my gums bleed from time to time. I've become forgetful of obvious facts like what day it is or why I'm heading somewhere. Before I seemed to fit perfectly inside my body, but now I'm its unhappy tenant, plagued by mould and damp and bad plumbing. Instead of fixing it, I'm receding into the ever smaller inhabitable corner: the bedsheets are mildewed and cling to me wetly in the night, there are snails on the windowsills and mice prowling the oven. If I let my corner get any smaller, eventually something will give. I'll restore myself through the constant clicking of the light switch on and off. My grief started as a mental thing, but is now a bodily thing, and will soon leap the barrier into the outside world and take control of every slow beat of my days.

And perhaps that's been my excuse: that I'm powerless. All the while that I'm cowed in my dwindling little corner I'm excused from – from everything. From taking responsibility. From taking control.

I've taken to *resistance training*. Which is to say *lifting weights*, though I'm not sure which phrase is more odious.

I started very lightly, impersonating the movements of the burlier men – reclining on a padded bench, pressing a pair of dumbbells towards the ceiling, up and down. I started too lightly – a nymph-like five kilos – then immediately doubled that, pushing ten kilos on each side. It seemed straightforward enough, and I even ventured twelve kilos and tried a few different movements, such as the *chest fly*. The whole thing felt satisfying and easy, so I tried fifteen kilos on each side, and my arms trembled with the weight, and I grimaced as I lifted them, but it was certainly preferable to the tedium of running on the spot.

The next day I was very sore, sorer than my exertions seemed to warrant. But the day after that was true agony. It was like the bands of my chest had dried up tight. I could barely put on my shirt.

This is called Delayed Onset Muscle Soreness (DOMS).

"Themes for Touchstone" continues across many pages of my wife's manuscripts. After about three pages, the key is revised from F major to B-flat major. The time signature remains the same. F major and B-flat major both share the flattened B, but B-flat major has an additional flat: E.

The change takes me a while to get accustomed to – I keep missing the E♭, playing E natural instead (E♮).

These sketches are considerably "jazzier".

In my frustration with that unwelcome extra flat, I look back over the development of the piece and I notice there are three preceding pages I've missed, not headed "Themes for Touchstone" but just hastily labelled "touchstone" in the top corner of a page. They are not in waltz time, but 4/4.

The very first fragment attributed to the Touchstone commission is a single bar on a single clef:

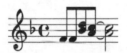

I look at the progression of her thoughts and try to assign them a day in my memory, or make one up. I imagine what she's thinking as she draws the marks. I imagine her face, her look of total concentration. I imagine the weather outside. I imagine her gnawing hunger, her shifts in posture. The pencil marks are thickest and blackest where she's least certain – or so it seems to my eyes. I imagine being back there with her.

Angela reiterates her concern about my weight. My back is good, my injuries healed, mostly, but she brings up the matter of my weight as more than a professional concern.

"I've begun to worry about you."

I admire the construction – *I've begun* – not *I'm beginning*, which of course has never begun. She is forceful, in her way, even if that's what I find unattractive in her. There is a push-iness, there. She wants to barge in on my mind. I imagine the bluntness of her questions is usually an effective battering ram.

"What did you eat this morning?"

Again, not *What are you eating?*, in general.

"I've lost weight, because of my new exercise regime."

She pauses, actually writes something down. Without moving, I try to peer at her notepad, but it's impossible to see anything. She frowns.

"It's good you're exercising. I'd like to talk about that later. What did you eat this morning, though?"

For some reason, I feel like a prisoner, in an interrogation. The meal, which I vividly recall, is a secret to some crime I've committed, or commissioned, perhaps. I swallow, as if I'm swallowing a bite, having mouthed it off the fork. In front of the television – the 24-hour news. Straight from its black plastic carton – not even decanted, to spare the washing up. It was an occasion that even I knew was desperate, in that it had the appearance of desperateness, even if I felt none – except for that awareness of how it would appear to an outside observer.

That I would be judged a sad case, even if I didn't feel it sad. I sensed that this might be how mad people felt, dimly, before slipping finally into their mania.

"It was a microwave meal." The utterance actually caught in my throat. I took off my glasses to knuckle my eyes. But Angela didn't appear moved by the confession.

"For breakfast?" she asked. "What kind?"

I shook my head. To name it, somehow, was beyond my powers, at that point. Because it brought to me an even more pitiful scene – at the supermarket, in front of a bay of microwave meals, making my selection, eyeing the carefully photographed images on those cardboard boxes, imagining the tastes that were packaged therein, perhaps even imagining the very scene of their consumption – in front of the television, the 24-hour news. And each with its own mocking description, as you might read from the menu of a restaurant.

"Why won't you tell me?" she asks, and she has thawed a little, taking pity on me, perhaps.

I shake my head again.

"I find it too sad," I struggle to say.

She is bemused, I can tell, but tolerant of me by now, as am I of her.

"Tell me why it makes you sad."

Because, I try to say, I don't feel, or don't think I feel, altogether so lonely. But when I come to describe it, I feel sad, as if for someone else.

I don't say: My wife would tease me. I can't say: She'd laugh at me, accuse me, call me a fool, bring me to my senses.

I have purchased a *sparring dummy*. In fact, I paid extra for the next-day delivery option, which was costly, given the thing's size.

I believe the two delivery men were surprised by my age. The senior's name was Ian – he was perhaps only ten years younger than me, whereas his colleague was a youth. Ian seemed to have a fairly developed opinion of my purchase – I was gratified by his enthusiasm.

It was only when they laid the box down in the front room that they – and I – could size up the state of my home. I was suddenly alarmed by it, by my negligence, by the parade of half-empty mugs and glasses, the unhoovered detritus gathering around the table, and the overloaded bin which had up until then remained invisible to me.

"We can install it?" Ian said. This was before I was aware he was called Ian. "Usually we install them," he said, turning to me, his friend resting one arm on the box, looking at the room, at my mess.

I thought I should turn the lights on or at least open the curtains – wondered that I hadn't already – preferred the half-dark.

I went to the box, tried to gather their attention to it.

"Is it so difficult?"

"Not if you do them for a living. This one has the force-meter, though. You'll want to make sure it's properly set up."

I had no idea where I wanted it. The box was by the bay

windows, so I told them they could install it there, and perhaps I'd move it later.

"Move it? You won't be moving it once it's all together. The base alone is over a hundred kilos. This one's good because it's solid, you don't have to fill it with sand or anything like that, like some of them. I don't think you'll want it so near the piano, there. What sort of training did you have in mind? You usually need a lot more space than this. I suppose you'll have to just do frontal strikes. Some people put them in their garden."

I sensed he considered me a lunatic. Perhaps he rambled in defiance of the dark mess we all stood in, which in silence might become morose, or even sinister. But there was something in how he said *You usually need a lot more space than this* – something I interpreted as a denigration, though it was probably my sensitivity about the room – but it made up my mind.

"Upstairs, then, I have just the place," and I smiled.

The youth closed his eyes. I wondered how many deliveries they'd made already this morning. How many heavy items they'd hauled up people's staircases. How many homes they'd denigrated with Ian's easy talk. But Ian himself nodded, appeared pleased to be hauling the box with the youth, and they took many breathless minutes to inch it up the stairs, while I looked down upon them from the landing, and turned the light on when they were halfway, as if marking some milestone.

It's in the bedroom. There's less space, if anything, but there's no piano or windows to break.

If you can imagine, it's a slightly purple-hued torso and head, completely limbless, sitting on a heavy plinth. Its physique (apart from missing all four limbs) is fabulous – its abdominal muscles, especially, are defined with deep ridges. Excitingly, it has an LED display where its eyes might be. The total effect is that of a space-age Greek marble.

The LED lights up when you strike the thing, displaying the force of the blow in Newtons, like a score. The display can represent four figures, presumably up to a mighty 9,999N, which I imagine is akin to being struck by a car. When they'd completed its installation, Ian launched a wild haymaker at it, rocking it madly on its base, and it beeped in acknowledgement of the blow, and we all looked to the display which shone 1421. He beckoned the youth to try and he declined, laughingly, though I suspect it may have been politeness, to either Ian or myself – Ian as the record-holder, myself as the owner.

When they were gone I took a cheeky swipe at the thing and it beeped and showed 510.

I dream of delivering a one-ton punch.

In Computing there is the concept of *abstraction*. Abstraction is when the programmer is shielded from the *implementation details* of a function or method or process. Abstraction is a desirable trait of a program or library.

For instance, a library that enables the programmer to interface with the internet via HTTP might have a function called, simply, *get*.

As a programmer, I might invoke this function like so:

SomeHTTPLibrary.get("www.google.com/ncr")

Or, in an Object-Oriented paradigm, it might be:

some_HTTP_object_instance.get("www.google.com/ncr")

As a programmer, I have no idea how the *get* function works – I need only consider it in the abstract (that it indeed "gets" the contents of the webpage), and can consider the process on a higher level – whether or not the request is successful, for instance, or what to do with the response.

This abstraction is common throughout human invention, as seen in the controls of a microwave or a car. The steering wheel is an abstraction – it could just as easily be a lever or a rein.

An Oyster card, too, is an abstraction. As is the trigger of a gun.

Now when I reminisce about some happy moment of course I feel as if I have Angela on my shoulder. She's neither my good nor bad angel – my indifferent angel, perhaps. My judgemental angel.

Sometimes I'll be at the sparring dummy, or running, and at some point my mind will demand some diversion, so I throw it a memory, like a log on the fire – and now I feel as if Angela is watching the memory too. It's not an entirely unpleasant feeling.

I was in the gym yesterday and we were warming down after a long training session. My shins were very sore and we were all in the so-called Plank position – that is, poised for a press-up that is never performed. There isn't much to think about in this position, except how slowly time passes sometimes, and the growing ache in the torso and shoulders. So of course a memory can make a fine distraction in these Plank moments. You have to pick on a subject quite at random, or otherwise risk failing to conjure anything except the notion of your own discomfort, and so yesterday I thought about cleaning the school desks with Paul, when he was in detention. I remember how amused he was by me, when I started spraying the desks with the foaming cleaning fluid and wiping away what appeared to be strata of graffiti with a rag. He asked me, "Don't they have someone else to do that?" And I told him we didn't, and we shouldn't need one anyway. "But we do," he said. "Need one." I looked at him meaningfully, and said clearly we didn't, we already had someone, and he gave me another incredulous look and asked if I thought I'd get through all the desks in the school on my own. "You'll never finish," he said. And I said, "I don't intend to."

But the problem with such fond recollections is that they run out too quickly, and then you're left back in the Plank moment – with the pain and lactic acid. The Body triumphing over the Mind.

So what I tried after that was a game: I imagined that, for every second of pain I suffered, ███ suffered with me. So when my midriff was scorched and my whole body shook feebly, I felt not my own anguish but his. Rather than shrink from the pain – rather than wish it would stop – I became overjoyed by it, fanatically sought to prolong and enhance it, so that I was finally alone, singularly braced in my Plank, shaking and dripping and everyone watching me.

To the Man Who Killed My Wife,

Revenge would be if I killed your wife.

Revenge is when the act is committed against the actor. Sometimes the act itself might be meaningfully mutated – for instance, if instead of your wife I ██████████████████████ ███████████████████████████. That would still be Revenge, because the Act, in the Abstract, will have been visited upon you.

That is: you killed someone I love, *therefore* I kill someone (or some) you love.

I believe you do love people, or are capable of love, and the evidence is in the love you have for yourself.

But Revenge, in such cases, isn't Right. The Bible makes a claim that *the righteousness of the righteous shall be upon him, and the wickedness of the wicked shall be upon him.* But I have no interest in Godliness, and no pretence of exacting any biblical sort of justice, so I leave Vengeance to silent divinity and instead I seek what is Right.

I have considered the matter at great length. I understand, now, that there is no philosophy that can satisfactorily reconcile the following: *A man causes suffering to a million souls, and receives none.*

To my knowledge, there is no ideology that can accommodate such a state as Right. Though admittedly I'm no scholar and may be ignorant of the diverse theologies of the world. My best understanding, therefore, is that your continued impunity is an *ideological omission* – such that has enabled *a man to cause suffering to a million souls, and receive none.*

I'm angry with my daughter. I even brought it up with Angela. For once, she took my side.

Amy visited me. She said she'd spoken with Granddad and that he mentioned I hadn't visited in over a week.

At this point I had to explain to Angela that I'd been distracted by my hobbies – that in order to enliven my existence I'd taken to a variety of new hobbies, and taken to them quite thoroughly.

"What kind of hobbies?" she said.

Exercise, cardiovascular and resistance training, just starting with martial arts, and the music, of course, both practical and theoretical, and computing as well, and networks and a little programming.

Angela nodded, wrote something in her notepad and underlined it, and asked me to continue my story.

My daughter's arrival was a surprise. She didn't ring me beforehand. She came straight from the hospital, straight from seeing my father, her granddad. It was pouring down outside and her hair and face were beaded with rain. She never carries an umbrella with her. In this aspect she takes after me.

Her first words were an accusation: that I hadn't been to see Granddad.

I was going to warmly invite her in; I hesitated.

"That's right," I said. "I haven't."

"Why not?"

She seemed content to have the conversation on the doorstep.

I beckoned her inside.

"Can I get you some tea?"

She blew an exhausted puff of air. She said, "Yes, please."

She passed through the hallway, unravelling her scarf from her neck and lifting her handbag from her shoulder. She dumped her things on the sofa in the living room, stood with a wide stance looking around her, hands on hips like a trouble-shooter. I waited a moment by the living-room doorway, feeling my existence under scrutiny. She said, "It stinks in here, Dad."

At this point Angela wondered whether I was perhaps relishing too much the details of the telling. She said so, after wondering.

The truth is, I was myself revisiting the memory.

"I want you to get to the point," she said. "The argument," she said.

"We argued about my piano-playing."

"How?"

"Perhaps it started when I observed her standing in my living room."

I told Amy I'd been busy with my projects, then regretted calling them *projects*. Oddballs have *projects*. That was the look she gave me.

I told her I have to keep busy, and she nodded and asked me whether I was taking care of myself. I told her good care, and offered to show her my sparring dummy.

"I don't want to see your sparring dummy, Dad."

"Most people would be curious," I said.

"No, they wouldn't." She was looking around the living room (which I'd mostly tidied up. I sensed she was trying to detect my negligence from the bits and pieces that remained).

The truth is, I said, that I was exercising more than I ever had. I was probably fitter than I'd ever been, in some respects. And I was keeping my wits sharp, with music and computing.

"Computing?" she asked, eyebrow full-high. "What are you computing?"

I thought about it. "All sorts," I said.

"Granddad's very ill," she said.

"I'm aware of that," I said.

I told Angela it had been probably eight or nine days since I had visited my father, in the hospital. His doctor, the brilliant youth, had moved on – though I didn't discover where – and had been replaced by a less brilliant, more senior (in age, at least) doctor. Though this had nothing to do with the hiatus in my visits.

"It's not fair to leave him alone for so long."

"Then you should visit him more," I said.

It was a bad thing to say. It was a bad thing to want to say. Her expression was very bitter, after that.

"I visit him as often as I can."

"I daresay." Unnecessary. Completely unnecessary.

"*Piss off.* I'm trying."

"Please don't swear." Why? Why not swear? These inert ripostes kept dropping from my mouth – except they weren't inert, for her. My daughter tells me I am being negligent, that she is trying to be dutiful, and I nod and tell her not to swear.

"Fuck off. *Don't swear.* How about don't be a shit? And bloody – *tidy up* a bit." Her anger was threatened by laughter. "You're turning into a bachelor." I was relieved by her laughter.

I told her I was sorry that I'd not visited him, that it was good she was concerned for her grandfather, and that with regard to tidying up I made no promises. She smiled at my attempt.

"He's so ill, Dad," she said. "I don't like it." And then it was nearly tears again.

"I know," I said. "I don't, either."

"He's going to die," she said. For some reason the saying of it alarmed me. I was anguished by it, even. I didn't reply. She looked up at me – I'd stood up, for no purpose, except as if to walk away from her statement.

I said: "He's been deteriorating for a long time. Perhaps he'll get worse, perhaps he'll get better. We can't help it either way. I should spend more time with him. But every time is a cost. As you know. Perhaps I've needed some respite."

She nodded solemnly. "Some time to live like a bachelor," she said.

I was still standing. I offered her some tea, I think, at that point, the tea I hadn't got round to, or else I just went to the kitchen. She didn't follow, perhaps out of sensitivity.

"But that wasn't your argument. About the piano," said Angela.

"No, that was what we spoke of just before the argument. It wasn't an argument, really. I suppose the argument was everything before. When I brought back the tea from the kitchen, my daughter was on her phone. Partly to draw her attention, I suppose, I told her I'd been playing some of her mother's songs, or trying, and sat down at the piano, and lifted the fallboard. She stood up, phone lowered at her side, still glowing. She stood behind me as I turned through the pages of my wife's manuscript."

"What songs?" Amy said.

"They're all mixed together. I've just tried some of the easier bits, so far." I turned the page to "Themes for Touchstone", the latter pages, after the transition into B-flat major. I started playing, just some notes on the right hand at first, to remember the movements, then I brought in the left hand, played a few bars, paused, played them again. After the second iteration, I realized I couldn't confidently continue any further into the piece, so I stopped. I turned the page, and then another, and then asked Amy if she remembered this one, and again after settling my hands into place I started ineptly, played a few slow bars, then started again a little more smoothly, reached the end of the stave and stopped.

Now, my playing I know was second rate – it wasn't a performance. I suppose I wanted to bring her into the room with the two of us, with just a few phrases, like repeating something she'd said; one of her sayings.

But when I turned to Amy, she was laughing. I was surprised, more than upset, at first. I didn't ask her what she meant by laughing, didn't immediately realize it was me she was laughing at. Then she reached over my shoulder and closed the manuscript.

"Sorry," she said. "It's just weird, seeing you play."

But I can't imagine that was it.

"What kind of laughing was it?" Angela asked.

"Suppressed. Like a giggling schoolgirl."

"You're like a child, Dad," Amy said, and she left the room for the toilet, and I closed the piano's fallboard, wondering what she meant.

Today I went to see the monument in the park, and I contemplated the victims of that terrible day.

Terrible, still, isn't the right word.

The monument is a thing of beauty. It is Art, I suppose. Perhaps the only art to have touched me in my whole life. And not just because I lost my wife, I don't think.

I don't have much reason to pass that way, so when I go there it is to see the monument. I stand in front of it, on the path, and think of the time between then and now. I think of my wife and the different lives she could have led, except for that day. I imagine she never met me: never lived with me: never had cause to take that particular train on that particular day. The bombs explode, but she's not there. Instead she's with someone else – her husband – when the news breaks. She imagines what it's like to lose a loved one, she and her husband talk about it, how awful it is, how fortunate they are. And where am I, in this different outcome?

I'm alone, perhaps. In front of the monument, maybe. Thinking about what it must feel like, to lose someone. Wondering, perhaps, what it's like to have ever had someone to lose.

It was a while before the Sultan affair came to a head, perhaps a matter of a full term.

The woman who would later become my wife came into my office one evening, in quite similar circumstances to our first meeting, and told me she intended to resign.

I can't remember what I'd been working on at the time – it was quite late, too late for her to still be at the school, certainly, and probably for that reason she treated me with a degree of informality. I believe she'd made up her mind completely. She was standing, still, just inside the doorway. She looked happy.

"I'm so sorry to hear that," I said. I capped my pen and laid it on the desk. "Would you like to sit down?"

She did so.

"Can I get you a drink? I sometimes have a scotch around now." I looked at my watch theatrically.

She smiled. "I'm not much of a whisky drinker."

"I'm afraid my supplies are roughly limited to scotch. Otherwise there's tonic and soda water."

She thought about it. "I'll go for some soda water, then. Please."

"I'm sorry to hear you're considering leaving. I'm afraid you've caught me a little off-guard."

"That was my intention, probably. I don't want you to talk me out of it."

I handed her the water in a cut-glass tumbler. Our hands touched very briefly. I myself had gone for a scotch and soda.

"Is it foolish to ask why you want to leave?" I asked.

"Not foolish. Forgetful, maybe. But I don't think you've forgotten."

"Is it still the matter of discipline?"

"Yes, I'm afraid so."

I took a pondering sip. She was resting her glass in her lap, on her crossed leg.

"What do you make of Sultan?" I said.

She tried to remember who he was.

"He's in one of your Year 8 Music classes. He's become a trouble to me." I think I softened my thoughts when I told them to her. I tried to represent myself in the best possible light, perhaps.

"A trouble?" She gave a slow half-nod. "He's one of the troublemakers in my class. But not the only one." She sipped her fizzy water.

"I think he's dangerous," I said.

She raised her brow at my severity. This was before Sultan's atrocity, of course, and I never suspected he'd do something quite like that – back then I was speaking, I think, more in terms of Sultan as a destabilizing force, as a threat to my reputation, as a concern that needed to be handled with intelligence and wisdom and, possibly in equal measure, haste. And I believed, at the time, that I could muster any two of those virtues, but not all three.

"At his best, of what I've seen of him, he has a certain dark charm. A sick kind of humour, sometimes." I rolled the whisky in my glass. "Also, he's relatively fearless."

"He seems quite afraid, to me. Though they all do, somehow."

"How so?"

Her gaze lifted to the ceiling and I was momentarily quite free to look at her. Then she looked at me directly again.

"I don't know," she said. "They all want attention or something, a kind of attention I can't give them. Reassurance."

"I think you romanticize them."

She didn't react. I think mentally she'd also resigned her professional pride before entering the room.

"Do you think there's anything we could do to address the issue of class discipline?" I asked.

She smiled and shook her head, almost girlishly.

"I think we gave it a good go," she said.

"There's really nothing I can do to change your mind?"

She smiled, paused provokingly.

"Nothing," she said.

I nodded and took a quick sip, perhaps to bolster my courage.

"Do you have another job offer?" I asked.

She shook her head again. "Not quite. But I've got some freelance commissions to tide me over, through a friend of a friend."

"What kind of commissions?"

"Arrangements. Giving a pop song a makeover for a string quartet. And another is some pre-production work for a West End play, where there's singing involved."

"A musical?"

"Hm – the singing only happens twice in a hundred minutes. A little too po-faced for a musical."

"How can any of that compare to conducting the keyboarding talents of your Year 8 class?"

She laughed, at the freedom of putting it all behind her.

"I'll miss some of them. Very few, though."

I finished my glass, absolutely to steel myself, by then.

"I do have one more question, if this is to be your exit interview," I said.

I think she knew what I was going to ask. Her gaze was unnervingly direct, almost provoking.

"Will you go to dinner with me next Friday?"

Angela refers to the destruction of my wife and the near-destruction of Paul as *terrible things*. Almost universally, that is her chosen phrase, to point at those events from the appropriate distance. She says I have to accept I had no control over those *terrible things*. I must accept I bear no blame for them – but, also, that there was *nothing I could have done*.

I asked her, "What things can we control?" and she said:

How we treat other people

How we treat ourselves

which I thought a pat answer, and then I thought the whole line of reasoning pat and recycled, possibly the answer to all grief and loss: there's nothing to be done. *Don't blame yourself, don't blame others.*

But I've looked over both calamities, plotted in my mind their lifecycle, their geneses through to their bitter conclusions, I've mapped in my mind enormous flow-diagrams to describe these occurrences, and in between the arrows and boxes it appears to me there were many chances for me to avert catastrophe.

I understand the argument *vis* Paul: that he is(/was) his own person, that in any case even if I did influence him towards his course then this influence was refracted and indirect. Hence, *uncontrollable*, in Angela's paradigm.

But just because a given factor's effect on a given system is *complex* does not make it *unmeasurable*. It only means we must try harder to quantify it. Take the following, heavily simplified scheme:

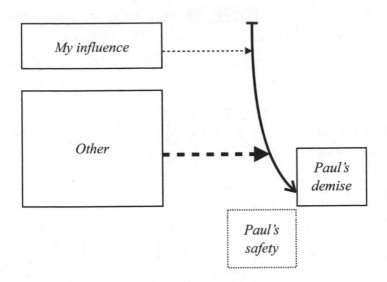

In such a scheme, it's not possible to discount the effect of my actions, even if others' actions are of greater force. Even if the force of my influence was negligible (which I don't believe), I can't absolve myself of the greater effect: my participation in such a trajectory – effective or not – renders me morally culpable. Further, it's hard to argue that my actions weren't key in the particular circumstances of Paul's demise. What did I manage to teach him? Only the basics: conscientiousness of a sort, and some discipline. Without which, his doomed career in the army was a non-starter.

So when Angela tells me I had no control over the *terrible thing*, she's wrong or lying. It comes down to this: had someone murdered me, or had I been stricken with a fatal illness before I met Paul, I don't doubt for a second that Paul would have avoided his catastrophe.

And likewise, my wife: had she never met me, she'd be alive today.

And then there is ███████. This is where all my calculations take me – what was the force of his influence? And – it follows – if I blame myself, to what degree shall I blame him?

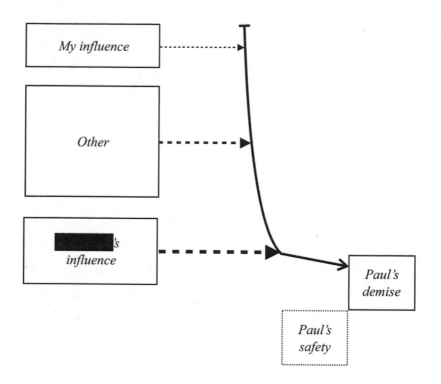

I gave blood today. There were forms and questionnaires – far more bureaucracy than I'd expected for a voluntary process. I even began to feel nervous at the sight of the machine that samples your finger blood.

Finger, heel or sometimes earlobe – these are the unappealing sites they can draw such samples from.

The nurse asked if I had any questions and I asked how often a donor (*a donor*, in reference to myself, I'd adopted their parlance) might give blood. She told me that it's healthy to donate up to four times a year.

It took me a moment. "Thirteen weeks?"

She tilted her head.

"We recommend at least twelve weeks between each donation," she said, and then nodded.

I'd read it was eight.

I asked where a person might purchase the required instruments to sample blood – syringes, vials, blood bags, that sort of thing.

"Oh, I'm not sure, to be honest," she said. And then she dared it: "Why do you ask?"

I smiled what I hoped was a guileless smile – I looked at the poster on the open door that led to the hallway and the passing aimless chatter of the orderlies. The poster said, though I'd read it previously and now only contemplated its colour (light blue background), "unfortunately, no amount of antibiotics will get rid of your cold."

(This is not the hospital I visit my father at.)

I sensed she would welcome an obvious evasion more than the truth, and since I had no plausible excuse, I said: "I was just curious. Lately I've been wondering a lot about the supply chain." I was still looking at the poster on the door, now at its pink, abstract hand, laden with capsule pills – and when I glanced at her she was no longer looking at me.

In the waiting room I caught the eye of a few of the other donors, all of whom appeared intensely relaxed, which relaxed me. I admired them for their altruism. One by one we were called, with about a five-minute pause in between.

Afterwards, I was despatched to the refreshment area: a table in the corner of the reception, with some plastic chairs for sitting. Two of my predecessors were standing there with styrofoam cups in their hands – a rugged woman with a pink complexion, and a man with thinning hair and a large jaw, the type you might expect to excel at mountain climbing, a kind of physical wisdom suggested by his structure and bearing.

The woman was still there when I exited the toilet, though now sitting – still only halfway through her digestive (I imagined she was savouring it). I would have preferred her not to see me after my change of clothes, in my running attire – I felt I'd exposed too much surface area to her judgement.

I ran home, about three miles. I kept a moderate speed and felt fairly normal, until I reached my home and felt very sick when I stopped – worsened by the stillness of the air inside, and I went to the kitchen and drank water from the tap and retched a little into the sink, and then went to bed and lay staring at the ceiling, trying not to throw up.

I wish I could hear you play the piano again. I wish you weren't dead. Sometimes I tell myself you aren't. But you are.

On the so-called Dark Web you can purchase guns, though mostly they try to sell you drugs.

I found one vendor, persona PSwiles, who sends you the gun in multiple packages. You must assemble it yourself, though the site offers several instruction manuals on how to assemble your weapon (and links to appropriate YouTube videos). The download links for these manuals are all accompanied by a note telling readers to ensure they aren't connected to the internet when opening the files. The guides themselves are littered with disclaimers to the effect that only "professionals" should attempt weapon assembly, and the authors (who are, of course, anonymous) take no responsibility for the health and safety of those heeding its words, nor the safe function of their weapons.

Several users of different fora have provided testimonials for PSwiles, though they could be mere mountebanks, in on the con. One reads: "Took longer than expected but received final delivery this morning. Assembly went smoothly, just followed instructions. Would buy from them again."

I imagine both scenarios: the happy degenerate, unwrapping his gun parts, assembling his gun – the relief of the completed weapon in his hands, the satisfaction of a purchase fulfilled – finally posting his brief endorsement, perhaps with the weapon sitting next to his keyboard. And then I imagine the other: PSwiles – just some boy perhaps, in his suburban bedroom – inventing these tales under various personae, all of it baseless, an elaborate complex of invention, based on researched scraps and personal whimsy, based on other such sites offering other such services – and are they, too, mere mountebanks? Is there any single one of them who truly offers what they claim to offer?

Another reads: "All packages arrived together (not sure what's the point then??) haven't assembled yet but seems legit."

I think it's time we considered "where we are" with your therapy.

(She said "where we are" as if with quotes.)

I think we've made good progress, but perhaps it's time for us both to recognize the limits of what that progress is.

(Something very close to that. *The limits of what that progress is*. Something like that.)

The process has been a long one, and it can't go on indefinitely. It's not helpful for you, and I'm sure you want your Wednesdays back. It may be the case that therapy itself can't take you "the whole way", as it were.

(Again speaking with quotes.)

That can be the case, quite often. So I think we should recognize the need to *wind down* the course of your therapy, to work through those last knots of trauma, so that you yourself have a better handle on them. Then I think it may be appropriate, in your case, for me to refer you to a psychiatrist, who can prescribe you antidepressants and perhaps other medication. I know you want to avoid medication, and that's why I want to hold off and work through it as far as we can. But it will be best to recognize I think we've come to the limits of how this process, this therapy can help you.

It takes me a moment to understand her.

"Well," I said. "Before you break up with me, then, there are a few memories I have – some from quite long ago – which I want to talk about with you. I think you're right, sometimes it might be the old memories that affect me more than I'd thought."

There was a time (briefly) I was a policeman. I've mentioned it before, passingly.

I probably would have been a policeman my whole life except that a young man drastically changed my outlook. He was a seventeen-year-old Asian male, a *man* by my standards then, though easily a boy as I see it now.

There was a domestic disturbance in an ethnic neighbourhood – I won't say which – and I was dispatched to the scene along with my senior. I remember it was cold, because I wondered at the time whether this Asian family felt the cold more than I did, and whether that was any factor to this dispute, on any level, the way a person's diet can affect their mood.

I remember the inside of the house had a kind of dusty quality all the furnishings were old-fashioned, the carpet especially, old and fusty-looking English style.

The young man (or boy) was waving a hammer around. The father and he were arguing heatedly, speaking perhaps in Hindi or in some other Not English. And the young man was gesturing limply with the hammer.

Behind the father was the door to the kitchen, closed, and it was clear that the father was guarding the door, and a moment later it was clear that the hammer was intended for someone beyond it – such was the direction of the boy's hammer gestures.

Stun guns didn't exist at that time, or anything like them, so we had our truncheons out and our left hands forward to say, "Calm down or we'll whack you." We were willing to smash both father and son, given that they were both men, and family, and so whacking the one probably meant whacking the other in any case.

Their argument continued, undimmed, until the boy struck the wall quite powerfully with the hammer, putting a large hole in it with a puff of plaster dust, and we took it as a declaration of war and raised our truncheons to have at him, but as we did so he saw sense and dropped the hammer and stood quite still.

For whatever reason I was charged by my superior with calming the two men down, while he attended to whatever was behind the door. So at length I got the father and son into the living room to induce them to explain what they were up to. I suggested they both sit down, but the son refused, and so I stood as well, holding the hammer inverted, its heavy head downwards, so as to lay claim to it while neutralizing its threat.

The father was trying to explain the predicament, but spoke zero English, and the son just shifted his weight from foot to foot and I was wary of him.

After a few minutes my senior came to us and asked me to "Keep an eye on the two in the kitchen", and he said it in such a way as to suggest there was no danger there, and as I passed by him he mentioned quietly he'd already requested an ambulance. But mostly I remember my confusion as I approached the kitchen door and heard my senior loudly addressing the men with the unforgettable statement: "I need to get to the bottom of why you attacked your mother with a hammer." Loud enough so that I was prepared, a little, for what I saw.

I rather overdid it. I took two pints of blood. And I ran to the hospital.

The nurses looked at me as if ready to point me to A&E. Presumably such was my colour.

I felt very ill – I got caught in a spiral of being nauseated by the thought of how much blood I'd taken. I think the mental aspect quite took over. I was sure I would vomit – that was the other thought. The sickening volume of blood, the certainty of throwing up. My limbs trembled enough that my fingers practically flickered.

I sat by my father's bed like this, without talking. Eventually I did make it to the toilet, to a free cubicle, to throw up, to get it out of the way, more or less. I felt more ready for sleep – more dim-witted and leaden – than I've ever felt in my life before.

But then I decided: this is exactly why I did it. I stood up straight, enough, struggled to focus, struggled to balance on my teetering gait.

This is what it will be like, I told myself.

When they shoot you, if you live, if they've shot you well and you're still alive, this is what it will feel like.

This time, I thought to myself, *you're lucky*. You've treated yourself to the toilet, to throwing up. You can treat yourself, this time. All you have to do is stand up. All you have to do is walk, one foot in front of the next. Don't look down. Don't drop your head. Keep your balance. All you must do is walk to your father's bedside and sit and be still.

And so I did.

And when I thought again of the two pints in the bags, a delirious pride swept over me, and I said,

"Hello, Father. You know I love you, in my way. And I'm grateful to you. I'm very grateful."

I believe he was sleeping at the time.

Another teacher, another time – another exit: "You're clinging to some old-fashioned ideal." "The world doesn't work like that any more." "Your methods [*methods* being my word borrowed by them in their attack] are way out of date." "You're holding the school back."

Holding the school back! When I was the only thing holding it together. At first they all believed in me. Then it was most of them believed in me. Then I suppose for a long time it was held in the balance, half and half, teetering back and forth, and of course I felt those breezes of discontent, but I kept my head down and stuck to my ideals.

If my ideals proved wrong, they were entitled to chuck me. With my blessing, even. But all the while my methods worked, what right did they have to complain?

One boy I let suffer because I thought it important. I considered his suffering a kind of lesson. That's Bad, isn't it? But perhaps not Wrong.

He was launching fireworks at other pupils. He didn't originate this practice – none of them ever originate anything, these things just occur somehow, they become customary, without any inventor or originator. It doesn't go: one boy launches fireworks at other boys in the playground, he is the first. I suppose one time one boy brings a firework into school. Maybe he lights it on the heath, or not at all. He originates the practice of bringing in fireworks. Another boy originates the practice of throwing waterbombs, perhaps, at the other boys eating their sandwiches at lunchtime. At some point another boy combines these two separate customs and a new custom begins – but did he really invent it? And then the next year a completely different boy performs the rite.

What I'm saying is, the boy throwing fireworks – he's not a villain. He didn't devise some new sinister practice to torture his playmates with. He just enacted an annual ceremony, that of launching fireworks in the playground, of sending a screeching rocket into a crowd of boys or tossing bangers at their heads. To see them flee, I suppose. Or to see the power of it, to see a hundred boys cower. To perform an action with such a wide radius of effect. For the few boys who conduct the ceremony of the fireworks it is, possibly, the very peak of their worldly joy.

But it was irresponsible. That word again – *reckless*. The stupidity of boys is to look no further into the future than the firework's detonation. If someone were to actually get hurt, they'd regret it – I have no doubt about it. That angered me. That weakness. To not see the consequences, and to be surprised and upset by them.

Well, one boy blew up his hand. My understanding is that he was trying out bangers and had taken to "cooking" them – which is to say, holding them with the fuse lit until they were ready to serve, as it were – so that they would detonate in the air above the other boys' heads (in military parlance this is known as an "air burst"). I presume he took it seriously and he was a talented athlete, so I don't doubt his timing or concentration. But I suppose the fuses were inconsistent in their length or in their burn. He hadn't necessarily used the right fireworks for his intentions.

The explosion cut a deep trench into the palm of his right hand – his throwing hand. He mercifully retained all his fingers, though the action of his tendons was irreparably damaged.

Would his tendons have been saved by prompter medical attention? I honestly don't think it would have made a difference.

But the fact is that the boy was taken to the school nurse cradling his hand. She was in the process of calling for an ambulance when I entered her office and gestured to her to put the phone down. When she put her hand over the receiver I told her that we wouldn't wait for an ambulance, that I'd take the boy to the hospital in my car.

When he went to get in the car I told him he was to sit in the back. He climbed in, looking forlorn with his right hand hugely wrapped in bandages, and, after starting the engine, I turned back in my seat to face him and told him to unwrap his hand and that he should leave his bandages in a pile next to him. He asked me why and I told him the air was good for it, and he said he'd rather keep it bandaged and I asked him did he want to go to the hospital or not? I told him I wasn't taking him to the hospital with his bandage on, so he'd better take it off. He was confused, but started to unwrap his hand, tentatively, and I let him take his time about it. He was a little sickened by the sight of his injury and I reversed out of the parking spot and we started our journey. I suppose I did a few laps around the same block before commenting on the terrible traffic, but he was too distracted by his hand – either the pain or the sight of it – to notice we were going in circles. I found a parking spot by the kerb and parked up awhile without saying anything. After a few moments the boy asked if we were going to the hospital and I turned back in my seat again and I nodded and asked him how was his hand? It actually looked a little charred, or else the wound was just congealed and blackened. It was dripping into his lap. He said it hurt. I asked him if he really needed the hospital? He asked me what I meant. I asked him again. He looked at his mangled hand as if it might not be as bad as he'd thought, but he didn't answer. He said it was hurting and he'd like to go to the hospital, so I pulled out and drove us there. I parked in the hospital car park and checked my watch. He looked at me in the rear-view mirror. I told him we were here, turned back in my seat again to face him. He nodded. I waited, asked what the matter was. I feigned realizing he wanted me to go in with him and got out of the car, and he got out, too, and then I stood a moment to see what he'd do, and then I held him by the shoulder and said:

"You have two options. The first option is we can go in together and I can lecture you and berate you for the foolish injury you've committed against yourself, and for endangering the other boys. And afterwards you'll get two Saturday detentions."

He was grimacing. Blood was dripping down his arm and I guessed he'd made a mess of the back seat. I don't think he cared much about Saturday detentions at that moment.

"Or the other option is that you can say, 'I've made a mistake, and I'll see to it,' and you can go in there on your own, and there'll be no lecture from me and no detentions. You just have to walk in to where it says A&E – you see it, there? – and walk up to the receptionist and say, 'I've injured my hand.' You don't have to say how, though I guess they'll be curious, and they'll ask you your name and address, and they'll see to your hand quite quickly, because the wound is quite bad, as you say."

He was gripping his wrist tightly, perhaps to stem the blood. The asphalt was specked underneath him. I sensed he wanted us to go together, but didn't want to say. He nodded and asked, "Which way is it?", though I'd already pointed it out moments earlier. I lowered my head to his eye-line and pointed to the red sign in the distance.

"Just there."

He looked at it as if it were very far away.

"Now, will you be OK on your own?" I asked.

He nodded, hollowly. He was still looking at the red sign.

I squeezed his shoulders firmly. "*Good lad*," I said, and he started shuffling towards the red sign, still grasping his wrist.

"One moment," I said to him, and he turned.

I went and reached into the back seat of the car – which wasn't so bloody, so that I was grateful to him, since he must've caught most of it in his lap – and got his discarded bandages.

"Drop this in the bin on your way, would you?"

When the soldier conducts war games against a pretend enemy, there's a real enemy in mind, but not a real war. The soldier prepares himself for the necessity of a war that he hopes can be avoided.

So when I plan to strengthen myself, and when I consider such things as weaponry and killing, and things like my *intended victim*, it's not murder I'm planning but my preparedness for it.

Because forgiveness is meaningless unless it's a choice. There can be no forgiveness by default.

The gun I ordered was a Beretta M9.

The vendor's stock was very limited – he offered only the Beretta M9, the TEC-9, or the MAC-10. The Beretta was the cheapest (which matters, given I'm not convinced I'll ever see my purchase) and the other two options seemed far too crude, more for adolescents than grown adults.

I paid 1.8BTC, which is about £800 at the time of writing. I have 0.2BTC remaining in my wallet.

A teacher instructs a boy that he has detention for speaking in class. The boy replies – and this is the first problem – "Why are you singling me out, when other boy X was talking first?"

How often did I instruct my teachers on this scenario?

Before I was a headmaster, I taught History and Geography. I would also often take PE classes with great relish. The truth is, I personally didn't care much for any subject. Not when I was of school age myself – and certainly not when I taught. School, in my eyes, is for three things: Literacy, Numeracy and Good Sense. These aren't subjects in themselves, of course – rather, they must permeate every subject, everything must lead back to those three virtues.

I suppose that young man who battered his mother with a hammer was a positive influence on me. He taught me that I didn't want to spend my life fighting against degenerates: I wanted to stem degeneracy itself.

And where better to come face to face with degeneracy than at a boys' school? When better to instil rebellion in people against their gloomy destinies than in their youth?

In order to teach any lesson, you must first grapple with the question: why should anyone care? This was always my first item on the agenda, teaching-wise. In the first lesson of term, I'd invite students to voice what they considered subversive opinions. Children will predictably boast of their ignorant, bigoted viewpoint if you give them the slightest encouragement. So I'd start a discussion, a sort of Who Here Likes History?

sort of thing. The few who actually raised their hands identified themselves as the ones I could leave to their own devices – I'd mentally note their faces, perhaps ask them their names, ask them why they liked History, or acknowledge and praise their worthy attitude.

But inevitably, within a few minutes, I'd hear my cue from one of the majority: I don't care about History. I don't care about things that happened ages ago.

Sometimes they wouldn't say exactly this. I might have to question them, lead them on, or outright misquote them. But in any case that is where the lesson proper would begin: History isn't about things that happened ages ago.

History is not about the past, I'd say.

Sometimes they'd roll their eyes or frown. This is when I might make note of the belligerents of the class.

History is how the past is told to us. Julius Caesar, Henry the Eighth, Napoleon – who here believes these men actually existed?

Suspiciously, they'd raise their arms. Sometimes I might stress *actually* too far, and I'd have to goad them to raise their hands. There'd be excitement in the air, at the theatre of it. Sometimes, one or two students wouldn't raise their arms at all, would obstinately refuse, perhaps getting too worked up in the game I was playing, trying to win without even knowing the rules – without knowing they stood no chance. And of course, it was necessary to question those boys, to make fools of them for not believing what was patently true, to render them as imbeciles to the others, so that the others would feel on my side, on the right side, and so easily, too. Such sacrifices are made daily in classrooms across the land.

But sometimes – rarely – a boy or girl might say, under questioning, something like: "What's the difference between one of those and Jesus or something?"

Indeed, Jesus and Caesar were contemporaries, I'd say. And Jesus is more widely known, universally known. Historically of far greater influence. Who exists more, of the two of them? They are all figments. They don't exist. At one point perhaps they did. And now their existence is told through words. Pictures, perhaps – paintings, et cetera.

History is important for only one reason, I'd say. The children would like that. Any sniff of bombast or over-generalization, any outrageous declaration or promise of a hidden truth and their eyes would widen.

I remember once I managed to quell a class by loudly stating: "God – is – dead." Everyone hushed, except two sniggering boys, and I picked the weakest-looking one and demanded of him: "What does it mean?" Of course, no one had the faintest idea what it meant, so they kept quiet. Then I carried on with the lesson. This was in Geography.

But my line in History was: History shows us how people lie.

There are wars, of course – most of it is wars. But that is just the constant backdrop. You'll learn about crossbows and trebuchets and weapons of war and technology, and how technology changes everything, always. But take any war, and you can read about what happened, often from what is known as *primary sources*. I might then ask the class if anyone knew what a *primary source* was.

You can take two accounts of the very same battle and they will contradict each other.

So – and here I paused awhile – which of them is lying?

In Transit:

Deliver to:

Meath Trim

I'd pause again, for as long as possible. I'd eye the students as if they could possibly answer my impossible question. And then I'd say:

Let's find out.

And then I'd continue with whatever dreary lesson plan I'd concocted, handing out the greyed photocopied sheets and setting them their numbered exercises.

And to the teachers who were asked: *Why are you punishing me, other boy X was talking first?* – well, it often happens. I admit I took what might be called a Scorched Earth policy, in my day.

A boy says, "James [or Mark or whoever] was speaking first."

James or Mark may or may not protest. But, after making note of the protester's detention, I ask, "Is that so?"

And they say, "Yeah," obviously.

"Just them?"

"Everyone was talking, not just me."

"Everyone? It wasn't everyone. Do you mean four or five others were talking, so that it's unfair to single you out?"

At this point it may be necessary to hush any rising excitement (sometimes with a click of the fingers, though only if one has the snapping power, the right timbre to their click).

The accused would say, "Yeah," obviously.

Then I turn to James or Mark and say, "Were you talking?"

And they say, "No," obviously.

At this point, the first time, I thought it nice to return to my very first theme. A kind of recapitulation. So I said,

"Well, what does History teach us?" Pause. "One of you is lying." And I opened it up to the class, I even asked for some first-hand accounts, asked those at the back who weren't near enough to be witnesses to evaluate the evidence. The class agreed it was likely both of them had been talking, though who'd been first wasn't determined. I used the incident to illustrate the difficulty of determining the truth of matters, even in such confined quarters, even in matters of the just-past.

But when a similar possibility came up a second time, and I asked the question, "What does History teach us?" the accused boy answered, "That you're a dickhead," and I had to raise him out of his chair by his collar and entertain the rest of the class that way. So I didn't ask that question any more.

Instead I'd return to the accused and say to him, "James [or Mark] says he wasn't lying. Do you think it might have been Rouf or Michelle you were thinking of?" (Rouf or Michelle being students I was fairly sure had been talking at some point, but not enough to warrant attention.) The accused then usually incriminates one or both of them, in the hopes of being given a more lenient sentence.

Then I would say, "Excellent," and write down Rouf, Michelle and James, or Mark's name on the board.

There would, of course, be uproar, from the newly condemned. This had to be cut off immediately with more stern threats. But then the important part was to return again to the accused.

"Who else?" I'd say.

And the accused would slowly begin to realize their error. They might shrug or say, "I don't know."

I'd shake my head: "You said four or five others were talking. You'll give me all the names you can remember or you'll be in detention every day next week." The whole classroom would tense. And I'd extract the necessary names, sometimes arbitrarily demanding another, insisting on it, able to treat the accused arbitrarily now, because they'd lost solidarity with their fellow classmates – could be abused without consequence, with no effect to the class's sense of justice – until I was sure the accused was now rendered a villain.

My threat, of course, was outlandish. I found my more biblical threats were the most effective. I once menaced a boy with a month of detentions. His look suggested he'd never conceived of such depravity.

Angela has summarized my classroom strategies as *divide and conquer.*

"Is this why you struggled to engage with your daughter – because she was an only child? You wanted to rule her, but didn't know how? Had no sibling to pit her against?"

She said there was a *fascist streak* in my approach to discipline. That I maintained order at the cost of an individual's dignity or self-respect or pride or whatever. *Self-esteem.*

She is beginning to understand me, perhaps.

Part of my gun arrived in the post. Two of the packages arrived at once. I picked them up from my PO box. They were fairly small cardboard boxes, equal size, nondescript, except for the StorePAK branding. They were quite heavy for their size. I took them home in the holdall, paranoid and feeling people's eyes on me. I put the kettle on and took the packages through to the living room and opened them ineptly with scissors (they were heavily sellotaped). Inside were several bubble-wrapped items (these heavily sellotaped also), and an oily machine smell that got stronger as I proceeded with my task. I'd already tried to familiarize myself with the exploded view of the Beretta M9; the instructions advised against "partial assembly". That is, I had to wait for the last package to arrive, and for that reprieve I was glad when the parts spilled out on to the table, some of them frighteningly precise-looking, suggestive of a finer type of instrument like a camera or a clock.

Still waiting for the last package to arrive – the final piece of the Beretta M9. After fourteen days I'm determined to make contact with the vendor, PSwiles – or try to. This was, though, as much as I expected. £800 gone, and a lesson learned, perhaps?

Sultan became a problem to me.

I'm prejudiced against the memory of him, of course, because of that first time I met him, in the Music class of the woman who would become my wife, the woman whom I probably was already in love with – and he smirked at me. Do I remember it so vividly because of simple masculine pride? Or was it good instincts?

My reputation had to be fastidiously guarded and maintained. A smirk was an attack against my reputation, as I felt it. Even if I was the only one who saw – all the more dangerous, if I was the only intended audience to the challenge.

But a reputation is more easily maintained than built anew – which is what my wife was finding, before she was my wife, when she was a Music teacher, briefly, before she packed it all in to write jingles and musical arrangements, and occasionally compose her own scores in the intervening peace between commissions.

Sultan didn't respect me. As far as I could tell, he didn't respect anyone working at the school. He tolerated some. I believe he liked some of his teachers, even – he was fairly well behaved, merely roguish in his English lessons, for the love of his teacher, Mr Parsons. Many boys loved Mr Parsons. He charmed them – and if his students did wrong, his displeasure was always punishment enough. But even as Sultan loved him, as the rest of them did, he held him in contempt, as he held all of us in contempt, in his way.

My greatest crises always happened when my reputation failed me. It was, in some ways, the decline of my reputation that ended my career. It was in these moments that, I admit, I resorted to my physical presence. I am tall. I can lift them from their chair, I can handle or restrain them. Often, just the touch is enough to alarm them, to make them fear what the limits of this contact might be.

But not so with Sultan. He openly challenged me. When I grabbed him by the arm to take him out of the class, he shouted at me to fucking get off him. He electrified the other boys, even as they feared and hated him.

What is one meant to do with a Sultan? I never discovered. Sultan threatened my reputation, and brought disorder to those around him. I isolated him when I could, to limit his damage to my school and my character, and I was building a case against him for permanent expulsion. But I never found a cure for a one like Sultan.

It was in a Chemistry class one day that he threw nitric acid in a boy's face. You must imagine, beyond the incident itself, the impact such a thing has on the social fabric of the school. Excitement and fear spreads. Violence has entered the school. An Atrocity, even, has been committed. Indeed, for weeks afterwards violence reigned – boys fought, where before they'd only cuss, and the severity of the fights deepened, some using weapons, throwing chairs or using the edge of a bench against their opponent's head. The classrooms had been rendered unsafe, and every boy's mind tilted towards violence.

The victim's wounds were thankfully superficial, despite the chemical burning his cheeks and eyelid. His eyesight was mer-cifully unaffected. The Chemistry teacher, in the wild panic of the moment, had shouted to one of his trustworthy students to get the teacher next door, and then had taken the boy to the back room, where he washed the boy's face and applied a wet towel to his burns.

First, you have to imagine how the panic takes hold. Sultan chucks some acid at another boy, who at first flinches and shouts as if at water – at a discomfort and a disrespect – and this shout isn't enough to capture the attention of the class. Rather, it is the witnesses on the same bench, their gasp and alarm, which spreads, until all the boys are looking at what has happened – the victim quietly scowling, unsure of the nature of the danger he is in – and then, in a few moments, the teacher is able to ask the boys what has happened, and then ask of Sultan himself, "What did you do?"

And Sultan, now, just looks at the empty test tube in his hand, as answer. And that is when the teacher attends to the victim – that is the moment of "wild panic". Because the boys panic only after the teacher.

I try to imagine Sultan, at that moment, still in the class-room with the other boys, after the teacher has taken his victim away – basking, perhaps, in their dawning awe, in the teacherless room. Or was he himself awed by his own actions? By the new extremity he'd reached? Or the extremity of the consequences, for the simple flick of a test tube?

The young victim never returned to the school. He was scarred, an ugly chemical burn scar, which might relax over time if he were lucky. And mentally, no doubt, too. But he was otherwise unharmed. I spent a great deal of time with the boy's parents in the days afterwards. I think they understood it as my penance, and absolved me, in time.

And when Sultan was finally isolated, again – now in a classroom on the ground floor, away from the havoc he'd created, just the two of us in the classroom whose windows showed only the staff car park beyond – I noticed that his fingers had been burned, too, the index and middle finger and thumb, severely enough, his wounds untended to. And I imagined the foolish grip he must've had, gripping the test tube high around its neck, like he was strangling the thing. It occurred to me, then, that he hadn't planned his atrocity. That he hadn't even considered it enough to alter his strangling grip. And strangely I think that was why, in the end, I dealt with him so severely.

The third package arrived, but it didn't take me long to realize the parts were wrong – I now had two barrels, but no trigger piece. An £800 lesson, after all. I suppose I should follow up with PSwiles again. As a matter of principle, I should explain his error – or the error of his organization, which may or may not be more than him and his garage.

Am I tainted by PSwiles?

Sometimes I think, *What would she say?* She'd be frightened by my thoughts, maybe. Upset and disgusted, maybe. Uncomprehending, even. Perhaps she'd say these thoughts of mine don't belong to the man she loved. They're a different man's thoughts, she might think.

All it would take is one look from her, to set me right.

I'll fill out PSwiles's contact form this afternoon. But I need an alternative means of procurement.

She asks me how I dealt with Sultan. I'm working up to how I can tell her.

I say, "Do you want to know for professional reasons?"

"Yes," she says.

"Or because you're curious?" I say.

"Perhaps it's a significant episode," she said. A *significant episode*.

"Which should we talk about first, though – what happened to Sultan or what happened to the boy with the hammer? They're connected, of course."

She considers this. "Is this a game to you?" she asks.

"I'm telling you my past. How is that a game?"

"Why are you offering a choice, like a game?"

"I don't want you to forget about the boy with the hammer," I say. "What I did to him and what I did to Sultan, they're connected."

"And what did you do?"

"To... ?"

"Tell me about Frankie," she says.

Now – *this* is a surprise.

"Is it just a name? In one of your first Self-Expressions, he or she is on the list. I think it's a *he*. But you've never mentioned him."

But there's still ground to cover, about my daughter and wife. And Paul. How he and my daughter got together – surely that matters? And how they fell apart. And my advances in computing, if anyone will listen.

"You know," I say, "when I think about it, I'm quite proud of my abilities, of how I'm coming along with my piano, and music theory, and especially learning about computers, which I know is dull, but if you took a moment to understand I think you'd appreciate that it's wonderful, really, that a man of my age can still learn, like a boy, practically, though sharper and less sharp in different ways. But you don't seem to care about any of that."

Her one brow is raised again, above the frame of her glasses.

"Do you know the technology your Oyster card works on?" I say. "Do you know it's just a number that you're holding up to those readers?"

She doesn't care. She wants the battles. She wants the History.

Frankie isn't a battle, though.

I met him at a support group, a little while after I lost my wife. It was a busy occasion, though sombre, at a packed community hall.

In the immediate aftermath of the bombings the police put me in touch with a number of organizations that could offer support – as well as arrange counselling if I felt I needed it. So, in a way, Angela is in parallel to Frankie.

One charity arranged this support group for victims and their families, the bereaved, in the community hall on a weekday afternoon.

People talked about their experience of the bombings, but mostly they remembered the dead and celebrated the living, or tried to. There were several rows of chairs, set back a bit from the stage – and no one got on the stage, but instead stood in front of it and said what they would say.

It was an informal affair and there were many breaks between the scheduled speakers, where it was intended that you would mingle with other people whose experience was comparable to yours.

I'd asked Amy to come with me, but she said it wouldn't help her, and I understood what she meant. She was glad I was going, though, and I suppose a little surprised. And I remember arriving, in the grey rain, and not being sure if it was the right place, understanding it was indeed the community hall, but hesitating until a family of six passed me and entered, and then

I saw the small notice, smaller than was helpful, perhaps out of respect: SURVIVORS SUPPORT AND REMEMBRANCE GROUP, penned on A2 white card.

That handwritten sign nearly sent me directly back home. I distinctly remember my aversion to it – the dubiousness of it.

This was very soon after I'd lost my wife, before I really understood what that meant, and I had wished she could be there with me.

But I did go in, after a few moments' hesitation, primarily to get out of the rain.

And it was in one of the many breaks between those survivors' talks that I went to what was probably described as the *refreshment table*. It was much the same as the one I encountered when I later gave blood, if you remember? Except more expansive, with greater choice, and even home-baked treats, which was heartening, and the money you gave went to the charity, but you needn't give anything at all. But it had the same white linen tablecloth as at the hospital, the same paper plates and plastic foam cups. I poured myself a black coffee, mainly for the smell.

And I met Frankie. He was an alarmingly shabby-looking man. That much hasn't changed, I suppose. His teeth are scant and discoloured, one of them points right at you, so much so that you have to look at it, as if to see off its challenge.

At first I didn't understand what he was saying. His speech was altered, perhaps, by the abstract arrangement of his teeth. He was asking after the circumstances that brought me there.

I told him how I'd wished my wife could be there with me, today. I told him about my wife. It was in the spirit of having a go, I think.

Frankie had taken to eating some kind of cake with pink icing on it, and I more or less fixated on his untotal mastication of it, as I told him about my wife and how I'd been uncertain about coming, or rather had come and then had had second thoughts.

He was very moved, eating his cake. He told me he was getting some tea, and shuffled to the other end of the refreshment table, and I followed, after dropping a few coins in the tin.

He told me, over the course of his brief meal (he started on a second cake with the pink icing, forsaking all others), that he, too, had lost his wife.

They hadn't found the body, he said. They hadn't identified it. It's a great trouble, he said, because of her estate, there are legal problems. But it's difficult in other ways. But sometimes I think she's still alive, somewhere.

It had been a matter of months, by this point.

I was anguished by his story, of course. I felt the sadness of my own situation, was reminded of how bad it was, but I was still capable, I think, of reserving some of that sadness for him, for his lost wife.

"I like to think," he said, after finishing the second cake and pulling focus on his steaming tea, "that she used it as an excuse, you know? I'd prefer that, in a way – that she'd just left and started a new life for herself. I could live with that."

That often comes back to me: *I could live with that.*

But at the same time, he said, you have to get on with life, don't you?

"Do you?" I said. And I really wanted an answer – I felt he could answer me, of all people.

"You do," he said. "Of course you do."

And I understood, then, that I probably did.

My shins are so tender, bruised blue and purple. Sometimes I wrap my fists too loosely and I sprain my wrist or bruise a knuckle. My body recovers too slowly, so it never recovers, because I never let it.

My whole body hums with a raw kind of pain. Not like the pain of a cut or a burn or an impact. I am, now, able to distinguish between them. This good pain is recovery. I am, now, always recovering.

To myself, yesterday:

   I'm stronger than you were, because of the efforts you made.

To myself, tomorrow:

   You're stronger than I am, because of the efforts I make.

The first time my superior took me to the pub was after the boy with the hammer had been taken into custody (I think it makes sense to tell things in order, perhaps).

There was what happened between me and the boy and my superior officer, and then there was the pub after, a winding down.

We met two other colleagues, both older, more senior than me, though not drastically so. I won't tell their names. But it turns out that Ian, the deliverer of the sparring dummy, looks and sounds a bit like my superior (or as I remember him), so let's call my superior officer Ian.

After what happened with the boy with the hammer I was in a vulnerable state and Ian invited me to the pub, and it was either a kind of encouragement or else an exploitation. I suppose I was to choose.

"Mike's had a hard night," he said to his two colleagues, and by this it was understood they would buy me drinks for the night.

This was a long time ago, in an era when public houses were different enough. The air was rich with smoke, the bar area was thickly carpeted underfoot – the carpet itself seemed even then from a different era – and it was loud and there was no music, except for when the jukebox was playing, and the jukebox itself was considered rather an American thing, which was both in its favour and disfavour, like an heirloom from a wealthy but despised relative.

We stood at the bar. It appeared that the three of them knew the young boy serving the midweek crowd, because he was the son of the proprietor. There were one or two vacant tables we could have taken, but I think we were all glad to be standing, me especially, since I felt more comfortable being on my feet, since I felt very uneasy being still and I imagined I wouldn't sleep when I got home, because I'd not be able to lie down in the first place to sleep.

I remember not saying very much and getting very drunk. They weren't the type to drink quickly, exactly, except for the first pint, which was taken like medicine, drunk in two or three pulls. And then after that they enjoyed their drinks with the most leisurely but frequent sips, almost rhythmically, never letting their lips dry (one of them had a healthy moustache and would lick it from time to time as if to taste it).

They talked for a while about aimless things: each other's wives, about the boy serving us, who would drift into and out of the conversation, and about some of the foolish villains they'd caught. I got the sense that some of their tales were quite old. They kidded with the moustached one about his "bodybuild-ing", at one point demanding he perform a feat of strength, though he declined. But their talk would return now and again, elliptically, to the boy with the hammer, speaking of me with phrases like: "He looks shaken up now, but you should've seen him with him," or "Don't trouble him, he's tired from his exertions."

It must have been six or seven pints down when I lost track of their meandering talk, and when there was a longish pause, as two of them were taking another sip and the one was licking his moustache, I said, "When was the first person you beat up?" I believe I was addressing Ian, who grimaced comically and told me to bloody pipe down, and they laughed at my indiscretion as if at a child. But I persisted, saying, "No, tell me, you must have all done it," though I modulated my voice to what I slurringly considered a covert level, though loud enough to be heard over the general din. They each tilted their heads in thought, except Ian, who shook his head and said, "Well, I've never bashed a paki quite like that," and they nodded quite solemnly. The one with the moustache said, "Well, I've had to be forceful with some in my time," and they nodded at that as well. "You have to be," one said, "some people are bloody animals." I said, "He smashed his own mother's head in with a hammer," and Ian scowled and said we mustn't poison the mood. The moustached one patted me on the shoulder and said again people were animals, some of them, at least, in which case it was no surprise they might smash their own mother over the head with a claw hammer. He added that *claw* very effectively. "You mustn't take it too hard," Ian said, though I didn't know whether he was referring to people's animality or my nerves. "Sometimes you need to be forceful." "It's the only language some people understand, isn't it?" said one. "But let's not go on about it and spoil the mood."

I meet up with Frankie only occasionally. I pity him. I certainly pity his situation with his wife, who still hasn't been found or formally identified. He was told that after a certain time had elapsed he could apply for a death certificate. But until that time, there were the complications with her estate.

But I pity him for other reasons. For his general dishevelment, I suppose. For his irregular teeth, his apparent lack of hygiene, his simplicity. He seems to accept things as they are: his physical condition, his benighted life. He is beset by bodily complaints – either it's his feet that are paining him or one of his joints, or a single red eye or itchiness here and there, or some other skin irritations. I remember one time he had a very severe limp, and when I asked how it happened he said he wasn't sure.

He was born to suffer. Or so I feel when I spend time with him. Perhaps that's why I only meet him occasionally.

Because of his financial problems I often give him money. Usually just twenty pounds or so. I can spare it, since my outgoings are increasingly sporadic, so that I can easily spare a twenty when I see him, and afford my next expense when I receive my pension. And what is charity, anyway, without sacrifice?

I believe this is part of the reason Amy dislikes him. When money is involved she is ruthless. She is – not quite the opposite to me, but close. I am casual with my money. The fact that I haven't spent every penny I have is mostly on account of not being very interested in its spending. Amy is the sort who sets reminders for when her bank account's interest rate is due to revert to some near-zero value, the sort who negotiates with her insurance company, who threatens her telephone provider with abandonment if her demands aren't met. It surprises me, in a way, since neither myself nor her mother ever demonstrated Amy's level of financial control. But, then again, neither did we ever make as much money as her.

Angela's take is this, which I tend to agree with: that among Amy's peers in her adolescence the prospect of riches ranked above all other ambitions. When she in fact went on to make more money than her peers she provoked their resentment and bitterness – while myself and her mother, having never ranked riches as any particular kind of goal, and perhaps feeling any talk or recognition of money, especially large sums of it, was vulgar, never really acknowledged Amy's achievement.

In any case, this is a long way of saying that Amy distrusted Frankie's relationship with me, being that money was involved. They met only once (which was quite enough for her). She said that Frankie gave her *the creeps*, and *perved* on her, in their brief encounter. I believed in Frankie's capacity to *perv* all too well, but I considered it more of a general animal instinct, completely without malice or even intent, like a dog salivating at his master's food.

But Frankie has a fascinating history. It's one which I've only gathered slowly. One day he was over for tea and spotted my computer screen and looked at it quite brazenly, so that I only watched him in astonishment – and he asked me if I was learning Perl. I was amazed by his question and asked him if he was familiar with it. He said he wasn't, really, that he barely knew any *scripting* languages. I couldn't tell whether there was a hint of derision in that word.

Unbelievably, it turned out Frankie at one time made a living writing compilers for x86 chipsets. I've never quite reconciled this former Frankie (*fF*) with current Frankie (*cF*), so some days I imagine *fF* was a completely different person, suave and professional and immaculately groomed, and other days I imagine he was exactly the same as now, except perhaps younger and better washed (possibly).

So now and then, when he's in the mood, I'll induce Frankie to teach me what he knows about computer programs and networks, though his manner of thinking is so foreign that I understand only the odd fragment. What's most important is that I let him sit down at the keyboard and type (though I wish it weren't necessary), and then afterwards I have his workings to learn from. Most of my understanding of memory management comes from Frankie, and sadly, too, my first encounter with inline assembler instructions. His programming style is so dense, so unaccommodating to the human gaze, that I must always rewrite his material with more generous whitespace and friendlier variable names (if I can fathom what his functions are doing, that is).

And always when I've finished I find myself missing him and wanting to discuss some point of his code with him – even though I know his answers would be terse and mystic, if he chose to answer at all.

In the book *Hacking for Dummies* by Kevin Beaver, there is a disclaimer that reads:

> If you choose to use the information in this book to hack or break into computer systems maliciously and without authorization, you're on your own. Neither I (the author) nor anyone else associated with this book shall be liable or responsible for any unethical or criminal choices that you might make and execute using the methodologies and tools that I describe.

A dense and ambiguous (not to say naive) passage. For a start, Beaver would do well to leave such fraught concepts as Choice well alone for his purposes. But still, I respect his drawing a distinction between "unethical or criminal" choices. But even there, there is the question: "unethical" to whom? – Beaver should take care to define his terms.

And I can't help but think that Beaver is resorting to wishful thinking, here. If we were to unpick these caveats, I think a more accurate phrasing might be:

> The publishers of this book would like to assert all necessary and appropriate legal protections with regard to non-liability, etc., while clarifying that no such protections exist *vis* responsibility.

Hacking for Dummies is currently in its fifth edition.

Hacking Wireless Networks for Dummies, also by Kevin Beaver, is almost identically caveated, except with an addition:

> If you want to find out how to maliciously break into wireless networks this book is not for you. In fact, we feel so strongly about this, we provide the following disclaimer.

(The following disclaimer reading more or less as above.)

The less said about Beaver's strength of feeling the better – but *Hacking Wireless Networks for Dummies* is over ten years old (with no new editions), so instead I've gone with *The Hacker Playbook 2: Practical Guide to Penetration Testing* by Peter Kim, which includes many examples and practical tips for using the tools in the Kali Linux distribution.

I've created a business persona. I believe it will greatly simplify my procurement pipeline.

To begin with I wrote up a list of companies that I presume have huge security expenditures. My hypothesis was that a company's security spend is a function of (a) its size (personnel-wise), and (b) the instability of the territories it operates in. My list therefore ended up with a lot of energy companies I'd never heard of (and some I had). I falteringly investigated their procurement channels and the security firms they engaged. Up until now I'd been contemplating the problem of how an individual might acquire weapons; my angle, as it were, was wrong, and I was banging my head against the proverbial wall for some weeks.

Of course, the answer is that an individual shouldn't attempt to acquire weapons. That would be, in most cases, illegal. Instead the weapons should be sensibly purchased in the regular fashion as a transaction between corporate entities. The benefits to using these regulated channels for such a purpose are manifold: we can rest assured we're getting a better product, with all the appropriate manufacturer's guarantees and service agreements.

And so I devised a persona to undertake the necessary transactions.

I thought there was a poetic rightness to the name Philip Swiles. It's funny where these ideas come from, sometimes. The main purpose of Philip Swiles (Oil Executive) is to serve as a credible identity under which to attend the Defence and Security Equipment International (DSEI) fair at the ExCel Centre in London.

In order to furnish Philip with the appropriate paperwork and other bona fides, I've purchased what's known as a "shelf company" (not to be confused with a "shell company" – a far more dubious enterprise). My shelf company is called Elcock Crest, and I think it will specialize in Petroleum Security (or PetSec, on the business cards). It will possibly be some kind of subsidiary to a much larger petroleum company, for which it will manage Pipeline Security (PipSec) and the Conflict Resolution Task Force (or simply the Task Force). I imagine the Task Force requires a steady flow of fantastic ordnance, particularly for their PipSec engagements in the Niger Delta.

Dear Angela,

This is my fifth attempt at writing this letter. <u>It is NOT a "Self-Expression".</u>

There is a man I hate. You have to understand my reasoning. I can't skip straight to the end, though I want to. Because I want you to hate him too.

When the time comes, I need you to forgive me. You, or anyone. But let it be you.

The MP5 is a fantastic sub-machine gun, manufactured by Heckler & Koch.

The Germans make excellent weaponry, due to their historical biases. The MP5 is used by special forces units throughout the world. It was used by the SAS during the celebrated Iranian Embassy siege. During the siege, the SAS soldiers shot surrendering terrorists. It was understood the time for surrender had passed. They fired what are known as *double taps*. Proficient shooters fire in *double taps* and do not use fully-automatic fire, though the MP5 offers a variety of fire modes. The MP5N is a specialized version of the weapon adopted by the American Navy SEALs. The MP5N trigger group, in addition to semi-automatic and fully-automatic fire modes, also has a *three-round burst*. This is when the gun fires three shots with every trigger pull. Some trigger groups also feature a *two-round burst*. With the *two-round burst* one imagines it is possible to pretend one is an SAS soldier performing *double taps*. The American Navy SEALs were responsible for the assassination of Osama bin Laden, though to my knowledge they did not use the MP5N during that operation (reputedly they used the HK416). During that operation, the Navy SEALs crashed a helicopter *en route* to Bin Laden's compound. The Navy SEALs have a crest or insignia, known as the SEAL Trident, which is of something like a bird carrying a trident, an anchor, and what appears to be a musket, in its claws.

The Navy SEALs, as you can imagine, are a bit of a joke.

Elcock Crest will be a Private Military and Security Company (PMSC). These sorts of enterprises range from solo ex-military consultants to fully fledged militias (indeed, some would better be described as private militaries).

Imagining my own private military, I was reminded of a brief interlude in one of my history lessons which touched on the magnificent British East India Company. Imagine a company so big, I said, that it had the power to declare war! Never was the profit motive more powerfully unleashed.

I realize now I was foolish to consider it an historical absurdity. If companies no longer declare actual war on countries, it's surely because war is so costly, and companies nowadays are so unpatriotic. So instead of (Royal) British Petroleum acquiring territory for the Crown in valorous corporate warfare, the task is instead delegated to the national instruments of domination. Nevertheless, in the broad category of Violence Up to but Excluding War, there is much need, and indeed much *value to add*, in providing security to companies who might otherwise have their businesses menaced in dangerous locales (by the Niger Delta Avengers, for instance).

The un-entrepreneurial among us might ask: What does it say about my company that I need a platoon with automatic weapons to protect it? But the businessman instead asks: What is the relative risk profile of leveraging armed personnel in achieving my business aims?

Favourable, is the answer. Guns reduce risk to the business

by increasing the cost of engagement by hostile forces. When you have weapons, you eliminate a whole category of threat (namely, banditry). In doing so, guns reduce the cost of doing business.

In my application for Section 5 Authorization from the Secretary of State, I (as Philip Swiles) listed Elcock Crest as a "Freight Forwarder". Being a new applicant – and therefore lacking prior business invoices, contracts, etc. – I (as Swiles) attached half a dozen unsolicited letters of enquiry from potential customers.

Freight Forwarding seems the most plausible explanation for Elcock Crest's almost complete lack of commercial premises (though I've found a good spot near Park Royal Underground Station which might suit).

Consulting the handy key in the documentation, as far as I can tell the authorization I'm requesting must cover all the below:

Section 5 (1) (a) – weapons which are so designed or adapted that two or more missiles can be successively discharged without repeated pressure on the trigger.

Section 5 (1) (ab) – any self-loading or pump-action rifled gun other than one which is chambered for .22 rimfire cartridges.

Section 5 (1) (aba) – any firearm which either has a barrel less than 30 cm in length or is less than 60 cm in length overall, other than an air weapon, a muzzle-loading gun or a firearm designed as a signalling apparatus.

Section 5 (1A) (e) – any ammunition for military use which consists in or incorporates a missile designed, on account of its having a jacket and hard-core, to penetrate armour plating, armour screening or body armour.

Section 5 (1A) (f) – any ammunition which incorporates a missile designed or adapted to expand on impact.

I feel once Elcock Crest has a proven track record, I might be inclined to later stretch to:

Section 5 (1) (ae) – any rocket launcher, or any mortar, for projecting a stabilized missile, other than a launcher or mortar designed for line-throwing or pyrotechnic purposes or as a signalling apparatus.

And having now seen it, I can't help but be tempted by:

Section 5 (1A) (a) – any firearm which is disguised as another object.

Amy was fifteen by the time she went out with Paul. He was sixteen.

I think Paul may have been wary of courting her, given she was my daughter. Perhaps I'm imagining that. In any case, eventually rumours started going around the school that Paul was having sex with the headmaster's daughter.

I don't believe he started the rumour, since, in a way, he was its victim too. It was an exploratory kind of gossip, a kind of gossip that probes a topic, ambiguously. It could have resolved in various ways: that Paul had conquered the headmaster's daughter, and by proxy the headmaster himself, or, conversely, that Paul had been snared or domesticated – emasculated, even – by the headmaster, by the proxy of his daughter. Much of it hinged, I believe, upon the attractiveness of the girl in question – as to whether a boy was conquering enviable territory or ceding their manhood – and this added to the complexity of the issue, given that it was easier in the boys' collective imagination to picture the headmaster's daughter as an ox, and the possibility that the headmaster's daughter might be desirable was problematic, both in that it threatened to glorify me, and also had the grotty whiff of incestuousness, like admitting one's feelings for a cousin.

After the gossip – and my wife's discovery that Amy and Paul were interested in each other – the first real evidence of their affair, which was hardly evidence at all, was a change in Paul's manner towards me. There was a new awkwardness between us, as well there might have been. For all he knew, he was being scrutinized from both ends – discussed between myself and his girlfriend (if they indeed referred to each other by such designations at that time).

Paul was, as it would turn out, in his final year at the school. Year 11 – approaching the summit of Key Stage 4. By then his manner and status had changed quite considerably – he was well liked by the teachers, especially those who didn't teach him. I don't believe my preferential treatment of Paul had any influence over the staff one way or the other, and in truth I'm not sure how much rein I had with regard to his increasing maturity. But I must have played some part.

How much better it would've been had I left him to his own devices. Had I left him to be largely tolerated and ignored, detained and allowed to rot – until, finally, at the summit of Key Stage 4, discharging him unto the world, like a domesticated animal being let free to fend for itself, its natural instincts chiselled away, and no cunning or resourcefulness drawn out in their place. Paul would have disappeared from my life, another unnotable failure – of many, I'm sure.

But as it turned out, during my long intervention with Paul I managed to inspire the loathing of Paul's RE teacher, Mr Spirakis. I would have alienated, too, the whole RE department, except that it was comprised entirely by the one person. Because it came to a point where Paul justly refused to attend any more of my detentions. Over time, they'd become shorter and more frequent – really they were my way of keeping tabs on the boy. I instructed his teachers to send him to me on the slightest grounds. In the early days they had grounds enough.

Eventually I was spending perhaps half an hour a week

with the boy, sometimes more, sometimes less – a ten-minute detention here, sometimes just a brief five minutes. The better his outlook became, the shorter our detentions became, and, finally, the more unreasonable they seemed.

I'd thought we'd both fallen into our routine quite comfortably, but one day the penny dropped and Paul entered into his detention – the sole detainee, once again – with a rebellious spirit. It was only the second time in all our exchanges that Paul had invoked his mother – but with her, this time, his father too.

"My mum says it's unfair that you're always giving me detentions for no reasons."

I didn't answer the claim, feeling momentarily betrayed.

"My dad wants to speak to you about it."

I nodded. It took me a few moments, but eventually I came out with something – something like, "It's true that your behaviour is much improved – I've come to see myself as something of a mentor to you – It's only my concern over your future," etc. Things like that, the thin clichés, true though they were.

He hadn't even sat down – he was standing by the doorway, still with his rucksack on, a single strap drawn diagonally across his chest, as was the style in those days. It was foolish of me to be saying anything to him, since he was mostly looking at his shoes, and around the room, and wanting to be off, and waiting for me to finish speaking, but since I had no real grounds to detain him – since I had no reason to keep him except the personal, moral one – I couldn't demand he sit and listen, so instead I blew those airy clichés at him, more than anything to excuse my own behaviour.

But I salvaged my position as he was leaving – I rose and

called after him, as he was striding down the hall, and I said,

"I'll make a deal with you."

And he stopped, and turned, and asked, "What?"

"I'll make a deal with you," and I was talking loud enough that I'm sure the English department could hear.

He slackened. "What deal?"

I didn't fancy us shouting to each other like this, but there was no way I was going to walk to him. It was clear we were at an impasse. I'd hoped the mention of a "deal" would pique his curiosity. But Paul was, by his very nature, an uncurious soul.

"No more detentions. And you get one lesson off, every week." So, it turned out, I resorted to a kind of money-back guarantee to finally draw him back.

"What do you mean?" He was smiling quite childishly, and I pitied him his lack of cynicism.

What I meant was that I would maintain my role as Mentor to him, but the mentorship would be conducted during Paul's school hours. Which meant nixing RE (obviously Paul suggested he sacrifice a double period of Maths to better be mentored by me).

If I alienated Spirakis by making such a judgement (I remember vividly his indignant suggestion that the period of omission should change from week to week, but I insisted that consistency in such matters was vital) I don't believe he found much solidarity with the rest of the teachers (and, as I mentioned, he had no department to fall back on, or to rally), and I suspect if anything the other teachers felt pleased not to be ranked bottom of the pecking order.

But in these mentoring periods every week, we never even touched upon the matter of my daughter. To be honest I wasn't particularly interested – Paul didn't strike me as such a bad choice. (And if anything I wondered whether it was Paul's parents who should be concerned.)

Rather, in these periods, I only glimpsed the possibility of their relationship in how he discussed the world. It was fairly clear to both of us that university wasn't his port of call. And I did nothing to pretend it might be a good option for him (of course I so wish I had now, no matter how false it would have been).

"Some people think I should," he said, in regard to applying for university, and I could only assume this was Amy's voice, given I couldn't imagine his parents or friends voicing that opinion. Funny to think that in those days Amy took university as the default path, only to deviate from it so wildly later.

I told him he should consider it carefully, meaning that he shouldn't consider it at all. "What subject would you study?" I'd ask, whenever the issue came up, and he never had an answer.

I thought, basically, that he should stick it out and get some A levels, and then find a profession he could start at the bottom of and work his way up, with the new diligence I hoped I'd inspired in him.

"You might even consider the police," I said.

The things Paul liked: football, rugby, a variety of television programmes (especially comedies), computer games (in particular football games) and little else. Lazily, I told him he might want to aim for some career in the periphery of sport, either writing about it (though he had no imagination for writing) or directly dealing with athletes (such as physiotherapy, an idea he half-toyed with) – and sometimes I took the other tack and asked him whether he could direct his energies to the media industry, perhaps working his way into one of the production companies that made one of the many television programmes he watched, though he always seemed incredulous that he could ever be admitted to the premises where such magic occurred, let alone feasibly have a career in its production. And as for the computer games that vied with the television programmes to take up his evenings, he dismissed any possibility of working on them with the appeal that they were made "by nerds", a summary with which I could only agree.

Such was my ineffectual careers advice.

Dear Angela:

    <u>This is NOT a "Self-Expression".</u>

    I can't skip straight to the end even if I wanted to. I want you to understand my reasoning. I don't want your pity,

    I don't want you talking me out of it. It's not possible. This letter isn't going well.

In terms of combat effectiveness I must obviously use the MP5. As I've said to myself many times, the MP5 is a fantastic weapon. For my purposes there is arguably none better.

And yet I am drawn to the FN SLP MK 1.

Fabrique Nationale is a Belgian company. They make some of the finest small arms in the world. At first you might think this strange, given Belgium's reputation, but you must remember that they, too, have their own particularly brutal historical biases. FN's fine array of guns must be, in their way, a hymnal to this cultural heritage.

Initially I looked into Remingtons, particularly the 870. But I decided against a pump action, and in any case it would seem Remington's manufacturing standards have slipped and it is the older-model 870s which are more sought after. Whereas I can most easily source new weaponry, either direct from the manufacturer or from a licensed wholesaler, in the guise of a transaction on behalf of Royal Dutch Shell.

Of the autoloading shotguns I've looked into, the SLP has very much taken my fancy.

I should have visited my father in hospital today, but I had to change my plans on account of a short-notice appointment scheduled by the Ealing Firearms Enquiry Officer.

So instead I took the train to Park Royal Underground Station and went to 28 Concord Road, where I have a small office which I rent for £200 per week. I spent a small fortune fitting powerful locks on the front and back doors, and the windows. It's a small space: a boxy room, with a desk and bare shelves, a very old Dell computer that someone had left there and which is thankfully just a prop since, when I timed it, it took a full nine minutes to boot. There's also an over-large photocopier that, as far as I can tell, is involved in some kind of revenue share scheme, and which I wasn't allowed to remove (I was given a bad photocopy of some catalogue page explaining the charges for using the unwanted device). There's also a more spacious back room, which serves as the armoury, but as yet is only home to four large gun cabinets (BS7558 compliant) and two ammunition cabinets.

The computer was still booting up when the FEO arrived. He asked me if I was Philip Swiles and I nodded and thanked him for coming. He enquired about the nature of my business, but I could tell he didn't have a head for such things. I told him the majority of the business was comprised of various overseas entities, that Elcock Crest was primarily concerned with forwarding shipments to these larger (non-existent) enterprises. I showed him the gun cabinets, the pair of keys for each, which he used to test the locks. He banged firmly on the exteriors of one or two of them, as if this might simulate the action of a break-in. I believe he was disappointed there were no weapons on the premises.

After he'd left, after his meagre inspection, I sat in the boxy office with my back to the huge photocopier and thought about my father in hospital, and regretted not seeing him. I had an overwhelming urge to plan a visit tomorrow – though I knew I wouldn't go.

I'd like to see him. Without climbing into that pit every time.

I imagine filling those cabinets with weapons.

The DSEI fair was fantastic. Of course, we didn't have time to see all the exhibition zones (Frankie was disappointed not to spend longer in the Naval Zone). It was my fault. I got chatting with the exhibitors in the Security Zone – which, despite having a preponderance of stands dedicated to cyberwarfare, nevertheless absolutely thrilled me with the variety of firearms on display for special forces units (and, indeed, it was really an eye-opener as to the state of play in tactical equipment). One exhibitor in particular – representing a smaller, independent firm – was incredibly helpful to me and seemed to possess a knowledge of the industry far beyond the remit of his own business. I especially enjoyed his authentic pronunciation of *Walther* and *Herstal,* and how it contrasted with his native English – he seemed to speak these German fragments with a respect and nobility entirely absent from his usual patter. He even gave me a few ideas for incorporating combat knives into my tactical mix. It was only Frankie's increasingly despondent looks in my direction (he wandered off here and there, but never out of sight) that finally drew my conversation with the exhibitor to a close.

I spent a long time admiring the shoulder-mounted rocket launchers. Frankie was strangely unmoved by them when I pointed them out, preferring the huge armoured personnel carriers parked on the perimeter of the Land Zone, so much so that he happily posed for a picture in front of them, beaming jaggedly at the camera while the attendants looked apprehensive.

There was one battle rifle, with a unit price of about £75,000 (I asked), equipped with a camera attachment for shooting around corners, and a top-mounted cannon for firing airburst rounds intended to eliminate targets behind cover (and that's not to mention the array of undermounts available for firing assorted grenades and shotgun cartridges).

Though I was a bit disappointed, after we arrived back home with the contents of the various goody bags handed out by the exhibitors – too many pens and rubbers by far. Frankie got a chunky, felt-tipped marker styled as a high-explosive grenade, which he's very taken with (mine was a disappointing chaff grenade, which he made fun of me for).

Dear Angela,

How many times have I started this letter?

I'd like to talk to you, one day, as if we'd never been client and therapist. I wonder how we'd get on?

Imagine we'd met in a café or bar, somewhere foreign (perhaps the proprietor only speaks Dutch). Imagine I've already run back and forth in my mind, pondered and ruminated and so on before we'd ever met, so that when I sit down at your table I can begin clearly and competently, set out my case, as it were –

If you could stop trying to fix me for a moment and answer me plainly, is what I'm asking, wouldn't you hate him, too?

The Bible would have us believe:

1) The world is unjust
2) It is not our place to enact justice in the world

That is, there is a Just God and our deserts will be met in heaven or hell (a crudely binary choice, it seems, but I'm sure that's just the necessity of the retelling). Therefore, there's no need for justice on earth. Indeed, to privilege justice on earth is to sin – because it implies lack of faith in God's divine justice.

Similarly, to grieve overlong is to sin, for the same reason.

Strange to think I considered myself Christian. But I realize I was only Christian in agreeing that people should generally be kind. If you were to ask me, "Do you accept Jesus as the saviour of mankind", I might say, "Why not? Someone has to be." But that is not accepting Jesus. Accepting Jesus is saying: "I accept men will be crucified on earth and God will (appear to) do nothing." So Jesus died for us, in the most brutal way imaginable, as an example, so that we might learn to accept injustice. That is Christianity's fundamental teaching, the supercommandment: Accept Earthly Injustice. Trade it for something higher. It should be on a tablet larger than all the others.

But I can't spend my life in this world building it up only to watch it burn. I don't have any strength to say, "It's all God's plan." I'm too attached to this world, too dug-in. If I'd known better, I would have kept back from it a little more, held it at a slight distance, to better detach myself when the time came.

But I can't. Without really intending to, I became a kind of father to a thousand children – not in the crude, worthless sense, but in the actual sense. We raised them, in that school. Some of them we pulled practically right out of the ground. And you can't raise a thousand children and not get stuck to this world.

The Bible tells us, "If any man love the world, the love of the Father is not in him."

Stark and plain. Well I do love the world. Or did. I loved it and the things in it. At the very least I loved it enough to try to improve it. I put my shoulder to the wheel – I raised fatherless children at that school, and I was a second father to the rest. I coerced goodness out of them when it was latent, and shielded goodness when it was menaced. I put my life into instilling the crudest raw values in them. And why? Because it's the world that outlives us, not the other way around. It's the world that carries on after us, and that might do so better, if we'd only let it.

So I'm not Christian. Even if I thought I was.

And if you'll tell me "Love not the world", tell it to my face.

Frankie believes in God. That's as close as I can get. I ask Frankie, in his opinion, what God might have meant by all the madness we've both experienced in our lives. I frame the question lightly, over the steaming kettle in the kitchen.

He just shakes his head and says he doesn't know. "We're not meant to know, I don't think," he says.

I think about that as I spoon the three sugars into his tea.

"I suppose not," I said. "But what are we meant to do about it?"

He looked at me blankly, so I continued, "This madness in our lives. What are we meant to do about it?"

He was eyeing his cup of tea, so I finished stirring it and handed it to him, which he thanked me for, and seemed ready to drop our conversation, so I took a moment, after I'd sipped my own tea, to try to reiterate my question without being insistent about it.

"Do you ever wonder if there's more we should do? If we've done something wrong? Or we're not doing something right?"

He licked his lips lizardishly. "I'm sure there must be!" he said and half-laughed. "All you can do is try your best," he said. "Isn't it?"

I wanted to say, *At what, though? Try our best at what?* but sensed the matter had been closed. Sometimes, in our early exchanges, I might have pushed too much, tried to steer the conversation too forcefully, and Frankie would recede a little, close himself off that bit extra, which would affect me quite profoundly for the rest of the day and I'd seek some means of reconciliation, even though he never acknowledged that anything had passed between us. So instead I reached for the bourbons (a late addition to my kitchen cupboard, more or less predicated on Frankie's visits, though I've started to get the taste for them too).

Today, Frankie is telling me about Cross Site Request Forgery (or CSRF) attacks. Last week it was Cross Site Scripting (or XSS) attacks. I don't ask how he knows about these things, and he doesn't ask why I want to know.

Frankie taught me: hacking is subversion. He told me about the classic hacks – the ones from "his day", as it were. He taught me about the stack and the heap and the buffer overflow. He described with great tenderness the genius of overwriting a function's return address, of mitigating compiler padding, off-setting attack strings down to the byte.

The first task, he said, is always to subvert the program. Wherever there's user input, he said, there's a chance – a slim chance – for subversion. Remote code execution is the grail – subverting the program to run *your* program. Once you're able to execute commands, the next task is prosaic by comparison: escalating privileges. Gaining root access. Frankie knows a few ways, has a cursory knowledge of the techniques, but his interest is in the subversion, in that moment of turning the machine away from its intended ends. As for taking control thereafter – power doesn't interest him. Or so it seems. So he told me about one of his favourites: opening a reverse shell through a bogus file upload.

Imagine it, he told me – the simplest of ideas (no buffer overflow this). The application allows users to upload pictures, perhaps to share with friends or simply to store them as back-ups. But instead of uploading an image, you upload a script. And the application (credulous fool) treats the script as an image, hosting it just the same as it would an image. And all you need do is follow the link to your hosted script for the server to execute your commands and forward a shell session to your machine.

He beamed devilishly at the thought, slurped his tea.

"And then what?" I ask. "Once you have the shell – once you can run your code?"

And nothing but an offhand shrug.

"The usual," he says.

By which he means: escalating privileges, taking ownership, gaining power. The usual.

Dear Mr Swiles,

It is my pleasure to conclude your first purchase with us.

I hope that you and your team are satisfied with the products delivered today. As I understand Elcock Crest is a freight forwarding agent, you'll see that I've taken the liberty of ensuring your delivery today is safely packed and ready for onward shipping in compliance with all necessary statutes and regulations at no extra cost to you.

At Bespoke Defence we emphasize our close working relationships with our clients and our manufacturers, and this means we can often seek arrangements which larger firms either can't or won't. For our clients that means a solution that better fits their needs.

When we spoke together you mentioned that your defence operations were scaling up due to the de facto militarization of the Niger Delta. While Bespoke Defence cannot directly offer any expertise in the region, we of course know of various key players who can, and we'd be happy to put you in touch with third parties who can help you fulfil your security requirements.

As I mentioned to you when we spoke, we mainly specialize in European small-arms manufacturers (though we're unable to

[continued overleaf]

sell weapons made in the UK due to licensing laws). Some of the manufacturers we have close ties with:

Benelli Armi SpA	Luigi Franchi SpA
Beretta Holding	PGM Précision
GLOCK	SIG SAUER
Herstal Group (FN Herstal)	Steyr Mannlicher GmbH Austria
HS Produkt	Walther
Heckler & Koch	

Though we are by no means limited to the above and also have good connections with manufacturers who produce a wide array of weaponry under licence. Similarly, we have great capacity to fulfil any orders for tactical equipment, particularly body armour and concealed explosive devices. As the state of tactical equipment is so fast-moving these days, don't be surprised if the best solution for your needs is one you haven't even heard of! (And, of course, that's where I hope we can help you.)

Allow me to once again extend my thanks for your business. If you have any questions or would like to discuss your security challenges further, don't hesitate to contact me via phone or email (details below).

Warm regards,
Liam Nestor

I came home one time to discover my wife was out, and Amy and Paul were in the living room – Amy had been playing the piano, and Paul listening, as far as I could tell. The piano stopped when I keyed the lock and opened the door, and when I reached the living-room doorway they both looked at me with vague alarm, the way lovers in a restaurant might eye a drunk who's bent on engaging them in conversation. I said hello to the both of them and went to my study to put my things away.

It was a little while before the playing started up again – I think I may have heard Paul encourage her to keep playing, though I'm not sure. In the brief glimpse I got, when I returned to the living-room doorway – before Amy realized my presence and stopped again – I had the distinct, powerful feeling that it wasn't going to last between the two of them.

It was just something in the way Paul was listening – some degree of boredom, perhaps.

I don't think it was common for Amy to play for him – in fact, the whole scene struck me as quite unusual. I won't pretend to understand the motivations of those involved, but I sensed the possibility that this was some strange ploy on Amy's part – even some kind of cruelty, perhaps – surely she could sense his boredom? It may have been a test, of sorts. Or perhaps I'm completely wrong – perhaps Paul just asked to hear the piano, having never really heard one played by someone he knew. In any case it seemed to me that there was some fundamental incompatibility playing out between them. So I left them well alone.

Angela, you test me when you refer to my *homosexual tendencies*.

It angers me more than I let on (I hope). Not because I'm bigoted (though I may be). Part of my anger is at your stupidity. I find stupidity aggravating. I find yours, in particular, aggravating, because I'm meant to take you seriously. Because after this long course of therapy I wish I could take you seriously.

Don't waste my time with your stupidity, Angela.

When we next meet I'll tell you. I'll tell you this, or something thereof:

1) You see my fondness for Paul and my fondness for Frankie and deduce, because they are male and because more than one of anything forms a pattern, that I have *homosexual tendencies*

2) This suggests I was in some way *grooming* (to use the modern parlance) Paul, or that I had paedophiliac desires

3) It also suggests I have similar (perhaps latent to your mind) sexual longing of some nature towards Frankie, even though his appearance (and odour and everything else) is repugnant to me and it is quite clear my bond with him is strongly emotional

4) I am beginning to suspect your Expensive American Education wasn't expensive enough and perhaps even was a Cheap American Education and that may be why

you didn't address the issue when I raised the issue of your Expensive American Education, because you were insecure/wanted to ignore or repress the thought of your Inadequate American Education and that in the course of this lacklustre schooling you learnt something about gender, such as one or two modules or something like that, and that is the sum total of your genius for analysis

5) You have one lens through which you examine everything

6) It is clear to me that you have no skill to stop me, which I realize or think I realize is what I hoped you'd do

7) If not stop me, then at least offer a convincing alternative that I might consider

8) But you have none.

"D'you remember that advertising jingle that your mother was upset about, because they put it through some kind of synthesizer?"

Amy didn't.

Do you think it pains your daughter to talk about her mother? Angela has asked me.

I considered it.

"Possibly," I said. "She's often reticent, whenever I talk about her mother."

Why do you think Amy closes down when you talk about her mother? was another question, perhaps it came before, perhaps it was a sort of lead-up.

Then afterwards, *Do you want to force her to reminisce about happier times? What you consider happier times?*

"Your mother was really quite upset, one time, when she saw the advert on the television. She hadn't been altogether so pleased with what she'd handed over in the first place, from what I remember. She thought she'd compromised too much and given them something really cheesy."

My daughter didn't say anything, glanced at her phone, tapped it, made it shine, briefly, before putting it out.

Do you think you've confused her avoidant behaviour with boredom? I can well see it, now. Angela has indoctrinated me, I'm turning into her: she's colonizing little parts of my mind, so that I look at my daughter idly tapping on her phone and I give it a tragic cast, saying to myself that she is not bored with me – as she has every right to be – but that she is avoiding *engaging* with the topic of her mother because it *pains* her.

Perhaps I do want it to pain her. Perhaps I want her to tell me it pains her.

But you don't tell her that it pains you? Angela might say. She lives in my head, now. Should I tell Amy outright? – force the issue? That would be her way. I'm not quite there, yet.

"And she saw the advert, a few weeks later, or maybe even it was months, I'm not sure, but she stopped what she was doing, momentarily, turned the volume of the television right up, too much, so that she had to then soften it a little – and then she softened it some more when it became clear her composition had been rendered by some quite dated-sounding synthesizer. I remember not understanding her disgust, even quite liking their crazy interpretation of it – in fact, I felt quite proud that her work had been *interpreted*, as it were – but she really hated it; she listened to the whole thing, then turned the television off – in case it might come on again, I suppose! Then she went back to whatever it was she'd been doing, laughing and shaking her head, decrying how bad it was, how *obscene* it was, that it had been cheesy enough in the first place without their *kitsch* keyboard getting involved."

Amy smiled unconvincingly at my retelling.

"I looked up the advert," I said. "Someone had uploaded a video of it, on the internet. Can you believe such a thing?"

She didn't say anything.

"Would you like to see it?" I said.

She took a deep breath, and said not tonight, that she really had to go, and she stood up and gulped down the rest of her coffee.

"Theme for Pirelli Tyres" went through several transform-
ations before the client was satisfied with it. It had what might
be described as a troubled conception. Part of this was caused
by the brief. The brief said something along the lines of: *the
music should describe a mountain-top scene, suggestive of
danger but also complete control, we have in mind possible
influences such as Russian folk. The score should be foreign
and yet familiar.* Accompanying this description (which was
not more than a few hundred words) was a hastily drawn
storyboard, which pictured a car careening around a snow-
capped mountain-top, and then through a forest. It wasn't
clear whether the advert was intended to promote a particular
model of tyre (I thought the inclusion of snow scenes might
point to some specific design or tread), but my wife insisted
that, in any case, it didn't make any difference.

In one cell of the storyboard, a strangely drawn bear threatens the car (as the car is entering the forest). The car is a
saloon-type car, which is able to manoeuvre safely but speed-
ily around the bear. The bear only appears in a single cell of
the storyboard because, I imagine, the artist thought that was
quite enough in terms of having a go at drawing any bears.

In her first attempt at rendering a composition from these
scraps, my wife took too seriously their request for something
tinged by Russian folk. She came up with a few bounding
phrases, which became the backbone of her doomed first draft:

When they heard it, their praise was more than equivocal. They belatedly retracted the Russian folk parameter, and I was very offended by the subtext of their reply, which hinted that my wife had somehow misinterpreted the brief.

She said – not entirely without satisfaction – that she'd known this would happen.

Apparently, this initial back and forth between herself and the client was part of her larger strategy. The Russian folk parameter, she'd already known, was a "shit" attempt at originality by the copywriter or the art director, or whichever of the pair had decided to involve themselves in the musical direction of the advert. The Russian folk parameter, she said, rang some sonorous alarm bells in her mind, because it was the kind of thing that was vague and nonsensical enough to haunt the entire commission. She gravely feared any unfulfillable requests like, *maybe a bit more Russian folksy?* – "as if it's some fucking magic dust you just sprinkle on top," she said (she swore often when it came to describing the thoughts of her clients, though mostly she was serenely tolerant of them, I thought).

In submitting three jaunty, folkish extracts – in isolating and emphasizing the problematic specification – my wife sought to eliminate the requirement with prejudice. By striking "Russian folk-ish" forever from their minds, my wife claimed more control over the remaining terms, and, she said, this early accommodation of appearing to change direction ultimately gave her greater freedom to set out the composition she originally had in mind.

Frankie likes my playing. He's very encouraging. The few times he's listened, he's been completely absorbed.

He always asks, "Your wife composed these songs?" and I never tire of him asking it – and I always marvel at his use of the word "compose", which is so unlike him, so that it seems a profound respect to her.

Whenever I pause or turn the page of the manuscript, or just turn idly back to him (I only play for a minute or so at a time), he'll nod smilingly, or else he'll ask, "Your wife composed that song?"

I'll nod, and then he'll say something like, "It's beautiful" or "I really like that one," and his liking it is always higher, to me, than any other accolade.

"She was talented," I said one time, just because I was at a loss, since really it didn't need saying, even my amateur playing could represent her talent enough, could suggest what it might sound like in the hands of someone competent. Very often I was at a loss after playing, or during.

"Does it make it better, do you think," he asked, "to have her songs?"

I shook my head.

"But, to have a part of her. Something that you can play and listen to?"

I tilted my head in apparent acquiescence, though I didn't think so. I don't like disagreeing with him. I often find the means to form a wonky accord with Frankie.

"It's a bit like a prayer, I suppose," I said. "But a prayer is said in hope for the life to come. Not for one that's gone."

"A eulogy," he said, another word as if plucked from the wisdom of the cosmos, so utterly beyond his regular speech.

I was inclined to remark *Elegy*, but thought perhaps he was right.

"You should put them on the internet," he said. "You should record yourself, and put them up for people to listen to."

I wanted to ask *Why?*, but instead I smiled and said, "A lot of these are probably still under copyright."

You'll never believe who I met: Ian. The senior delivery man.

I met him at a gym class. They teach a form of kickboxing there called Muay Thai (every instructor pronounces it differently).

He caught my eye early in the lesson. He was clearly an established figure there, a stalwart of a diverse crowd, young men and old men, one even quite podgy, so that I doubted his capabilities, and the odd very fit young woman.

There was an air of cliquish jocularity, so I kept to myself, except to nod to Ian from across the mats as the instructor was giving directions, and smile with my eyebrows raised as if to say, "Fancy seeing you here."

The warm-up was very extensive, so much so I had to defy the instructor's bellowing to avoid passing out.

"There's no point coming if you're going to sit on your arse!", etc.

The instructor was also around Ian's age, slightly younger, and even of similar build – so that it appears Ian is what the instructor will soon become: wider around the midriff, balder and mellower. But until then he screams at the slightest provocation, and the cords of his neck are often visible, and his circulatory system is very present, too.

I smiled at him from the depths of my stupor, on my knees (not my arse).

I was set to sparring with the podgy one, whom as I mentioned I underestimated. Almost immediately he struck me with his knee quite powerfully in the ribs – quite unnecessarily I thought – and I spent some time limping away from him as he continually launched kicks at me, and, of course, he came after me with all the more relish when he saw I was weakened.

Ian actually shouted encouragement to me then – having apparently decided not to bother with sparring, but instead to talk to one of the few women present, under the guise of instructing her on her kicking technique. But I barely noticed it at the time – because of my windedness, because of my half-stupor, but mainly because of the deafening indignity of being taken advantage of by the podgy man.

There is an etiquette for sparring. There is an etiquette, in particular, for sparring with a stranger. There is a necessary period of martial small-talk, as it were, where you trade strikes that are merely gestures. You spar *politely*.

But I was aware of Ian's presence just enough, and the thought of embarrassing myself restrained me. Because, by now, I've been to a number of these classes and met a number of people who, like the podgy man, spar rudely – taking advantage of my newness, of my meekness, of my age, of what they don't realize is my diminished red blood cell count – taking advantage of one they consider a novice.

I kept limping away from him and he kept launching wild kicks and grunting loudly with a vague *cho* kind of sound with every exertion, and when my ribs had recovered enough I stepped into his unpractised kicks and clinched him, and from there sought control of his head and was able to deliver three solid knee strikes to his middle, and even in those brief contacts I was repulsed by the bounce and warmth of him against the point of my knee, so that the third strike was the most hateful and he fell to the floor and I sensed that, perhaps, I'd need to find a different class next week.

After putting him to the mat I offered him my hand, and he took it, knowing he had no say in the matter now, and I lifted him to his feet before he was quite ready to stand, and he had to remain half-risen, with the air seemingly all beneath him.

"He's very good!" I cried to Ian, smiling, rubbing my ribs.

If I give Frankie forty pounds instead of the usual twenty, does it mean I feel guilty?

I always ask about his wife, though I know I shouldn't – I know, by now, I should have the sensitivity not to raise the issue, except perhaps by the lightest possible reference. So perhaps it is guilt – perhaps I only ask in order to see the same despondent shake of the head, to have the constant truth confirmed for me.

Does it make me feel better that he is suffering too? Without doubt. And why? And why do I demand confirmation, every time, of his wife's continuing absence? Because it reflects my own situation, perversely?

And do I hand over the extra purple note as penance for the asking? Or is that just the fee for the service he offers me? The price has risen, tacitly?

There is the other aspect, though – his trampishness, that he is so artless, so vulnerable to suffering, which he does to the maximum degree. That he resembles to my mind another failed schoolboy, the most extreme case, perhaps – completely unprepared for life and yet at the same time the most prepared, with the greatest capacity to suffer and take it in his (limping) stride.

That same despondent shrug – a shrug that would destroy me to make. His missing wife, his bad joints, his inflamed skin, his irritated scalp and his one red eye, they're all the same to him, one continuous blight. And my twenty pounds seems too slight by far – and forty even more so.

I locked Sultan in that room – only briefly – and I went to get the acid. I spoke to the Chemistry teacher, who was in a state of distress, and he was very helpful in explaining the chemical, what they used it for, the gist of the lesson plan, and he told me how severely he warned of the acid's danger to the class and the fuss he made equipping the boys with goggles and gloves, and it was his fault that some of the class had removed their safety goggles by then because the lesson was winding down, though he told them to keep them on until the very end, yet some didn't, and that made the ones who kept them on look foolish, so that more of them took their goggles off and he lost command over them in that respect, and then wished simply to bring the lesson to an end quickly, and when I asked him to show me where the substance was kept I believe he felt himself accused. I assured him he wasn't to blame.

I said: "Four years ago a boy called Pierre threatened another boy's head with the pillar drill in a DT lesson. But, further back than that, I remember a boy was stabbed quite viciously with a compass." (And I know now, of course, how dangerous even a pen can be.) "You can't supervise a boy's morality," I said, "only guide it, and the whole school bears that responsibility, especially myself."

He was relieved by this absolution, and didn't question it at all when I told him I was taking the nitric acid (in its large white plastic bottle marked with a skull and crossbones). I was going to give a reason, like "for when I discuss the matter with the police", but I saw it was unnecessary. He was glad to be rid of it, like of a cursed thing.

And I took it back to the locked classroom, with Sultan enclosed within.

He was standing at the back of the classroom staring at the wall. It had darkened outside, but he hadn't bothered to turn the lights on, or else preferred the dark.

I turned on the lights, and put my keys and the bottle of acid on the front desk.

"Sit down," I said.

And he turned, slowly, and went for a nearby chair.

"Here, at the front," I said, pointing.

And he paused, with his chair half-pulled out. He noisily scraped it back under the desk and slowly came towards me. I kept pointing at the chair I expected him to sit in and he did so. He looked at the bottle. He must have guessed at the contents, certainly the skull and crossbones were visible to him.

Perhaps he sensed something in me, when he said, "I didn't mean it."

I tried to work out what he meant.

"What didn't you mean?" I said.

He took a long time answering. "To hurt Garnet."

I thought about that.

"Perhaps you're sorry."

"I am."

"That's good. The problem you face is that you've harmed him irrevocably."

I pulled out the teacher's chair, but didn't sit down, instead keeping a firm grip on its back.

"*Irrevocably* means you can't take back what you've done.

You can feel sorry, but it's not enough," I said.

I released the chair from my grip, stood up tall and looked down upon Sultan, and I suppose he did seem apologetic, from above.

"I didn't mean it," he said. He was looking at his crotch and fussing with the lining of his pocket.

"You've spilt acid on your fingers," I said. "Sit up straight."

He half-straightened.

"Did it hurt?" I asked.

He looked at his injured hand, at the red burns.

"A bit," he said.

"Would you like to be burned on your face?" I asked.

He didn't say anything. He looked at me, then the bottle, then his fingers.

"No," he said.

"But you've done it to someone else," I said.

"I didn't mean it!"

"If you raise your voice again I'll put your head to the desk."

He looked at me. I was half-inclined to do it anyway. I could feel, in my hand, the reverberation of his skull against the desk, travelling up my arm and into my own body, where I'd dimly share the concussion with him.

"What does *irrevocable* mean?" I asked.

Hesitantly, "That I can't take it back," he said.

"Good," I said.

I unscrewed the bottle top, and he watched. A slow wisp of smoke rose from the bottleneck.

"Which hand?" I asked.

He was calculating what I meant. "What do you mean?" he said.

"Which hand?" I said.

"No," he said.

"No what?" I said.

"What are you doing?" he said.

"Which hand do you want to burn?" I said.

"Neither," he said, and I could see he was taking me very seriously now.

"And which of your hands is 'neither'?"

"What do you mean?" and his voice was unsteady, by now.

"Which hand do you want to burn?" I asked again.

"None," he said again, densely.

I took a breath. "And which of your hands is 'none'?" I asked, evenly.

"I don't want you to burn my hands."

"I understand," I said. "That isn't in question."

"What do you mean?" he said. He struggled greatly to understand things. What I thought at the time was a delaying tactic I see now was genuine bafflement at his predicament.

He began to cry. "I didn't mean it," he said, but softly enough that his head wasn't in jeopardy.

"Listen to me. Stop crying. Stop crying, Sultan, if you know what's good for you." I still wielded the bottle, uncapped, in front of me. "You've said a great many times now that you didn't mean it. I believe you. I believe you didn't intend to harm anyone, or at least not severely. But you did intend to splash him, didn't you?"

He shook his head. "No."

"If you lie to me I will burn every part of your body from your head to your testicles. So answer carefully: when you threw that acid at the boy, you were in control of your senses, weren't you?"

He didn't shake his head, but he cried, "I didn't mean it, though!"

I stooped over him and he flinched, and I said, "Be careful, Sultan. What you're saying is ambiguous."

I straightened.

"*Ambiguous* is when it can mean more than one thing," I said. "What you mean is that you didn't intend any harm by it."

"Yeah!"

"Don't raise your voice. Stop crying. *Stop crying!*"

He didn't quite stop, but enough that I had his concentration.

"You acted foolishly, and though you meant no harm, harm came of it. You didn't intend that harm, but you bear the responsibility for it. The harm is yours."

Then he whimpered "I didn't mean it" quite pathetically and I had to stop myself pouring the whole bottle over his head. He'd probably learned his lesson by that point, whether or not he'd reform his ways – whether or not he was capable of any meaningful kind of reform.

"Now you must face up to that responsibility," I said, "though you didn't mean it, and though you wish you could undo it. It is, as we've discussed, irrevocable.

"Now, which hand?"

The hand that he finally, tearfully pressed down on to the desk, quite bravely enough in the end, was his left, and afterwards the desk bore a partial outline of his fingers, where its surface had been masked from the corrosive, enough so that over time the peculiar mark became looked upon as a kind of omen, whether or not anyone really understood its relation to

Sultan, the timing of its appearance after Sultan's atrocity – whether or not any of this was ever formally understood by the boys, or whether the teachers admitted it to themselves, there was nevertheless an understanding of what it represented, and, eventually, the good thing it meant.

I said to Frankie, "I'd like to visit you, some time."

I said, "I enjoy your visits immensely, but I wonder whether I'm always dragging you out here."

Dragging you out here, though from where I didn't know.

I said, "Well, as long as it's no trouble for you to always be the one to make the journey. To always be the visitor," because after all his meaningless agreements or his quiet nods that I should visit him, I'd come to think he might be ashamed of his hovel (which I assumed it must be), and then thought I'd been insensitive to bring it up so often, though in truth I hardly brought it up, except out of politeness and what I'd thought was consideration, given that he might have been travelling from goodness knew where.

"At the very least," I said, at one of his visits, "you'll give me your address. I'd like to send you a letter."

He looked put upon.

"Well, not really a letter."

We were both sitting in the front room. We'd come down from the bedroom, where I'd shown him the sparring dummy, performed a few demonstrative kicks and elbows, and invited him to prod or thump it, though I was privately glad he didn't, on account of his lack of hygiene.

It was still sunny outside, a golden mid-evening, and I'd turned the television on for us to watch the 24-hour news, so that there was something we could both attend to if our conversation waned.

Our conversations often wane, because our friendship isn't based on talk.

"I've been writing down my thoughts, as part of my therapy, you see," I said to him, as he glanced nervously at the television, at the news that was softly going on in front of us.

"It was my therapist's idea, to begin with. But sometimes I write things which aren't meant for her. I'd like you to read a little of what I've written," I said, and he appeared uncomfortable, and so I reassured him, "but I don't want to make it awkward, or force you, which is why I'd like to post you a few pages. You wouldn't have to make a performance of liking or being interested in it. You could read them entirely at your leisure," I said. "Or not at all, even. It'd reassure me, somehow, just to send them to you."

"I'm not very good at reading," he said.

"I think you'd understand," I said. "More than anyone," I said.

He shook his head sadly. "I'm really not very good at reading. Not good at all."

"But it'd help me, Frankie, if you even just read a page. I think you'd understand, and you might be able to help me, with my wife, with how desperately sad I am."

He looked at me very sympathetically, then. He looked upon me as I imagine I looked upon him most of the time – with a profound sorrow for what had become of him, compared with what might have been.

Was I manipulating him at that moment? Surely it would be one of our discussion points, were I to tell Angela about any of it. I believe I was more honest with Frankie at that moment than I'd been with anyone else for a long time. Since I last spoke to my wife.

"OK, then," he said, as if he understood the gravity of what I'd asked him, and, since I felt bad for being so honest or so dishonest, for swallowing Angela's dogma and assuming you can and should describe how you feel – instead of being decent and untroubling – because of all that I insisted I'd sweeten the deal, and perhaps I could consider him my editor, of sorts, and of course that was worth a little money, in fact editors get paid quite a great deal, I said, smilingly, turning towards the news which was still going softly, though I could feel, then, the warmth of his gaze upon me, and the point of his tooth as he smiled at the prospect.

"Do they?" he said.

"Oh yes," I said, still watching the TV, and perhaps it was the only lie I told.

Perhaps I'd always intended to visit Frankie after I'd got his address out of him. Angela would probably have me believe that – that there was some kind of neurotic destiny involved.

The fact is, about two weeks ago I sent Frankie a few pages of my notes, for his editorship. Just ten short pages to begin with, since I imagined he could only concentrate on reading in short bursts (if at all). After a week without any word, I texted him, asking if perhaps I'd got the address wrong.

He's slow to respond to communications of all kinds, despite owning two phones: a smartphone with a screen so cracked it has the appearance of frosted glass, and a so-called feature phone, whose purpose I've never discovered, but which I begin to suspect was simply the first phone he possessed and is loath to be rid of, and so the smartphone is simply a kind of supplement. After ten days there was still no reply (even though the messaging application showed a green tick next to my messages, indicating he'd read them – another habit of his which I usually grudgingly tolerate only because I've seen him typing with his thumbs and there is no sight more agonizing). I decided to check in on him.

I regret it.

Frankie's house was perfectly charming on the outside, an old terraced street. The paintwork was tired and there were cracks here and there, but in a way that is fairly harmonious on that sort of Victorian house – those terraced houses that fall into disrepair with a degree of grace, somehow, compared with newer buildings, many of which aren't designed to degrade at all, and so degrade horrendously.

So if, in retrospect, Frankie's house was a little more crumbly and cracked than the street in general, it certainly didn't strike me that way at the time, and I wonder if it's only after having been inside it that I've made that judgement.

The door, though, was a faded baby blue, almost sun-bleached, like the door of an old cottage in the Mediterranean. The letter box had a "no junk mail" sign above it.

A woman answered the door, only enough to show her face. A severe face, creased. A poor face, suggestive of neglect.

I thought I had the wrong address. I thought perhaps Frankie had fooled me, given me a false address just to dodge my request, to avoid being burdened with my amateur journals or whatever he might perceive I was offering him. It would have been fair enough. I would have understood that, I hope. But I was sure that after I'd mentioned the money, that I'd pay him £10 per page for his editorship – an idea he took great delight in – that even if at first he'd given me a false address he would have contrived some way to supply the correct one.

So that after the initial surprise and hesitation, I asked the woman if Frankie lived there. She immediately turned from me and shouted "*Frankiiiiieeee!*" down the hall.

He was surprised to see me on his doorstep. It was the most surprised I've ever seen him. He didn't immediately invite me in.

"I've brought some letters. For you. My editor." I held the brown envelope out in front of me. "Is now a bad time?" I asked.

"No, no, no. No, of course not," he said, without inviting me in. The door was still mostly closed, held like a shield against a door-stepping salesman.

I think I already knew it was the end of me and Frankie, then. Perhaps that's why I asked him, outright, "Can I come in?" and stepped forward, so as to give him no option – unless he chose to close his shield against me, which he wouldn't. I even pushed against the door, slightly, so that he had to step back to let me in.

"Do you have a dog?" I asked. There was a faint odour in the hallway.

He shook his head. I knew, by then, by his utter dejection, that it was all over between us.

The woman was banging around in the kitchen, and she even cried out, "Who is it, Frank? Does he want a cup of tea?"

I looked back at Frankie, who was still lingering by the door, the door still not quite shut, as if he were willing me back out of it.

"A cup of tea would be lovely, thanks!" I shouted to her, still looking at Frankie, who seemed to flinch at my words.

She called me darling in acknowledgement. "And how about you, Frankie?" she cried, banging something else, a drawer or a cupboard door.

He walked past me, towards the clattering kitchen.

I ambled to the living-room doorway and peered inside. It was "lived in", as they say. It was about as messy, come to think of it, as my own front room (except on those days when my daughter visits and I'm forced to do a partial clean-up). For some reason it was far less appealing in someone else's house. The upholstery was more dated, there was a greater degree of old soft furnishings. The curtains in particular looked appalling: half-drawn, they appeared to linger grottily at the window.

Frankie came back to me and quietly suggested we take a seat, and I went ahead, since I was already in his way.

I sank into the sofa; he sat on the gigantic reclining chair.

The woman's name was Debbie. She didn't make another appearance – seemed to have disappeared entirely into the kitchen, which had fallen silent after Frankie went to – presumably – have a word with her, perhaps briefly suggest she disappear for the purposes of avoiding an awkward scene.

So I never got that tea, in the end.

Was Paul a surrogate son to you?

He wasn't. But is becoming so, perhaps. In the intervening period between her asking that question and now. *Life moves on*, as they say. I can't keep revising my opinions to keep up. Should I rewrite Frankie out of the whole thing, given what's happened? But this isn't about that stump of a man – that execrable deformity of a human being.

Perhaps it's natural, after Frankie's betrayal, that I should seek to renew old friendships. So Paul has started to become a surrogate son to me, perhaps. Or is becoming a surrogate father, in lieu of my actual father, who's wasting in hospital.

I met with Paul again, and I had a strange purpose, which I had to take great care in working up to, I thought. When I saw him, he was even worse than before, I thought. I telephoned his mother beforehand to ask to speak to him. I spoke a little to her, spoke some preliminaries to warm her up, to make it seem less odd that I wished to speak to her son *out of the blue*, completely out of the blue, as it must have seemed to her, picking up the phone in that bleak flat (though all flats are bleak now, it seems to me), and so I asked her how she was getting on, she and her husband and her son Paul, how was Paul doing? and in her voice was a delightful note, almost gleeful, because it was *such a nice surprise* to hear from me, so that I was humbled by the pleasure she took in my phone call, and guilty at my long absence, though it wasn't necessarily anything to do with me any more, Paul's outrageous debility, except that in my way I'd caused it, obviously.

"I'm sure Paul'll be delighted to speak to you," she said. There was a long transition between her saying that and Paul actually speaking to me; through half of it I heard her walking (from the kitchen?) and huffing and puffing after a few steps and still seemingly holding the receiver to her face, despite saying nothing, just her breath, so that it was a sordid thing almost and I held my own receiver away from my ear, and then there was an interval wherein she explained to Paul that he had a caller, that his old teacher was calling and hoped to speak to him, and I couldn't clearly hear what was said, but focused on the noise of his voice, and my heart actually raced at that sound, of his voice, at the guarded uncertainty of whatever he was saying (something like *Why? What does he want?* I was sure) until there was another movement of the receiver and Paul coughed louder, and there was more movement of the receiver as he hoisted himself straight, perhaps, got the phone handset into a comfortableish position, listening to the endless rustle of its transit, until finally he said,

My name.

My throat was quite dry, and my lips practically glued shut, but I got out,

"Paul. It's nice to hear your voice."

He didn't say anything, but there was more movement, and I sensed he was dismissing his mother, perhaps with a wave of his free arm, and I wondered then whether he waved her away with his stump arm or his good arm.

"How's it going?" he said.

At least with Paul I had the good sense to call him first, I thought, before I went to see him.

I'd sat by the telephone for many minutes before I'd had the courage to dial that long number. I'd been exercising, had been thinking of calling him while I struck the sparring dummy, while I ran through the streets, while I lifted my weights, delirious, perhaps a little, from the blood I'd taken, just a little more than last time, so I didn't trust myself to speak to him, though I wanted to – was certain I had to, that he could lead me to my goal – so that I wanted to but couldn't, because I thought for sure I'd be calling like a drunk in my breathless, bloodless state, like a spurned lover wanting to be taken back, or else like an errant lover slurring for forgiveness. And all through my euphoric exertions – euphoric because of the idea I'd had, of Paul – I distrusted my capacity to speak sensibly to him, and then after my exertions I sat by the telephone and waited for my blood to return, or for my courage to rise, and I wasn't sure I had either blood or courage when I finally did pick up the phone, with all my euphoria gone entirely, timid and nervous and sick from all my exertions, since I'd really pushed myself far beyond what was sensible, and was ready to throw up and trying not to.

It was going all right, Paul said. Not doing badly. How were things with me?

I was hoping I could visit him, if he wouldn't mind too much, I told him.

"Yeah, sure," he said. "Why?"

"I've been remiss," I said. "I feel I've let our friendship lapse."

I could practically feel his eyebrows rise.

"*Remiss*," he said. "Of course not," he said. "Has anything come up?" he asked.

"No, no," I said. "But I've had some thoughts," I said. And I wasn't sure, then, how much to say, how much was kind to say.

"I've been thinking. I wanted to ask you about some of your training," I said.

"My *training*?" he said.

I sensed that he wanted to push me closer to the awful topic. To say, *your military training* and invite all the horror that was attached to it.

"Your military training," I said. "If you wouldn't mind, I'd like to learn what it was like. I've just started exercising for the first time in my life, properly, and I thought to myself, if there was anyone who could give me some pointers, it'd be you. If you don't mind." I was, by then, very pleased with the tack I'd chanced upon, feeling that my subconscious, my inner wisdom, had thrown me a lifeline.

"Oh, right," he said. There was a long pause and I thought he was trying to come up with some excuse. "Of course," he said. He hesitated, seemed on the cusp of saying something.

"It would mean a lot to me," I said. "But if you'd rather not, I understand." Again, I was sure it was my subconscious conducting the phone call by now, since it was the only thing capable of saying what I really meant, and nothing else.

"No, of course, I'd be glad to give you some tips," he said, and I wondered, for a long time after I'd put the phone down, how much he meant it.

She asked if I was keeping some kind of diary. "In addition to the Self-Expressions." Maybe she thinks she's on to me.

"Some of your notes," she said, "I think are for me. And some of them aren't."

She stared at me, which is my cue to say something. I nodded.

"That's probably true," I said.

"Are they to yourself?" she asked.

I nodded. "I suppose they are."

"Are they?" She smiled and was silent. Another of her golden revelations deferred.

Do I write just for Posterity? Is it just for vanity I write these self-revealing records? Or do I write these words for their soothing power? To feel momentarily less alone?

He was even worse than before, when I saw him, after being *remiss* and not visiting for – months? Perhaps more than a year, by then. I visited in the morning, late morning, because I wanted to avoid seeing him later in the day, when his spirits usually deteriorated, was my understanding.

His mother brought us both cups of tea, though he was fixed on his beer. I always flinch, when I see him again. By now the flinch is almost entirely interior, a psychic flinch, but I've no doubt he sees it. I would hate it too, so I bow my head in acknowledgement of his glowering derision.

"It's good to see you again, Paul," I said, and made for the sofa, next to his chair. His chair faced the television, which was off. His neutral posture was facing forwards, towards that dark rectangle.

"It's nice of you to drop by." He looked unwashed, unshaven, he scratched himself with his good hand. He hadn't stood up to greet me, though he was wearing his prosthetics. I could see the stumps of his legs were red where they made contact with the false limbs, perhaps due to abrasion or a skin irritation caused by the material.

And every time I see him again, and sometimes just when I look at him, the same phrase is spoken in my mind, and it distracts me from what I'm trying to say or think, until I, too, am thinking what the voice says, and I have to beg myself not to say it out loud.

Look what they did to you.

I once watched a boy in a computer room, leaning back in his chair, slowly rocking back and forth on its rear legs, crane forward to press the eject button on the computer, and then, when the disc tray (as I now know they're called) had presented itself to him, he struck it with the bottom of his fist, so that it snapped off, and the computer's casing shook with the force.

He hadn't originated this practice. But he'd been the first to demonstrate it in my presence. This was always the only way I saw such things – by stealth, by spying an open classroom door as I did my rounds.

I admit I was quite transfixed by that boy – leaning back in his chair, which was enough, most of the time, to draw my ire. It ruins the floors, of course – there's that. But mostly it is the arrogance, as if the classroom were their home. And I well knew what the boy would do, as he craned forward to press the eject button.

Of course, disc trays of that nature had something of a design flaw. Nowadays – where an optical drive is necessary – the fashion is to forego any such tray, with its inherent fragility and tendency to jam (or break), and instead have a slot-loading drive, where the disc is drawn into the drive either by the action of rollers or pincer-like arms (depending on the expense of the device).

But! This was well before such fashions.

I knew his intention, but nevertheless I watched him. As he was undertaking his enterprise, the first few faces in the class had looked up at me, and seen me and straightened, and begun turning to their friends to nudge them – and very soon, of course, the impulse of this silent alarm would have rippled all the way through to the boy himself with his disc-tray-destroying mission.

And, do you know, he actually looked up, as he brought his fist down on it, as the whole workstation clattered with the force of the blow, and I've wondered about that look – sometimes wondered whether it was negligent sentryism, that he'd abbreviated the process of first checking the coast was clear, then acting, so accustomed was he to rule-breaking, so pat had the checking become, so comfortable was he in his own home, the classroom, as he saw it.

But I don't think it was that, any more. I think at that moment, when he brought his fist down, and at the same moment looked up – the look was simple curiosity. He wanted to know what was happening, but not enough to divert his action, so that, as I see it now, the act of smashing the disc tray was akin to stubbing out a cigarette – something banal and necessary, the natural consequence of sitting in front of a computer.

And I still didn't say anything at first, after he'd struck the disc tray and snapped it uncleanly in half, at the exact same moment he set eyes on me, along with, by then, the rest of the class.

He quickly drew his chair forward and sat looking straight ahead, as if, like the tyrannosaur in the movie, I might not see him if he were very still. Or as if, if he didn't see me, he could be immune to my powers.

I did tell my daughter all about Frankie, in the end. She was very sympathetic.

"You were right not to trust him," I told her. "You were right." I rather over-stressed her rightness.

Was the matter of her being right important to you?

Amy expressed sympathy, perversely, for Frankie as well – as if before he'd simply been odiously desperate, and now his desperation was cast into a whole new realm.

Debbie was his girlfriend. Is there any point going over it again? Debbie was his girlfriend, and I remarked that he'd never mentioned a girlfriend – or actually I said, "I didn't know you had a girlfriend," because obviously his whole story had been about his AWOL wife. He just shrugged and affirmed that Debbie was indeed his girlfriend. At first I didn't comprehend the scale of his lie and was confused and thought to say he moved quickly, he had moved on quickly, though it wasn't all that quick actually and more it was a case of him having a girlfriend and never mentioning it that seemed somehow duplicitous. Then I realized that he'd never had a wife, obviously, and I wondered at that, so much so that I didn't have the vocabulary to express my surprise or even bring myself to address the magnitude of his deceit. I said, "What's going on, Frankie?" and he shrugged.

"Don't shrug," I said. "You really mustn't shrug, not at a time like this especially," I said, and he was very still, except he nodded.

"What about your wife?" I said.

He waited, as if for the question to go away, then he said, "I don't have a wife, really."

I nodded at that. I drew the brown envelope containing my notes – the ones I thought he'd understand better than anyone else – into the inside of my jacket. My jacket had an inner breast pocket, but it wasn't wide enough, so I just let the envelope rest there on the inside, against my chest.

For a while I was still waiting for that promised cup of tea, because having asked for it I had the dim notion it would be rude to leave before drinking it, and it took quite a while before I understood Debbie was not coming back, and I felt a strange affection for her, for just the few words we'd shared, and her calling me *darling*, and the fact that we both knew Frankie, or thought we did.

Paul has used the SIG Sauer P226 before. He shows me the correct stance and grip, though he can only hold it one-handed. He instructs me tersely, pulling and pushing me with his one good hand. His breath is of rank, stale beer, but if I look away he'll think it's his blind eye I'm avoiding.

"I remember these," he said, when I first got the gun from the boot of the car, out of its aluminium carry case. He rotated it along its barrel, in his one good hand.

It isn't deliberate. I didn't know the army ever used the P226. I selected it for its excellence. SIG Sauer is a Swiss arms company. Despite being Swiss, despite their historical biases, they make excellent weapons. I had considered the Walther P99, because Walther is a German manufacturer (the P99 is also an excellent weapon).

I'm glad I opted for the SIG.

We'd driven for about an hour. The drive felt long, and we didn't speak very much after the first ten minutes or so. I asked him if he'd ever been to Epping Forest and he said he hadn't. I said neither had I.

I didn't know you had a gun licence, he said.

I nodded.

I've found several new hobbies since I last saw you, I said.

The noise of the car engine was quite loud.

Tell me the end of what happened with Frankie, Angela said to me.

It ended as I said. There wasn't anything else.

And Amy? And Paul? And your wife? When are you going to tell me how you feel about your wife? *You've closed down, again*, she said.

I told her I wanted to be honest with her. I told her again about the man I hated. I told her about the colour of my feelings towards him (black).

She told me that I've been looking for someone to blame. That I am preoccupied with blame, far more than guilt, which, she says, is what most people are preoccupied with.

Well, I found him, I told her. The one to blame.

And what difference do you feel it makes? Blaming him? she asked me.

I thought about that.

"If you see someone do a blameful thing . . . there's a duty, there. Isn't there?" I asked her. Like when I asked Frankie, if we had to go on living – I really wanted an answer, I think. She asked me *what kind of duty?* And I told her that's what I've been trying to work out.

I thought that my anger was an emotional thing that might recede, once Reason took hold again. I thought I had to hold out until Reason returned. I was on that battlefront, supplies running low, watching each night fall and hoping Reason would come next morning. But I don't think that, any more.

I distrusted myself, my feelings in particular, and presumed they would change, like bad weather.

"I suppose you have done your job, after all," I said to her.

She looked unmoved, as usual – placid and all-knowing, as usual.

"Because I feel now I've come to a kind of peace," I said. I suppose I was getting a bit emotional. I was thinking of my father's imminent death, at that moment. That's probably where that word "peace" came from. "I understand, now, that my feelings won't change. Not in the way I was hoping, at least."

She asked me what I meant by that.

"Sometimes things are simpler than we take them for. I've spent my life trying to instil order. You'll take this as some kind of betrayal, but I must tell you – there were other Pauls, of course. There were other boys I tried to mentor, whom I thought *could be saved*. From their gloomy fates. Some of them I think I helped quite a lot. Perhaps I should dwell on those young men instead? But Paul happened to be the last. He was more a part of my life, on account of his relationship with Amy – but that petered out in the end, didn't it? There's a chance I've over-egged Paul's significance, that I've confused him for something he isn't. I talked about Paul to discover what I really felt. As if by talking about him I would uncover something, the key, the reason for my grief. But it seems obvious now that everything I've said has been spun from that sadness. I've shrouded Paul in all my feelings, leaving only the softened contours, the shadows, and none of the texture. I've described him as a kind of tragic figure, because that was the only material I had. And I've omitted the happier times with Amy, for instance – because it was beyond my focus.

"What it comes down to, now, is that I've been angry, *am angry*, and with good reason. I dedicated my life to Order, and was repaid with Havoc. That would make anyone angry. And in this life, as I see it, you have either to rot or to burn."

She said I was being dramatic again.

Angela's arguments:

██████████ only did what all politicians have to do. He made a hard decision.

There was no "right decision" (*right decision* being said as if in quotation marks; most of these arguments being said as if in quotation marks – most of these arguments announced as if printed directly from stereotype, the only thought put into them being how to sound the vowels, mere sound-sequences so bereft are they of intelligent thought).

You cannot blame ██████████ for terrorism, terrorism has existed for centuries, and though the particulars might change, there will always be those who wish to make political capital from a population's fear (this one I disregard almost completely – and further, I've worded it better than her).

But this is the one I mark, the one which makes me think perhaps Angela is wise, or nearly:

Your scheme is incomplete. If you follow the thread of blame all the way from the terrorist event involving your wife to ██████ ██████, then you cannot stop there. Who else is to blame? How many others? What justice is there in blaming him alone?

She has me. She definitely has me. A strong warm feeling rises in me as I come to understand just how much she has me. I almost want to cry with joy. It has been a long time since I've experienced this feeling, so long that it nearly strangles me with happiness. She has understood me. She's pointed out some intimate detail of mine better than I could, like describing a birthmark on my back. She has cast light on my thoughts, and I do my best not to cry with gratitude.

Who else is to blame? The question is enormous in my mind.

We all are, I tell her. I say the words in speculation, in case they might ring true.

"We all are," I say again, more certainly.

She looks at me.

"You're right," I say.

We all are.

My skin tingles along my forearms, along my right cheek and the back of my neck, and it's like my hate has taken a step away from me.

"I am," I say.

I was on the platform with my feet planted on the yellow line. Of course, I've imagined jumping many times before. I shift my weight backwards.

A train came in, and I didn't get on it, watched those that did (it was in the mid-afternoon, it wasn't busy). I took more pictures of the tunnel and track with my phone. Then I did another RF sweep to record the frequencies being broadcast as the train pulled away.

The platform attendant eyed me briefly again. I stared at him until he looked away, said something into his radio. I think I wanted a confrontation at that point.

What do you think it is that you're seeking, that you think you'll find in a confrontation?

"I think, by now," I say to myself, "I just want someone to come out with it."

With what?

"With whatever. Whatever they're thinking. Whatever they're offended by. Instead of thinking it and not doing. To stop being hypocrites."

Do you feel that's what you are, for what happened to your wife? You've said many times you felt you should act in some way, *do something about it*, in your words.

"I suppose that's right. I suppose I have been a hypocrite."

I turned to sit down on one of the wooden benches that line the platform, and there was a large man in a light grey suit sitting looking at me with what appeared to be warmth bordering on fondness, as if I were an old friend or a memory, then when I got closer his expression changed and he gestured to the track and said, "Two people have died here," pointing as if to the very spot.

I asked him what he meant by such a thing. I didn't sit down.

He scratched his nose and nodded and said, "One of them had a large family, five children. He worked at an accountancy firm."

I turned to the track, as if to a memorial. The distant thunder of another train started to blow through the tunnels.

"Who was the other?" I asked.

"A young woman," he said, hardly a pause between us.

I nodded.

"Twenty-one years old, drunk from a night out with friends."

"An accident?" I asked.

He shook his head. "By all accounts, no. The CCTV footage was quite unambiguous, apparently."

I wondered at that *apparently*. I didn't wonder, mostly, at the truth of anything he told me.

The train came in and we didn't speak for a while, but both watched it, and the people embarking and disembarking, and the slow wait before the doors shut again and it pulled away and disappeared and we were left with the memorial again, of the young woman and the family man.

"You're not getting a train," I said.

He took a breath and hoisted himself up from the bench. He had a plastic bag with him that didn't look like it was holding very much, possibly his lunch. His suit didn't appear inexpensive, exactly, though it was a poor fit for his girth, and I wondered whether it was cut for someone else, or whether he'd let himself go (which was much the same).

"Not here," he said.

"Why do you come here?" I said, rather presumptuously, though it seemed obvious he often did this, sat on the platform with his plastic bag with his lunch in it.

He shrugged lightly. "Someone should remember them," he said, and he left me looking at a blank space just above the tracks.

When Bad occurs in the classroom, the usual collective response from the boys is that deadly sin: Indifference. Because the ones who perceive the wrong are not in the position to correct it – or so they believe.

And how many times did I trot out that famed line to the boys, trying to dispel that Indifference?

When bad men combine, the good must associate.

How attractive it sounded to them, though a little oblique – the first clause clear enough to them even if strangely worded (which is what made it attractive), but the second utterly lost to them until we waded together through that phrase *the good must associate*. It unearthed to them the power of association. Even whom you stand next to is a choice – the choice of association, not simply a matter of finding some vacant spot, because there are no vacant spots.

I must have rehearsed it so often I forgot its meaning.

When did I ever consider my own position in the scheme of things? Because, in the end, bad men did combine – and what did I do? I stood and watched. I didn't even protest – but, protest failing, I still did nothing. Like everyone else. I *got on with it.* I let the black mark against my character be drawn and *got on with my life.*

And I have stood and watched till this very day. Most of my life has been standing and watching.

There were other options open to me, of varying degrees of violence. Protest and activism on one end – and attack, assault and murder on the other. I didn't do the former because they weren't convenient (nor effective) – and the latter because it never occurred to me. Not until now.

And if those other options had occurred to me I would never have done them because I considered myself moral. There's the hidden joke – how can a Do-Nothing ever be moral?

And there's a second part to that quote, a little too wordy for the boys' consideration (and anyway too long for their memory): *else they will fall one by one, an unpitied sacrifice in a contemptible struggle.*

I wonder: what's more beautiful, our piano, or my FN SLP MK 1 autoloading shotgun?

Before I'd touched it, I spent a great deal of time admiring it. Its shape, its blackness, its matte finish. It has a pistol grip, an ample stock, a very long barrel and piston, with an elegant front sight that crests gently.

The touch of it is even better. The action of the ejector port is especially smooth. It has a capacity of 8+1+1 shells, meaning it can be *lifter-loaded*, or *carrier-loaded*, so that the carrier can take an additional shell, with eight shells in the magazine tube and one shell in the chamber.

It is heavy.

Though I haven't loaded it yet, let alone fired it, I know it has a very quick action and can fire all ten shots in under two seconds, if your trigger finger is fast enough and your shoulder strong enough. It is a marvel.

Propped against the side of the piano, I see how well they go together, their matching colour and elegance. They are very beautiful. With the right maintenance and care, both of these objects will outlive me. By a long way, I hope.

I admire the gun next to the piano, and then I sit at the piano and admire its keys, and when I play something – just a mean-ingless string of notes – it is, perhaps, to the gun I'm playing, to whatever it has stirred within me. Joy, I think. That people can make such things – pianos and autoloading shotguns. That I could dedicate myself to piano-making or shotgun-making my whole life, and never make any finer than these. That I am blessed to possess such things and to know how to use them, and to understand them, in my way.

1) Politicians continually alter our Laws or seek them altered.
2) This indicates the Laws and Statutes are not fit for purpose.
3) The Statutes are an aggregate of multiple generations of politicians' best guesses (to be kind),
4) muddled guesswork (to be unkind).
5) The Laws are a function of society's values.
6) They are aggregate and high-latency (to be kind),
7) contradictory and slow (to be unkind).
8) The Laws are *low resolution* (they describe generalities).
9) Despite all of the above, the Laws govern society.
10) That is, they do not govern individuals (insofar as individuals can choose to ignore them or may be in ignorance of them).
11) We can see this is true because a person's morality doesn't change when they enter another country.
12) The Laws map imperfectly to circumstances (hence the need for specialist judiciary).
13) Therefore, criminal convictions may or may not correlate with a person's Badness or Wrongness.
14) That is, convicted criminals may be Good and Right, and those deemed without offence may be Bad and Wrong.
15) It is up to individuals to interpret and challenge the Laws.
16) It is up to individuals to govern themselves.

Before Paul left the first time, I didn't speak to Amy for a while, because I blamed her for his going – because I thought it was somehow within her power to stop him, even if it was beyond mine. And she, too, was frosty to me for a time, possibly because she had similar feelings about how I could have stopped him, or possibly it was for a completely different reason.

It always upset my wife when we had these spats. Thinking of how she must have felt, now, makes me very sad.

He wrote a letter to Amy in the middle of his training. Perhaps he was in Wales at the time or somewhere like that. Amy was in her first year at university (shortly to drop out), so I telephoned her to explain we'd received his letter. I left her a voicemail message. It was sort of in the early days of mobile phones, as far as I remember, and I didn't trust the concept of voicemail messages. Certainly, she never responded to them and she rarely picked up the phone in her room. Finally, I managed to speak to her and I asked if I should forward his letter, and she said it was fine, she'd already told Mum she'd be back home in a few weeks, she'd read it then. I told her it likely had information about Paul's imminent deployment.

"He's being deployed?" she said. It was the first she seemed to care in the least.

I told her I didn't know, but I suspected that's what the letter was about. And immediately her tone altered and she found a way to end the call.

I spent quite some time over the next few days and weeks

staring at that envelope, with the stamp of his barracks on it. It would preoccupy me; then I'd try to phone Amy again and she wouldn't be there or wouldn't pick up, and I'd ponder the contents of the letter, and then finally I'd get on with something else. My wife told me one time when I was staring at it, "It's probably nothing important, otherwise she would've asked you to open it." And, "She's probably been in touch with him, she probably has an idea what it says or else has already spoken to him."

I told her I doubted it, that their split had seemed quite final to me. Amy had seemed fairly cool about the whole thing to me. What did I know, though?

Perhaps I never did forgive Amy for her subtle attacks, her attempts to undermine my confidence or make me doubt myself. By the time she was going out with Paul, she had access to knowledge I lacked, and she began to play upon my fears now and then, especially when we argued, which was often. The fact she knew of those fears – identified them and understood them – perhaps that's what I can't forgive. No doubt Amy would say she takes after me. That such calculation is a bond between us – except I don't have half her skill for it by my reckoning.

One time: "Paul says most of the teachers think you're crazy."

And how would Paul know? And yet plausible enough. He was friendly with most teachers, by the end – by the time I'd tempered him. No doubt they were more casual with him than I was (did I envy them that?). It was possible that they bantered with each other in his presence, made jokes at my expense. Or even that they outright sallied against me, vented their frustrations, pointed fingers of blame in my imagined direction.

Amy must have known those kinds of attacks were the most effective, because I never had an answer for them. They'd come out of nowhere, quite often, which left me unprepared to retaliate, to deflect or counter.

"A lot of [the teachers] are thinking of leaving in the summer."

They didn't, though. But had they thought about it?

Your ambitions are all far too specific. You're not original in what you say, any of you – and far from the first to cast those stones at me. *Old-fashioned* is the favourite. As if *new-fashioned* is better. And every one of you who came to my office chucking in your notice with a lecture on how different things should be – you all made the same mistakes. You don't believe in Standards. You don't believe in Exams. You don't believe in measuring individuals, in fact you hold the individual to be immeasurable. That may be. But I never intended to measure any individual boy who passed through those gates, except to get the general sense of them. But even that was too much for you, you who'd rather throw away the measures and lavish praise on the ones you like or the ones whom you've most *inspired*. Well our job isn't to *inspire* and it certainly isn't to *foster fucking creativity!* In boys who come into school surrounded by the whole universe and yet you think it's *you* who'll do the inspiring. We have one job – and it's more important than whether some kid has a go at art or poetry (which is all you ever mean by *creativity*, so much that you've synonymized *creativity* with *artish nonsense*). Well let me tell you, by my reckoning boys wouldn't like *creativity* very much if they were taught it properly, indeed if Creativity were taught to a high standard they'd all go running. But still you went one after the other and lectured me on *group discussion* and all these other things which are poor surrogates for Effort and Discipline – Effort and Discipline, which are the unloving parents of

Creativity, except you don't see it – and all the while completely ignoring the one and only job we have, which has nothing to do with any individual boy or their capacity for lines of bad poetry – our one job which doesn't lie in the specific but in the general – our one job which is this: Stem Their Degeneracy. Stamp out their Latent Villainy. *Improve Them*, for God's sake! It's not hard! Their redeeming attributes are initially so scant we could hardly fail! And if we succeed there's a chance we improve the whole of our future, which to me seems an incredible miracle, a unique chance of our own – but to you – what? You'd rather gratify yourselves in thinking you might inspire Art in some small soul? You who don't know the first thing about Art and Artfulness and instead mistake it for any dead artish thing like pictures or humming. And when I challenged you for lesson plans, you gave me *writing music lyrics for the plots of Shakespeare's plays* –

FUCK
YOU

I filmed myself tying my shoelaces three times, tying a double-knot. Then I noted the average time: 13.1 seconds for both shoes.

Then I took two pints of blood and again filmed myself tying my shoelaces.

The task was completed in 15.3 seconds (outside the standard deviation of my earlier efforts).

And how much longer did this entry take to write? To type? To think up (not long at all, this one)? But I haven't been recording any such facts in order to compare. Perhaps I should, though there are too many variables – my bloodlessness just another.

Which has the greatest effect on these entries: when I take two pints of blood or when I forget to eat for a day? When I'm sad or when I'm angry? Tired or pent up? When I see ███████ on television or no? What combination of the above is the best? And worst?

I've imagined what it might be like to kill a person.

Of course, the imagination can't reproduce the precise emotional textures of such a scenario. I can, at any point, simply stop imagining – and so I believe a fundamental claustrophobia cannot be properly experienced in imagination.

Because I imagine it this way (apart from the grisliness, which will be shocking, the emotional development of the scenario is quite distinct in my mind): in the first moment, I have no hesitation, and indeed wish to commit the deed. I put the gun to his head. (It must be said I don't imagine him begging for his life or anything of the sort. These imaginings are to probe my own feelings on the basic matter, hard enough without those kinds of emotive flourishes.) So I imagine that I pull the trigger with something like relish. Sometimes with relish, sometimes with qualified determination – in any case, every time I pull the trigger it is with great certainty. With great necessity.

And then it's in the aftermath I struggle. There's the grisliness, for a start, especially if I've used the hollow-points (but again these are not quite moral details, I find – except that perhaps the manner of a person's destruction can be better or worse, that horrificness does perhaps have a moral velocity, but these are split hairs in comparison with the basic question I'm interested in).

So apart from the grisliness there is the sudden change: that I am now a murderer. And no doubt that change is rendered more frightening by the victim's extinction. I will watch him die in the most brutal way – and I will have caused it. And it is morbid not just for the obvious reason, but because it is inescapable – I cannot, at that point, undo what I have done. I am forever a murderer. I am, most likely, a Bad Person. Strange that you can live a whole life well, or well enough, and then invalidate it so quickly.

But then I wonder, what do any of these imagined emotions even mean? Do they mean anything? Just because I know something will be unpleasant – well, that's merely a matter of breeding. I've been bred to be soft, to value life, to preserve it. It's no wonder death will appal me. I imagine a sick feeling holding around my stomach. That claustrophobia that I can't fully appreciate yet. But these will just be responses – *gut reactions*, if you will. They have no bearing on whether something is Right or Wrong. Indeed, if the only reason not to kill is for fear of being a murderer, well, isn't that mere cowardice?

It is patent that killing can be Right, in the right circumstances. It is not possible to state otherwise and still be describing the known universe.

So if we exist in the circumstances where killing is Right, and *do not* kill – are we Wrong? If we live through a moment in which killing becomes necessary and don't kill, because we don't wish to be killers – because of what amounts to a matter of manners – we've failed to do Right. We've perhaps done Wrong, become Bad, or close. We've taken the Easy Option.

No one denies that those allied killers in World War Two were doing Right, on the whole. But what of other, more equivocal circumstances? It is, of course, easy (relatively) to kill when everyone is in agreement that you should, must, and without delay. In the case of the slaughter of World War Two, how many even considered their position, with the enemy sighted down the length of their rifle? How many evaluated their Rightness?

How many of them thought to themselves, "Though this is Bad, it is Right, and for the following reasons:..."?

What I'm asking is, how many went to battle and sought to kill and did Right only incidentally? Because they happened to be on a particular side?

And what if everyone says of killing that you shouldn't, mustn't and never – when actually you should? Once the world has reverted to its complacent default, isn't it the braver man who says, "You'll judge me negatively, but I must kill, and for the following reasons:..."?

Who decides what's Right? It doesn't come about from consensus or popularity. It's thought up by those who consider such things – but it exists as surely as my right arm.

The task is first to evaluate, most fully, the question of What is Right (given the circumstances)? And then to follow the conclusions to the very end, no matter how upsetting or frightening.

And I'm well placed to do it, because frankly the better parts of my life are past. Which is to say, if I'm to experience that sad moment of badness, of doing bad against my moral manners and knowing it cannot be undone, knowing that a particular aspect of my being is dead forever – well, it would be a kind of sacrifice, surely. The greatest and the worst kind, perhaps.

I opened Paul's letter to Amy, after I'd stared at it long enough. I admit I was jealous, from what I read there. I felt guilty, reading someone else's private correspondence, though it was my daughter's, and my guilt was mitigated by what I felt was my guardianship of both correspondents. Of course I was prying. But not knowing what was happening to Paul was making me anxious. And part of me felt that Amy might be negligent – that the letter might reveal something she later would regret ignoring for so long.

It started awkwardly, I remember. He said that he wanted to get in touch with her (Amy), because he didn't have anyone else to write to. Of course that hurt me, though I admit it would have been surprising for him to address a letter to me. Ours was never a letter-writing sort of relationship.

He wrote something like, *I have to thank you for helping me get out from all that.* It was in reference to his parents. He wrote that he hoped eventually she'd stop being angry at him for joining *the forces.* He said that he was going to be deployed. He said they'd all written their wills. He said he'd written her into his will. He said something like, *I don't want you to think you owe me anything and I don't have anything anyway, but I wanted to include you in my will for everything you did for me.* Again, I felt at least part of his thanks should have been bequeathed to me. I felt a little robbed, perhaps – disinherited?

He said he was scared and had been thinking about going to church. He said that he should have gone to university, *even a shit one, just to get out that way.* He better understood her (Amy's) anger now. He mentioned me, finally – said he understood why I tried to talk him out of joining the forces, could see it better now. But on the whole he was glad, he said, and he had to stand by his decision, and that getting shot by ragheads was probably better than being back home.

You can write to me if you have anything to say, he said. He finished by saying, *And say hi to your dad from me. He means well. You should try to hate him less.* That stung me.

I put the letter back in its envelope and put it in my drawer. I readied myself for a showdown, when she came back home in the holidays, when she began to carefully broach the topic of her dropping out. One morning I reminded her of Paul's letter as she was leaving the house (she was always leaving the house, it seemed), and she didn't hear me or she ignored me, and another time I caught her coming home and reminded her of the letter, asked if she wanted it, and she said yes, and I went to get it and she had disappeared again by the time I'd returned to the front hall. On a rare evening she ate with us I finally threw the letter on the dinner table in front of her, quite petulantly, no doubt. She eyed the open envelope but didn't pass comment – then she took the letter out and read it, once slowly or twice quickly was my guess, then she put it back in the envelope and finished her food.

I was bewildered. I was ready for battle, for her indignation, for her outrage at having her privacy violated. She asked me to stop staring at her and I felt that was the least I could do.

"If you don't mind me asking," I said, "will you reply to him?"

She told me it was none of my business, at which point my wife tried to raise the mood by telling Amy to be nice. Then she turned to me and told me to butt out.

I apologized to her then, for opening the letter, since I really didn't know what else to say, and then I left the room. In fact, I went to the bedroom and sat on the bed and tried to work out what on earth was going on in my daughter's head (something I attempted rarely, since it was fruitless).

When I went back to the living room Amy had gone, and my wife was playing the piano, and the letter lay there, still, half-peeping from its envelope. My wife was playing something melancholy, and perhaps that enhanced my self-pity. She must have seen me acting glum and at some point stopped playing, and I asked her wouldn't she continue, and she came and sat next to me and hugged me, and I asked her if she'd read Paul's letter, since I understood by Amy having left it there that it was by now discarded – trash in her eyes, perhaps – and there could be no harm in any case if her mother read it. She hesitated, but I think she felt the same way, and she read it, and I sat in silence for what felt like a great deal of time, until I finally looked up to see her regarding it, like a museum piece, and she said, "She doesn't hate you, you know," and I nodded and said she had cause if she did, and she dismissed that with a tut, and then she said that Paul had nice handwriting, that it was a good letter, and had I taught him that? And I said some of it, perhaps. Or most of it. And she asked me how I felt, and I said I was worried for the boy. Very worried for him. She hugged me and said that she was too, that we all were.

She asks me what I saw in Frankie, what I see in Paul – why I'm friends with these sad types.

I reminded her that Paul fought for our country, in fact nearly died for it, and she should perhaps show more respect.

"And Frankie?" she asks, as if the conversation were still cordial. As if she weren't insulting people I care very much about – as if I didn't care about them at all.

"Frankie has a brilliant mind," I said. "He may be simple, indeed moronic in some areas of intelligence. But aren't we all?"

She says it strikes her I'm drawn to pathetic types, people that need my help.

And if I told her the truth – all of it – would she be any closer to understanding? Any closer to rebutting my arguments? That Frankie helped me, taught me, sometimes for hours, things I'd never have known without him. And Paul likewise? Or would she concoct another cartoon to analyse?

"Paul and I go shooting," I said.

She waits for an explanation.

I didn't give one – let her imagine what she may, what it means that an old headmaster and his former pupil go shooting together. "He teaches me how to shoot," I said. "Occasionally – and I mean really very rarely – he'll tell me something, some little glimpse about how he's getting on. Some days, he told me, the pain in his missing legs is so bad he's immobilized. He just lies in bed, with his whole body clenched. Can you imagine that? Being immobilized in the first place by having no legs, and then stunned by phantom pains, like your legs are on fire?

"Is that what you call *pathetic*?" I ask.

So, Angela, the police came to my house.

There were two of them – they can't exist these days except in pairs. A young man and an older woman. The woman, the more senior, took the lead in addressing me on my doorstep. By which I presumed the young man was the muscle, so to speak.

My thoughts immediately went to my guns in the garden shed – not a helpful thought. I was briefly terrified that I'd left the SLP next to the piano, but remembered I'd since stashed it. Then, as I asked them for a short moment to make myself decent (they politely allowed it, though they could clearly see I was fully dressed), I closed the door quietly and stood behind it, gathering more useful thoughts as to what evidence might be lying around. Obviously if they found the guns that was it. But it was more important to consider the other ways I might be compromised. The fact is there was evidence everywhere, if they only knew what it looked like. The modified sparring dummy in the bedroom – the vials of my blood in the fridge – the computer in the living room was, of course, brimful with it – even my annotations of my wife's manuscripts at the piano were a sign, if they knew how to read it. But there were no paper printouts splayed across the floor, nor even any books with their giveaway titles (*Field Maintenance for Small Arms* or *Penetration Testing Essentials*) – all these things existed only on disk, and all it required was for me to close the lid of my laptop in order to shield it from their prying eyes. So I did that, and then returned to the door and opened it with what I hoped was a concerned smile, and invited them in.

And do you know the sad thing, Angela? I was almost pleased to see them. I was very anxious they shouldn't put me away, obviously, but all the same I felt a simple pleasure in talking to them, in the pleasantries, offering them some tea (they both said yes, milk and sugar), asking how their morning had been (not bad, so far). And then the senior officer said something that I could sense her junior was thinking but couldn't say:

"Woof, it's a bit messy in here, Michael."

That was, of course, its own kind of evidence – evidence of neglect, of not-quite-rightness. I briefly tried to calculate when I'd last showered, stopped short of sniffing myself.

"Yes!" I said, as if seeing it for the first time. "I do apologize. My daughter says I'm living like a bachelor these days." I hastily pulled the curtains wide to let some light in, feeling brightness would offset the dank mood of my mess. "Please, sit down," I said, sweeping some of the empty food cartons to the other side of the table. I took up two fistfuls of mugs, since I'd probably need to wash some for my guests. They both sat down with great hesitation.

The camaraderie I'd initially felt had vanished. I felt instead newly self-aware. The word *plight* popped into my head, as the descriptor of what was happening to me. Hastily washing out some mugs while the kettle was on – I felt intensely sad, as if for someone else. *You're in a state*, I thought to myself. I felt as if I was trying to win some friends, and failing.

When I returned to the living room with the mugs of tea (I had to awkwardly run back to the kitchen for my own mug), the junior was looking around himself as if he were in a museum or cathedral, while the senior smiled at me with what felt like a degree of warmth.

"Do you know what we're here to discuss with you, Michael?" she said, motherly enough.

Obviously I had a whole list in my head, but I honestly couldn't pick one reason in particular – so I suppose I looked baffled enough when I shook my head with an incredulous frown.

"Not at all?" she said.

I smiled at them both, one after the other. I decided I wanted to reclaim the senior status from the motherly copper.

"Why don't you tell me, and we'll discuss it?" I said, with more than a hint of Angela about me, I felt.

She nodded and turned to her junior, who was gratefully sipping his tea. At her gesture, he put the mug down and reached for a many-pocketed briefcase next to his chair. He pulled out a plastic folder with some printed A4 pages in it. Too ceremoniously, I thought, he turned the folder around to face me. I glimpsed the first line of text

Frankie you fucking CUNT

through the folder's transparent cover. I was confused by it, for some reason. I don't suppose I reacted very visibly. They were watching me closely, as I eyed the text, not really readingly yet.

"May I take it out?" I asked, picking up the folder.

"Of course," the motherly one said.

I took it out carefully, trying not to notice the next letter behind it (or the one behind that – or indeed the approximate number of pages they'd brought with them). The thing was, the pages were so crisp and clean, except for the folds in the paper. It seemed fake, somehow – I wondered whether they were the genuine articles or had been quickly printed out at the station this morning. Except for the folds.

Frankie you fucking CUNT. You deceitful piece of SHIT. I should give you a beating, except I'd have to touch your disgusting FACE. I should smash that one bent tooth of yours.
    I should headbutt you, you simple CUNT.

Short and to the point, I felt. I admit I was rather embarrassed. I was never one to have an argument in public. I felt very exposed.

After she'd given me time to finish, the senior one said, "Do you recognize this letter?"

But I'd started on the next one:

Frankie if I ever see your disgusting face again I'll fight you, even if it means touching you.

I lingered on the line, re-read it once or twice.

"And that one?" she asked.

I sighed. I nodded. I looked up from the page. I looked at them both, tilted my head to scratch my left temple.

"I wrote these letters," I said.

She nodded. The junior hastily took out his notebook and began writing – my confession, presumably.

"Am I under arrest?" I asked.

She raised her chin, looked down her nose at me, as if taking a reading. "Do you think you should be?" she asked.

I put the letters back in their plastic folder.

"I was very upset with him," I said. Once again, a dirty little prevarication: the past tense – as good as a lie, no, Angela?

"Making threats of violence is a very serious matter," she said. The junior was still scribbling away.

I nodded.

"Why did you write those letters, Michael?" she said. I was touched by her use of my name.

I considered that *Why?*, but struggled for anything succinct – struggled without beginning, *I met him at a support group, a little while after I lost my wife.*

"Mr Lefevre wasn't very clear on how you two knew each other."

"Pardon?" I said.

"Frank Lefevre," she said.

"Christ," I said. "Is that what he told you?"

"I'm sorry?" she said.

A line for my next letter flashed into my head

Name of a French aristocrat, face of a crusty SHIT.

"That's his name, is it?" I said.

She nodded, apparently not seeing the funny side.

I told them a little of my story, about the man I knew as Frankie. I think I gave honest testimony to the matter. At length, the junior completed his scribbling. I thought it was fifty-fifty whether I'd be booked or not. They explained the full ramifications of my actions, were things to proceed to court. A conviction, possibly a prison sentence (as if), heartache not just for myself but my daughter, too.

"All for some silly words," the junior said, as if he was stealing the next line. Then the motherly one asked if I was getting any help, making sure I wasn't lonely, and then I felt sure I was out of the woods, that I was getting off scot-free, as it were. We briefly discussed my hobbies. They gave me a caution. The senior told me, quite warmly, never to write to Mr Lefevre again, in any capacity. Never to contact him in any way. She was quite emphatic about this.

"I've moved on," I said to them as they were leaving.

She smiled at me on the doorstep. "Good," she said. "I hope so, Michael."

On one of those long journeys in the car with Paul I asked him – over the din of the engine and over the din of the wheels against the road – whether he'd spoken to Amy since his injury. Whether they were still in touch, after all these years.

Of course I knew the answer, from Amy's side. Perhaps I had no other way of broaching the subject of my family.

He shook his head. We were never that serious, he said. You were always the one for me, he said, and he smirked, or grimaced.

The last we spoke was after the bombing, he said. At the hospital. He swallowed at the recollection. He looked a little nervous, looked out the passenger window, stroked the stump of his right arm.

I have a feeling that's what *this* is all about, he said, not much over the car noise.

There was something about him saying it, talking about what happened, possibly for the first time in my presence – I was filled with a sick-feeling, heavy, like something terrible was about to happen that I couldn't stop. Like it was happening all over again.

It is, isn't it? he said, and then he did turn to me.

I kept my eyes on the road.

It's fucked up, what happened, he said, and I felt he could have been talking now about any number of things, that the sense of his words had lost their grip and his meaning had widened madly, even as I understood perfectly what he meant.

I'm drunk, he said, as if he was about to go on – but he didn't.

I nodded solemnly at the declaration.

I suppose Paul's first shot of the handgun was momentous, being the first time he'd shot a firearm since he was nearly destroyed.

If it was, he didn't show it. It has become something of a game to us, a friendly contest between us – because he's learning to shoot with the one hand – his left, which was the weaker – is literally handicapped. Not to mention his one-eyed vision, though I daren't ask him what kind of impediment it is.

I load the magazines with cartridges. I have four magazines. Each magazine holds twelve rounds. I use a magloader to make loading the cartridges easier. I don't like to travel with loaded magazines. It's mere superstition, but with guns I'm superstitious. Paul watches close by as I load the magazines, or shields me if it's windy, sometimes drinking a can; sometimes we have little cover from the elements, other times we can use the trees to hang our bags on; sometimes I'm loading the cartridges awkwardly in my lap, other times I'm using the fishing stool as a worktop, with my knees in the mud.

And so when it's Paul's turn, he shoots one-handed, with his left arm flamboyantly ahead of him, and he stands side-on, what I imagine is a reduced profile, and he shoots and curses, and if he does well he shoots the magazine dry and says nothing and doesn't move, except to check the chamber, and if he does badly he curses and curses and shoots quicker and quicker until it's dry and drops his arm to his side and keeps swearing. And I worry, then, about his legs, and foresee them flying off in his rage, or else getting stuck or dislodged. One time, in his anger, after shooting the gun dry he ejected the magazine and let it fall into the mud, and I had to reprimand him for his abuse of my property, and we had an awkward moment between us that was only resolved after we'd both sulked a bit, he with his can of lager.

Whenever he offers me a sip, I always take it, even if I'm not particularly in the mood. There's something of the camping spirit, slurping from the beer can in the wind. It's part of the symbiosis we've formed. He'll shoot his twelve rounds and I'll lean in to cup my hand underneath the gun and he'll eject the magazine into my palm, and I'll load the fresh magazine for him, and I'll rack the slide and he'll keep shooting. This was obviously on account of his missing right hand, initially. But occasionally he'll perform a similar function for me, pulling a magazine from his waistband and loading it into the weapon for me, though I still have to pocket the empty when he does.

He asks sometimes about the school, about teachers he liked or disliked and what I thought of them. He asked if I'd heard of a kid called Sultan.

There were gypsies by the monument today. They looked like a band of dishevelled picnickers. I asked them whether they knew what it was, where they were eating, where they were littering, but only their young man spoke English and he struggled to interpret between us.

I said to him, "Why is it that none of you has any common decency?" Which was a stupid question, cruel and pointless.

He took offence at my question, and then shortly afterwards they all did. I was ready to fight all of them, then. I wanted them to have a go, as it were. I was mentally rehearsing my strike patterns, the order in which I'd attack them – the brutal energy I'd reserve for Nana Gypsy in particular. She seemed the locus of my anger, for whatever reason.

If I asked Angela about that locus of anger – but why do I get the feeling that Angela is receding from me now?

I called the police and awaited them patiently, and then watched them send the picnickers on their way. And then, finally, I crouched in front of the monument, in case I might be forgiven.

My Frankie,

I'm not going to send this letter to you, since you'd go and tell on me. So maybe this is a Self-Expression, after all.

I'm angry with you, but my tender memories of you are not invalidated by what you've done. Your deviance needn't detract from those moments we shared. And maybe after all you were honest some of the time? It's possible.

Do you remember some of our kitchen discussions, our waiting-for-the-kettle-to-boil interludes? We discussed all sorts: religion, politics, childhood (in the abstract). We discussed with particular fervour what kind of biscuits I should stock my kitchen with (bourbon creams). I wonder whether you ever think back on those times? And the times I induced you to sit and type out your terse mystic C programs, with names like "h.c" (because, I finally realized, you aren't a programmer but an artist, and where others generalize you particularize, so that the programs you write *do* in fact express your personhood, knowable basically only to you and the compiler – and to me, because I did go through it all, line by line, and I came to understand your personal history – your extensive work in assembly languages, your very strange mind – through your penchant for bitwise operations, for shunning abstraction and delving directly into memory, for your passionate love affair with recursion, with nested conditional statements, negated Booleans and even doubly negated Booleans (heaven knows why).

You're a talent and a no-talent. You're simple to the point of stupidity, and acute to the point of brilliance. Emotionally, you're a seeming-moron. But I can't be entirely deceived in imagining you have some capacity for decoding people – if you were ever to show any interest in people, that is. You needn't listen to anything they say, only observe what they do. I really thought I might unlock that in you – a genius for spotting our patterns. Spotting my patterns. For debugging the errors in my logic. But I hardly got anywhere with you.

I should have been more patient. All the while I did you no harm, you did as I pleased. Was it that straightforward? Knowing the facts, as I do now, I see how predictable you are. You pursue the easiest path – and why not? For someone so beset by bodily complaints and generalized illnesses. I don't blame you. The only trouble I have is knowing what exactly goes through your strange mind – what you consider easy and what you consider hard. How much will I have to pay you to do something you don't want to do? Perhaps you're not so pre-dictable after all.

When I showed him the shotgun, he was deeply impressed.

"How the fuck can I shoot that thing, though?" he said.

The wind was up again. We were on the fringe of the forest, looking on to open ground, earlier than usual, and colder.

We have half a dozen large yellow plastic signs, by now, which state

DANGER

LIVE AMMUNITION DRILLS IN PROGRESS

GO BACK

I wonder sometimes what the police would make of them, if they chanced upon our perimeter. Of course, I've imagined an encounter with them.

I kneel down, facing towards the targets, and he rests the shotgun's barrel on my right shoulder. I squeeze the earbud tight against the drum with my left hand tucked under my chin, careful not to obscure his aim, but the shots' seismic force buzzes through my skeleton. I can hear his whoop even through the ringing in my head that continues for a while afterwards.

The dents the shots make in the steel targets are impressive, but, after rising from my muddy knees, it takes me a few minutes to shake off some elemental fear that has entered my spirit, to shake off the last gunshot echoes still tracing my bones – and there is even a degree of nausea involved – all of which seem completely out of proportion to the cause.

"That is fucking beautiful!" Paul shouts. He swears far more now than when I knew him as a boy.

I shoot the shotgun now and then, but mostly it is Paul's toy. I let him cradle it in his lap and load shells into the magazine tube, which he can do unassisted, and meanwhile I practise with the MP5, which Paul can't shoot because its barrel is too small to rest on my shoulder.

Shooting the MP5 is the opposite of shooting the SLP. Its recoil, in comparison, is a caress. Its report, too, is comparatively muted, though all our shots echo out like thunder.

It is when I fit the suppressor to the barrel and load it with a magazine of subsonic ammunition that we both experience a completely new kind of magic far removed from the brute power of the shotgun.

The only noise is the clack of the hammer and the ring of the steel target. There is no other noise. I shoot a few rounds into the damp earth to test I'm hearing properly – the hammer clacks and the bullets pat into the mud. I raise my aim to the targets again, and again the only noise is the beat of the hammer, the ring of the target. It is extraordinary.

The grey steam that rises from the barrel and ejection port, curling into the wind, seems to be part of a dark sorcery, a demonic exhalation. I am overjoyed, stunned and incredulous, and, at the same time, feel a dread in the pit of my stomach, a primal sense of evil, a fear of the gun and a superstition of it – as if it will turn on me, murder me in my sleep. I look to Paul, who is still sitting on the fishing stool, cradling the shotgun in his lap. He is staring at the protrusion on the MP5's barrel, the thick suppressor. He moves his gaze from the suppressor to me, and there is fear, too, in his eyes.

"What's that for?" he says.

I turn away from him, eject the empty magazine, check the barrel is clear, look downrange to the targets, into the wind. It starts to rain, and he says,

"Seriously."

I don't look at him, but I say to him:

"I don't suppose I've been entirely honest with you." I tuck the empty magazine into my ammunition pouch, and load another.

▮▮▮▮ has *leveraged* his position in office. It is understood that all politicians attempt this, but only ▮▮▮▮ has done it so well.

A lever is a simple machine that allows the user of the lever to exert force far beyond their own capacity. They work by generating a *moment* of force around an axis or pivot. This *moment* is directly proportional to the distance between the fulcrum and the line of action of the force. That is, the longer the lever arm, the greater the *mechanical advantage*.

Understanding the Law of Moments, we can balance a skinny child (A) and a fat child (F) on a seesaw. If F is twice as heavy as A, we must place A twice the distance from the fulcrum. This balance is known as *equilibrium*.

Likewise, with a long enough lever, A can hold the whole school (nA) in equilibrium. With an even longer lever, A can upturn nA.

So when it is said that ▮▮▮▮ has *leveraged* his position in office, it is understood that the lever arm is comprised of his time in government, by which he has levered his subsequent riches. We can see how he has exploited the *mechanical advantage* of his long spell in office, in order to achieve riches far beyond his effort. And we can understand that the fulcrum, in this case, is all of our backs. Because, of course, the fulcrum is all important. A lever is nothing without the fulcrum – because without the fulcrum there is no *moment*. So his subjects provided it. I provided it. He has levered riches every day across my back – and for how long? My wife was the fulcrum, too.

And many others. Those most exposed to the grinding force of that lever, they died. In their thousands. My wife was there, under that lever. Paul, too. And I was a little way underneath, perhaps, so that I wasn't caught in the brunt turn of it, but only caught in the aftermath, in the fulcrum's shedding of bodies, as it sheds and regenerates and the levering continues apace, so that there are bodies strewn underneath (too many to count). So I slid from the summit of that fulcrum with my wife and Paul, on to the pile, and I was alive and they weren't (and is Amy with us or is she still up above with the rest with the lever pressed to her back?). And from the size of the lever, and from the pile of bodies, it seems impossible that it is just one man levering away, except for the gigantic load that rises on the other side – the enormous riches that fly up so effortlessly. The riches themselves are near the fulcrum, to better increase the mechanical advantage (as the Law of Moments explains), so that everyone on the fulcrum can see the riches close by and be astonished and sickened by them. But for those of us who have flaked off and been shed, we're free in our way. Free to watch and wonder.

You can set up a Wireless Access Point on your laptop. You can name it anything you please. You can name it "Starbucks Free Wifi". You can observe the traffic of anyone who connects. You can do this every day for a week. You can stop that and do it less often – say, twice a week. You can try other spots near the institute. You can try the nearby Pret A Manger. You know his assistant comes here for lunch after you follow her from her office. You know the receptionists come here sometimes, too – but none of them eat in. None of them bite. One of the many pubs in the area is a better bet, many of them convene of an evening. But none cares for the Wifi at such hours. You can follow some of them home – you'd be surprised what corners of the city they come from. You'd be surprised how far some travel to the institute. You can go to their house on a Sunday. Sunday seems good. You can follow the family to the restaurant. You can tuck your chair in when they squeeze the baby's high chair past. You can establish your Wireless Access Point when you see the older child asking for the iPad. You can observe the traffic when "Stuart's iPad" connects. You can drink a coffee and an Earl Grey (variety staves off the boredom). You can spoof the Apple Sign-In page, though it took a while to get it looking right. You can redirect Stuart's son to your spoofed Sign-In page. You can actually see Stuart's password as his son enters it with clumsy, sticky fingers. You can write down Stuart's Apple ID and password. You can log in as "Stuart". You can try logging in to the email address associated with Stuart's

Apple ID. You can't believe your luck. You own Stuart's email address and Apple ID. You can – quickly now, they're getting the bill, attending to their screeching infant – contact Stuart's colleagues, apologizing for using your personal email, but it's a Sunday and you just wanted to quickly send this off. You can attach a poisoned Excel spreadsheet. You can wait and see.

"When are you going to tell me about that second time you hit Amy?"

I was momentarily taken aback. I admit, I assumed she hadn't picked up on it. Did I want her to? Is this what I'm reduced to – dropping clues, hoping she picks up the thread? How pathetic.

"You said twice in twenty-five years, I think?" she said. "But I think Amy is in her thirties? So what did you mean?"

How much, I wonder, does she remember of what I say?

"You'll think me a monster," I said to her.

She frowned. She rotated the pen in her hand – the expensive-looking fountain pen, the one she barely uses, except as a kind of prop, a thing to twist and rotate, a fetish to guard her against her patients' (clients'?) neuroses. Her father gave it to her upon her graduation from her expensive American education, between joyful tears and congratulations, and she struggles to actually find an application for it – this is the story I've devised for it, in my head. I might ask her, one day, as to the pen's provenance, though honestly I couldn't care less about its actual origin. (She has a talent for ignoring my speculations pertaining to her personal life, on the increasingly rare occasions she reads my notes any more. Sometimes it seems she merely looks at the page for an interval, to humour me, and so I don't look too closely at her when she does, in case it's true.)

"You regret the second time, more than the first?" she said.

It was a very stressful time. It was a terrible time. So, yes, of course. It's incomparable to that first instance. The circumstances were so much worse.

She asked me to carry on, if I could.

I shook my head.

"It was just after the bombing," I said.

Did this surprise her?

"Twice in twenty-five years," I said. "Well, she was twenty-five. It was terrible."

"You argued?" she said.

"Bitterly."

"What were you arguing about?"

I took a deep breath, thought back to that awful time, in the aftermath of losing my wife, of trying, and failing, to be strong – of failing so completely at that – and thought back to Amy, how bad it was for her, as well – how bad it was for the both of us in very different ways. And I had some dim idea I needed to be strong for Amy, that this was the expected course – obviously this was before all that mess with Paul, before his injuries, before I'd seen the strength of his parents in his near-destruction, so that I couldn't even draw on their example, but I more or less collapsed entirely, and could only look at Amy's suffering as a distant counterpoint to my own, and offer nothing – absolutely nothing – to her. Her sadness magnified my own. I couldn't look at her without thinking of my wife.

Finally, my father came to her aid – to both our rescues. He insisted Amy and I stay with him, and gave it the appearance it was his need, that he was suffering too (no doubt) and needed his family, when in truth he was forsaking his own sadness, judging it less than ours, even though the toll of it must have been enormous, and that not only had he lost his daughter-in-law, but he had to endure the distress of his son and granddaughter, and at an advanced age, so that it was little wonder that after it was all over he was utterly sapped and flattened by it, having taken as much weight from our shoulders as he could bear, more than, and finally being crushed after the two of us had just about escaped. And in those early days when I was allowed to retreat from adulthood, from the adult family home that could only remind me of her in its every surface and corner and item and odour, in those early days in the aftermath, which brimmed with sadness, which constantly seemed to overflow with grief, my relationship with Amy was stricken, and we looked at each other, in the quiet hallways of that old house, as if across huge distances of both time and space, as if I was looking at her into the past, or the future, or indeed any time other than the present. We barely talked at all in those early days, except to say "Yes" or "No" or "Perhaps", and certainly never spoke to each other except perhaps I nodded at a question she asked me, a very plain question like "Are you going to bed?" or "Have you eaten?" and I may have nodded or shaken my head and returned the question to her, "Have you?" or "Are you?", more or less to get it off my hands, to not be burdened by even the lightest query, but to reflect it completely so that I could focus all the more intently on my grief.

One or two people visited, somehow came to understand I was staying with my father, came to know where that was, and actually turned up on the doorstep on a grey morning to offer their sadness and lend their sympathy and support, or whatever, and I hid from them, and my father received them, and, by then, even Amy took it upon herself to meet with them, though neither of them really knew the visitors, they were family friends, friends of mine, nominally, but mostly friends of hers, being that basically all of our friends were really friends of my wife.

Strange to think, of all the fatalities on the Underground – that on this very platform someone has already died here. Your precursor.

They died by jumping into the train – or in front of it – by jumping into the space it was hurtling towards, jumping into its trajectory, into its promise, as if in front of a bullet.

But you'll be inside the train. You'll be showing around your client, another rich warlord, a chieftain, an exotic despot with a bottomless bank account. I almost admire your flamboyant cunning in securing a private carriage on the Underground. Such are your connections to the state apparatus, even to this day. There's a Scheduled Engineering Works that weekend, but there won't be any engineers on the track that day. They'll shunt a train just for you, and instead of thanking them, your people demand the driver submits himself to additional background checks. But I know something you don't: that driver has it easy; he'll do nothing except open the doors to let you on, and he'll take double pay that day. Pity instead the supervisor in the Service Control Centre – you have no idea how fiddly it is to run a single train around the track, and then to cleanly revert the software to its normal function. But he'll get paid double time, too, and you've promised to drop in an endorsement for Thales Rail Signalling Solutions so all is not lost.

So it'll be you and your warlord in a private carriage, except for the many security guards – it'll be like Soviet Russia, your own private train line, and perhaps while you discuss public investment you'll privately, secretly, revel in the fantasy that you always travel this way, on your personal railway, on the ████████ Line (what colour is it?).

And what about those security personnel? Do they deserve what's coming? And there's also, I regret to add, the warlord's photographer, who will take pictures, ostensibly reference pictures, but also because the warlord is something of a fan of yours, and wants pictures of the two of you together, though you've declined them before, always declined them, but have finally relented, what with the money so near.

One time I parked in Paul's estate and he didn't look like he was thinking of getting out, he had a very faraway kind of look, and I wondered if something was wrong, if I'd done something or if I'd missed something – I'm more sensitive to Paul these days, overly so, since sometimes it seems as if anything will set him off. One time it was even just walking too briskly from the car before he was quite ready – I think he had to adjust his legs, which he rarely had to – and I was only a few strides away before I looked back, but that was enough for him to say, "I'm fine, thanks," quite bitterly, and I wasn't sure in what way he meant it, so it seemed he meant both that he was fine and simultaneously was remarking upon my lack of consideration, so that I felt the force of his words equally in both directions:

1) I'm fine and don't need your help

2) You're callous and insensitive

Then he was quiet for a long time and didn't help set up and didn't even shoot for perhaps thirty minutes, but just sat shivering on the fishing stool, while I went through my drills, and he didn't even open a can as usual, so I just got on with my drills, and in the end it was only the progress of my drills that distracted him and he said after perhaps thirty minutes: "You're still too upright." And I stopped, and was glad of his comment and thought about what he meant, and perhaps slightly feigned not knowing, so that he got up and came to me and guided me with his good hand, told me to bend slightly more forward, to point slightly more. "Concentrate on your follow-up shots. You should manage the recoil better now."

So I wondered, parked up in Paul's estate, whether I'd said or done something wrong again. I pretended to be busy looking for my spare pair of glasses in the well in front of the gear stick, but I couldn't do that forever, so I straightened and turned to him and asked him if he was OK.

He said, "Can I ask you a favour?" and he was resting his chin in his hand, had his elbow on the door where it met the passenger window, like Amy used to do when she was similarly despondent (often).

"Of course," I said, not knowing in the slightest what it might be.

He lifted his head from his hand and his face was towards me, then, but he still looked out the windscreen. "It's a bit fiddly," he said, and at that moment I assumed he needed me to perform some sexual act for him. Then he said, "It's a bit awkward, at home, and I'm not sure really how to go about it, but I was wondering if you could help, maybe, with me getting a flat of my own. With the council, I mean," and he looked at me then, finally.

"Accommodation?" I said quite lamely. I was, I suppose, a bit slow on the uptake.

"It's a bit awkward, trying to bring it up at home. With Mum and Dad," he said.

I didn't ask him whether he'd spoken to them about it.

"There should be a few people I can contact and see what they can do," I said. "I presume I'll need your details, National Insurance number and the like. Perhaps you can give me the necessary bits and pieces next time?"

"I have them," he said. And he heaved himself out and

shambled into the estate, and while I waited for him to return, I turned on the radio (tuned to the BBC World Service) and listened to a brief section on marauders in Africa, then turned it off when he came back. He came to my side and knocked on my window, by which I understood there wasn't to be much discussion on the matter. I wound down the window and he offered a handful of loose documents to my face, which I diverted on to his vacant seat.

"I really appreciate it," he said, by which I understood he considered it a matter of some urgency.

"Not at all," I said, and he patted the roof of the car, either as a means of affection or else to dismiss the vehicle, as if from a checkpoint, and for the first time he watched me drive out of the estate, which I can only believe served to heighten whatever feeling he was experiencing, of being stuck there. I eyed him in the rear-view mirror and felt a little derelict to be leaving, except that I had my mission, but even so it seemed that sardonic utterance of his resounded through my head – "I'm fine, thanks."

Sometimes I get a good string of days together, life-like days. But then the next is the worst yet, it seems.

I spent an eternity in bed, yesterday. I lifted myself out, finally, frail and beaten, like a hermit emerging from out of the mountains. By the time I was out of bed the sky in the window was just turning, readying for dusk.

This, I know, is an unnatural grief.

I went for a short walk outside, skirted the high street, as the sky got dark and the streetlights took hold. There seem to be more homeless people than ever, or I notice them more. I worry I might see Frankie in a sleeping bag, now, since I stopped giving him money, but I doubt that's really likely. I worry I might see Paul there in a sleeping bag, now.

What's left, then, after my evening stroll but to return home and eat something? The television is on while I eat. I lie in wait for him. I crave his appearance on the television. On these kinds of days his face is the one thing capable of galvanizing me, capable of pulling up my spirit. On these days if I see his face I can compel myself to extraordinary feats at the sparring dummy or with my dumbbells. On those other days, when I don't see him, I can slip back into bed and lie there for eternity until sleep.

I try to think back on every website I visited, on every internet search – I've been diligent, or so I thought, in anonymizing my web traffic for anything that could be considered suspicious. So what could have tipped off the police?

The more I try to remember what I did – when and how – the less certain I am of anything, the more I distrust everything, most of all my memory – and soon enough I'm willing to believe I repeatedly searched for ███████████'s address in a normal browser, or that the Tor browser itself is a government trap, or that there was some setting I'd simply forgotten to enable like a fool.

I must have slipped, somewhere. They can't see through walls or detect ill omens in the transmission of encrypted IP packets over the wire. They can only detect what's exposed. So I've exposed something unwittingly, somehow. The only trouble is I'm not capable of rewinding the last six months of my life (or have they known longer?) to replay the moment or moments I exposed some telling signal to them. Perhaps my application to the Home Office for Section Five authorization put me on their radar. It seems obvious, now. I'm so desperate to remember anything that might explain my detection that I start inventing memories, and believing them. And even my familiar memories get distorted by paranoia's creative influence. And once I've replayed the corrupted memory in my mind, I'm not sure I can retrieve the original, but instead can only reimagine it entirely, deliberately avoiding the paranoiac flourishes, like a contrived re-enactment.

And in this crisis of recall what scares me most is the idea of losing my memories of her – of falsifying them by the act of recollection. Or that I have already – that everything I remember of her has become a bad soap opera, that actually I have nothing real of her left, not even the image of her face, of her saying a simple phrase, of her back and her neck when she sat straight, playing the piano – that it's all made up, that I may as well have never lived those days at all.

I try not to mention to Angela, today, that there is a surveillance device or *bug* attached to the underside of my car, in one of the rear wheel wells. Perhaps I'm calmer about it than I realize, because she doesn't pass comment on my distracted state of mind. Or maybe she did and I was too distracted to notice.

I do tell her, however, about my trip with Frankie, though it seems so long ago. To the DSEI. I call it the DSEI, without explaining what that is, as if she might not notice. I allude to its location at the ExCel Centre, in case it might legitimize the activity in her mind. If she hasn't ever been to the ExCel Centre herself, no doubt she'll have heard of it in relation to various benign expos and conferences. But obviously I can't get very far in my tale with Frankie without reference to some of the exhibits there.

She is very confused, at first, and perhaps I have been more distracted than I imagined, because she actually doesn't understand a thing I've said. She asks what the DS Thing is, in reference to the story's very first sentence. So my intention to gloss it is undone by my inept and distracted storytelling. You were with Frankie? she asks, and it takes me a moment to realize the scale of my failure to convey meaning.

A few months ago I went with Frankie to the DSEI at the ExCel Centre in London, I say (though obviously I cannot pronounce that capital C in ExCel).

And after that there's no getting around it. She asks, "DSEI?"

The reason I bring this up, I say to her, is because actually I met someone there. At the conference. (And I realize again I'm incompetently saying what I'm trying to say and now it must sound like I've *met someone* in the romantic sense.) Not romantically, I don't mean (as if I might salvage this scrap of a retelling).

The DSEI is an arms fair, I say. They exhibit weaponry of all kinds there, much of it quite spectacular. There are no prices anywhere to be seen. I checked. That is how much these items cost. I went to this fair with Frankie (I omit the *why* of that, let her assume it's for companionship) and we had quite a nice time (and I'm even aware of how banal and unhinged that comes across as it escapes my mouth). And while we were there, I spoke to a few of the exhibitors, and one man in particular. And this morning I was just speaking to this man, who is a defence contractor, he represents a fairly small firm. And the reason I was speaking to him is because I was asking him about a particular model of surveillance device. The reason I wanted to speak to him, and did, about that device is because I believed I had discovered one attached to the underside of my car in the left rear wheel well. I didn't tell this person – whose name is Liam, by the way – I didn't say to Liam anything about the left rear wheel well of my car, or that that was where I'd seen this device. I was just asking him about the device in general. About this particular model, because I'd taken a picture of it and discovered enough about it on the internet – without removing it or even touching it – to get its name and manufacture, and pretend to Liam that I might be interested in purchasing some surveillance devices of the nature of the one I'd found underneath my car (though that detail, as I've said, I didn't tell him). So Liam told me all about it.

I was about to get going on the technical specifications when Angela halted me properly (she had, while I'd been saying all the above, been interjecting with a word here or there, like "What?" or "OK" and "I'm not sure I understand").

"I'm afraid you're going to have to slow down," she said.

"I realize I've told this all a bit backwards," I said. "I suppose I'm a bit distressed."

"So you went to an *arms fair*?" she said. She is even more incredulous than I'd imagined.

I shrug, and say that Frankie saw it advertised, and had read about the protests and controversy in a free newspaper and we got talking about it, and he expressed curiosity, and then I thought it'd be interesting too (I think it was the detail of the "free newspaper" that sold it to her, if she did believe it).

In any event, I think she believed that people could go to such a place with innocent intentions, out of mere interest in the things people get up to.

"But you're going to have to explain about this device. This surveillance device?" she says. The tone of her voice suggests there is a great distance between us, a great distance between what I understand and her understanding of it, and I feel anxious at the prospect she'll never understand. That she'll remain on her side and I on mine.

I describe to her how I came to discover it – first with the periodic interference in my car's radio signal, and my growing annoyance with that insistent sound over the past few weeks, the intermittent pulsing sound that interrupts the news bulletins, and my growing anger at my phone, especially after I'd turned it off and the pulsing interference carried on all the same. I told her it was funny in a way, that I thought I was being crazy and paranoid, looking *underneath* the car after looking everywhere else (what was I even looking for? the origin of an electromagnetic field I didn't know was there? had I even thought it through at that point?).

Of course it makes no sense to her, she has none of the necessary information. To her, an old retired headmaster is confused and distracted and frightened about someone spying on him. There are too many details, all at once. She perhaps doesn't believe there is such a device under my car, and briefly I wonder if that isn't for the best. I've given her the facts, in a strange order, which isn't anywhere near enough for her to understand my state of mind. To understand the predicament I'm in. So I decide I must furnish her with an organizing principle, something that will place these strange and surprising events into some kind of order for her.

"In a strange way, I think it's these Self-Expressions."

Her look is one of – what? confused alarm? mixed with satisfaction or relief or something like that? She's back in familiar territory, with my Self-Expressions. We are well-versed in discussing them. Her confused, worried look is one she might aim at a malfunctioning domestic appliance, rather than a deranged man. It's then, with her look, which I find reassuring, that she's closer to understanding me, and I decide I must now cede more to her, as part of the negotiation.

"Some of my Self-Expressions," I say, "were quite extreme," I say. "I mean, violent. I talked about ███████."

I have to pause, to let her understand the gravity of what I'm about to say.

"I wanted to try to express my feelings about him. To see if I might get rid of them, perhaps. Or come to an understanding about them."

"How extreme?" she asks.

"Very violent," I say.

She appears to consider this, perhaps sketching in her mind the possible boundaries of *very violent*.

"Anyway," I say, "I may have made a mistake in publishing one or two, just excerpts really, in an online forum. Without removing ██████████'s name from them. I've deleted them now, of course," I say (in case she might try to look them up), "and I forgot all about it, except to keep those Self-Expressions to myself. But then I went with Frankie to that fair. And I wonder if someone somewhere hasn't got the wrong end of the stick, if you catch my drift."

I like to imagine that Angela's expression was one of dawning clarity. But maybe she was just happy for any explanation.

"If that's the case," she says, with an incredulity so undisguised it suggests perhaps she does believe it, "it sounds like you should just explain the misunderstanding."

I nod vigorously at that.

"Ring the local police station, tell them what you think is happening. I'm sure they'll be able to put your mind at ease. They may be able to explain what it is you've found under your car."

I nod, more slowly. I'm enjoying her capacity to restore a sane interpretation of the world.

"After all, isn't it more likely to be something quite mundane? Or even a kid's prank, at worst? And if you have wound up on someone's list because of something macabre you've written, well, that's not a crime. But perhaps it would help," she says, "if I could see those Self-Expressions."

I nod more vigorously again, though inwardly I'm practically beaming.

"They're quite gruesome," I say, because I sense extra hype will heighten her pleasure in reading them. "And I don't know if they're really how I feel," I say. "But they *are* honest."

She looks satisfied – do I flatter myself to think she's a little excited at the prospect? To test my theory, I say, "I know you won't, but you'll have to promise not to judge me for them."

"Of course not," she says, "after all, I'm the one who started you on them. And you mustn't take them too seriously, the things you write, even if they're very dark indeed. Sometimes you have to get it out. That's what they're for."

I smile at her, at the simple rightness of what she says, but mostly at the undeniable anticipation in her voice. Because I suppose she did indeed get me started on them. And now, finally, they are bearing fruit.

██████: I'd like to clash heads with you.

I'd like to headbutt you, repeatedly, and collapse the structures of your face.

I'd like to torture you with my body, with some of the locks and holds I've practised for you – this one, the *armbar*; that one, the *Achilles ankle lock*. I'd like to invert your joints.

Your collarbones, in particular, I'd like to break.

I'd like to rip the smooth vents of your face – your nostrils, your mouth, your ears. I'd like to put your teeth in disarray.

I'd like to put my knee to your neck and pop your Adam's apple. I'd like to rotate your feet and hands out of their sockets and displace your kneecaps. To very finely shatter your coccyx.

Your organs I'd take great care with. To burst your lungs each in turn. To burst every sac, every alveolus, and your ventricles and atria. Or else, at least, to puncture your kidneys and liver, to disrupt their normal function, to disperse urea throughout your bloodstream, to disperse and divert your bloodstream in unnatural courses, out your empty eye sockets and tatty nostrils. I'd like to mix your innards, form with them a kind of slurry. I imagine the smell of you, in such a state. I imagine you in a pool of your own insides, a flowing viscera with face and arms.

The brain I do my best to preserve.

Then, finally, once you've reached this ideal state, I tell you that you're forgiven, and I shoot the remnants of your face so that it explodes wetly in a wide halo.

You degenerate. You abscess. You snake. You scum – you for-
nicating excrement – look at your tainted family, sprung from
the taint of your degenerate seed – from your toxic spunk –
rendered from the detritus of your genes, the catastrophic base
pairs of your DNA. You're a cosmic mistake. An evolutionary
error. You're an emptiness. I hate you with an elemental hate.
I hate you with the force of the universe. I breathe in this hate
from the leaves of the trees. It's whispered in the rain, this hate,
in the wind that presses on my face, in the occasional birdsong,
which is in the key of this hate. This hate teaches me, guides
and instructs me, pushes me like a loving parent to excel, to
outdo others, to learn from it and grow far beyond it, to hate
you more than just with hate itself, to bring my whole being to
bear on this one act of hating you, to fold my outward-pointing
senses inward. The whole of Knowledge is a mere scaffold for
this hate, its vector every technology, human and animal, from
a bird's nest to an offshore oil rig, its expression is in every
physical force, it hums and shrieks in the magnetism of the
poles and in every detonation across the face of the earth. To
kill you isn't enough – but to summon the whole force of the
universe to erase your presence from every plane, to revise
every shadow you cast, every creak and reverberation you
emitted, to wipe out the very trace of you, cell by cell, atom by
atom, to perfectly excise the structures of your existence from
the cosmos, to eradicate your lineage and delete your worldly
imprint, to undo every misdeed and utterance, to reconstruct

the universe in your joyful absence, in an everlasting celebration of your non-existence, in the jubilant, God-blessed ecstasy of your never-having-been.

Angela reads this other kind of Self-Expression with a keener interest. She seems to breathe more deeply as she reads it, as if she's breathing it in. When she finishes (or I presume she has finished), her eye rests at the bottom of the page for a few moments. For many moments.

Then she nods.

I swallow.

"Did you feel better, after writing it?" she asks.

"I'm not sure. Perhaps a bit, for a while."

"And how did you feel, as you wrote it?" she asks.

I consider this. "Hard to say. I was concentrating. Whatever concentration feels like, I suppose."

"Was it hard, to concentrate on it?" she asks.

"No. It was like... solving a problem. The problem of how to make a man suffer."

"Do you think it's real?" she asks.

I look at her quizzically.

"Is this what you want to do?" she asks.

"Possibly not," I say, and Angela shakes her head as if I've given the wrong answer.

"Do you know what I think?" she asks.

I don't say anything.

"I think you have to be honest about your thoughts as well as your feelings. I think it is honest," she says. "Perhaps more honest than any of the others. Are there any more like this one?"

I say there are, and she nods, is pleased.

"When did you write them?" she asks.

"Not long ago," I say, and she likes that.

"And some of them recently?"

And then I nod, as if copying her, feeling this is what she wants. "Yes, quite recently."

And at the end, as I leave, she asks if she can keep this one, and I pause, thinking it a kind of evidence she might use against me, but I tell her of course she can – without asking why, knowing well enough, perhaps.

Liam, my weapons sales rep, put me in touch with a surveillance expert, Klimt Spurman, who ran me through the technical specifications of the particular Wireless GSM Bug found under my car. I conducted the conversation under the pretence of being *in the market* for such surveillance devices, under my persona of Philip Swiles.

Unlike when I ineptly broke the news of the surveillance device to Angela, I was a little smoother with Klimt. Because this time I didn't bother to blend any of the truth with the falsehoods – I spoke fluently as Philip Swiles. So in describing my requirements to Klimt Spurman, I outlined the need to record audio (primarily) and occasionally track GPS information in a variety of contexts.

"I appreciate there's probably no one-size-fits-all solution," was a phrase I used. Pipeline protection was a small aspect of our business, but in any case for that sort of thing we were mostly using drones (I had to subdue Spurman's excitement at this, sensing he had a lengthy pitch up his sleeve regarding surveillance drones) and I was waiting for the relevant evaluations to be completed before I could pursue anything much in that realm, so my main interest for the time being, I told him, was recording the contents of discussions and phone calls that took place in our offices, our lobbies and corridors and possibly the surrounding environs. Devices that would fit discreetly into our lobby were ideal, given that many of our key suppliers, competitors and even members of government fielded calls there before being admitted into meetings.

"I want something that's fit for both the lobby and the jungle," I said. "Or close enough."

And that was when I described – with all Swiles's classic naivety – the model of surveillance device we'd used a few times in the past for such eavesdropping.

"I want to know its shortcomings, like battery life, does it have any anti-tamper mechanisms, is it prone to any kind of interference from other devices, et cetera, et cetera."

Swiles littered his sentences with *et cetera*, I found. All the while I spoke I was looking at the dingy pictures I'd taken of the device on my computer, the pictures I'd taken lying on the pavement, my head averted in case I should hide my face from whatever it was. I'd softened my every sound and even cushioned my breath in case it was listening to me. While I was snapping over thirty pictures of the underside of my car, I had the idea *they* were about to descend upon me, or would do if they detected me, and this was contingent, mostly, on how loudly I breathed.

When I finally ceded the phone line to him, Spurman rather lovingly recounted the technical specifications of the surveillance device. It was a *combined listening/tracking unit*. Further, it was *active*, which I gathered meant that it could transmit its data. It did this using conventional GSM technology, the same as mobile phones. Spurman was a little sceptical of such *combined* devices and recommended instead to get *separates* which avoided *jack-of-all-trades syndrome*. He said that often the *listening* part or the *tracking* part inexplicably broke. I forgave him his use of the phrase *set and forget*. He said that such *set-and-forget* devices (that is, devices that aren't intended to be retrieved) were not recommended, because even though they transmitted most of their data rather than storing it, and even though they could encrypt this data in transmission (reducing battery life), they nevertheless retained easily accessible configuration files that could be exposed by a person with the necessary savvy. And such configuration files could, in turn, reveal whereto and by what means the device was transmitting ("akin to a self-addressed envelope", he said, a phrase that was so resoundingly quaint I at first thought it was a quote from a Shakespeare play). He recommended instead devices with *time-to-live* (TTL) settings. Such TTL devices polled their remote parent at set intervals, and would wipe themselves if the connection was irretrievably lost (after the specified *time-to-live* value of course).

I felt frustrated that I couldn't share more with Spurman. That it was probably the police who were deploying these questionable devices. I very much wanted to laugh with him about it. I very much wanted his reassurance. *They really should speak to me about their inventory*, he might say, laughingly.

In my conversation with Spurman, I hadn't actually got round to asking him how one might surreptitiously remove the listening device without arousing suspicion. I was desperate to give no outward sign of knowing what I knew. The effect was almost suffocating.

I admit I procrastinated on this matter – two immobile days of anxiety, of fearing the hex on my car and that its power might spread further. My online searches for any schematics or documentation for the devices had returned nil, and somehow I couldn't bring myself to telephone Spurman again or contact him in any way – it wasn't plausible, I thought, that Philip Swiles would be so needy.

But after two days of profound anxiety that my every move was being watched, that they would swoop upon me at any moment, I finally summoned Spurman in my imagination, where we might discuss things quite freely. It was a brief discussion – in truth, it occurred as a continuation of our last conversation, so that there was no plausibility issue of Swiles getting back in touch. In the revised version of the conversation, Swiles has reached such a stage of familiarity with Spurman that I simply ask him outright: "And if someone were to ever encounter one of these things and want to get rid of it without arousing suspicion, how would they do that?"

Spurman's answer is reassuringly simple.

"Hit it with a hammer. They go wrong all the time, just go dead or just stop transmitting."

It's so sensible – so upliftingly straightforward – that I abort the imagined discussion immediately. The very idea revives me – especially coming from Spurman.

I telephoned Amy, asked her if she might consider joining me on a day trip to the seaside. To Brighton, or Eastbourne, maybe? To Beachy Head, to get blown around by the wind together awhile? I felt bad for her, that she had to say no, that it was an essentially unreasonable request, and at such wild short notice, and possibly gave her the wrong impression about my state of mind.

I was only asking her to join me so that she might give me strength, that she might distract me from my situation, from my pressing fears of the surveillance device clinging to the rear left wheel well of my car. Of being watched and eventually swooped upon. I was using her as a kind of emotional escape hatch (or trying to). Perhaps I had in mind some kind of fantastic healing would take place on a pebbled beach somewhere, and we'd unite and throw all our emotional malfunction to the waves.

Good for her, for declining such a miserable offer. She was kind and said she'd come another time. I was touched by that, and dimly I was excited and looked forward to the occasion, dimly even dreaded the arguments we'd have to dodge (or might our discontent be blown clean off Beachy Head?).

So instead I dedicated the next day to the task, alone – this job of hitting the thing with a hammer. I decided on Eastbourne, mainly because I thought it would be deserted, which would suit my mood. It could have been anywhere, really, but I thought the sea air might be a plausible context for the device's failure. I drove an hour in silence, very aware of the thing beneath me, listening and transmitting. I imagined a red dot traversing a map on a screen somewhere. Then I put the radio on for the next two hours, because I began to think my silence was suspicious.

I stood and watched the tide go out, was buffeted by the big winds, spat at by the sea spray. For forty cold minutes I thought exclusively about the device attached to my car, and imagined how I might knock it out in a single blow. Then I imagined what it'd be like if Amy were here with me, thought what a stupid idea that had been, to multiply my own misery like that. And then I took the letter from my inside pocket, the one from Paul to my daughter. I held it in front of me in its slack envelope, trembling in the wind. I thought about Amy and Paul and how little I'd done for them, and how much more I might have done. I walked further down the beach to where the water had retreated and thought about dropping the letter into the sea. The wind was such it could have blown the letter in any direction, even right back to the promenade, even right back into my pocket. So I held it up above my head to feel where it might go, and the air above was rawer than I expected and the letter immediately flew from my hand away out to sea, and then bombed into the water without a splash. At some point I started back, cursing myself for letting it get nearly dark, feeling a general regret and a growing hunger. At about halfway into my drive I began to intermittently stamp on the floor of the car. This was to indicate, to any listeners, a developing fault in the car's operation. After I'd stamped on the floor now and again over a period of about half an hour, I pulled over to a welcoming stretch of the hard shoulder and got out with my hammer. It was only half-light by then, so I had to use a torch for illumination (and I worried that the device might detect me this way, that it might blare like a klaxon and they'd swoop on me from the verges of the motorway), and then, with an awkward, underarm swing, I blatted the bug and it rather satisfyingly fell to the road, and I got back in the car and drove away and tried to spot the receding dot of the listening device in the rear-view mirror, but it was too small and it was too dark to see.

To you, the police,

At first I wanted to avoid all encounters with the police, certainly all violence against them. I wanted to concoct the perfect plan.

I thought that killing a policeman would render the whole undertaking unjust – not unjust, Wrong. I admit I still feel a kind of kinship with the police force.

But I realize now that you yourselves have a debt to pay down. You've killed civilians for no reason. Grown men, armed with the hollow-points, panicking like young boys, laying waste to people by mistake.

More than ten shots for a man who was pinned to the seat immediately in front of you. Did they teach you, I wonder, the *double tap?* I bet they did. I'm sure they took great pains to. And then you ran out and shot a man with hollow-points until his head was gone.

So let's see now, how well I fare, with my ten shots to yours. With my one man to your many. You'll be using your hollow-points again and you'll have to shoot me in the head, because I'll be armoured. In that respect we'll be well-matched, so against you I'll use the FN Five-Seven with extended maga-zine (30 rounds) and armour-piercing ammunition.

I don't reckon you'll manage to shoot me in the head. I'll be at a little distance – not pinned down at point-blank range – and there's a good chance when I take the first of you that you'll panic and shoot wildly, and your hollow-points will stop at my armour, if you hit me at all. I imagine there will be a lot of bellowing on your end, particularly when I hit you. I'll shoot you and my rounds will go through you, and I imagine you'll scream and panic all the more, and the wound profile will be such that perhaps you'll die bleeding, and I wonder then at the danger you'll pose, to myself and others, in that protracted interval between being shot and dying.

I'm looking at you, ▓▓. I only catch a glimpse here and there. I've looked at the side of your head a lot. But I see you full in the face now and then, most often when you're about to dial a number, or – better still – when you're reading one of the many emails you receive every day.

It seems so strange that I can't read those emails (though I've tried to) and yet I can watch you do so. Isn't it perverse? I try to glean their contents from your expressions. I just look. I almost rue it when you finish reading or when you raise the handset to your ear and the picture goes dark.

I fantasize, sometimes, in those moments, of pressing a button, or more likely a sequence of buttons, and blowing your head up, and – I fixate on this detail – blowing your hand up, merging your head and hand into a fine haze. I've considered the way. I might have one of your people deliver you my phone. That is the cleanest method, if I could compromise any of your staff (I know how thorough they are with the security checks on your devices – now *those* emails I have read!). Then one time when a dignitary telephones you, I let you both say hello, and perhaps I listen to a few self-congratulatory words, and then I press the button, or enter the detonation sequence, and pop open the champagne.

There are problems with this method.

I'd need to measure such a detonation of your head – such a commingling of head and hand. I'd need to verify the force readings. When the Americans dropped the atom bombs, they didn't just guess at their effects from the pictures of the aftermath – they recorded and measured their new devices, they validated their effects. Such measuring complicates the undertaking immeasurably. Should I simply trust my inside contact to give testimony of the explosion and its precise effects on you? Certainly not.

There are points in such a scheme's favour. The use of a bomb as a vengeful echo, as a recapitulation – as a reminder of why. To kill you and argue your death at the same time – you can't deny there's elegance there. But even that echo seems too much of an honour to you: for you to die like those you killed. Unacceptable. Better by far to crucify you upside down.

There is that other reason against it, too: that I want you to see me. That I want to be there, by your side, when you die. That I want you to know it's coming. I want you to know it's coming and try to escape it, and fail. I want you to be abject. Not a quick detonation you'll be mindless of – I want you to feel the anguish of a coming death. Even that is a mercy to you, a light suffering compared to what you deserve.

One of your homes is protected by two policemen. The guns they wield, I was surprised to discover, are HK G36s. Admirable guns. What kind of pitched battles are they prepared for, I wonder, to be armed with assault weapons? And can they shoot them? I'd like to find out.

A pair of sitting ducks on your doorstep. If I spent four bullets on them I'd still have enough left over to welcome the flying squad, after I'd been inside.

But I have a dreadful feeling that when the time came I'd give in to temptation and quite forego my gentlemanly standards, and establish the M249 Squad Automatic Weapon on a bipod inside your front hall.

It is a useless thing, a machine gun in a hallway – except for the surprise I can see in the policeman's face, in that slim fraction of a second before the trigger is pulled. It is a kind of gift, that moment – where the policeman sees the barrel of a belt-fed machine gun in the hallway of ███████████████, expensively photographed portraits hanging on the walls – the glass in their frames soon to glint in the repeating flash of the muzzle. How long does it take a person to realize there really is an M249 pointing their way at the bottom of the steps? Do they ever?

Why do you think you're more concerned with Paul's well-being than your daughter's?

Why are you more capable of looking after Paul than your own daughter?

And, lastly:

Why are you more capable of looking after Paul than yourself?

I was explaining that I seemed to be able to approach the issue of Paul's housing more efficiently than I could do my own. Such an issue, when it pertains to myself, seems exhausting – rebuking my energy supplier, rebuking my internet service provider, rebuking the council about the rats (surely someone else cares enough to complain?).

When it comes to my own petty frustrations (of which there are many) I inevitably become infuriated in the process of trying to parameterize my problem into the necessary bureaucratic mould – isolating the necessary data: finding the correct department, consulting old correspondence on the matter, noting my account number (sometimes there are many), trying to find a recurring name to address my complaints to (wishing there was one), trying to incorporate the matter of a phone call into a letter, or else trying to conduct the phone call in the first place.

With Paul's housing the process is far more free-form. I phone the first number I can find, speak to whomever answers me, take their name and explain I'm recording the conversation on account of my quite poor memory, but my secretary types up all my tapes at the end of the week, and would it help them to have a copy?

I speak to half a dozen people at the council and the housing association. I lie astoundingly about virtually every detail. I fabricate at every turn. If they corner me on some detail, I am outraged and insist it is their records that are to blame. I say whatever is necessary at the given moment. I hound and harass and demean them. Or else I encourage and beg them, play upon their heartstrings if I sense a welcome note there. The rules quite simply don't apply in any sense whatsoever.

It doesn't feel like I'm lying or manipulating or cheating. Because all those things, it seems to me, are directed along the adversarial axis – one against another. But somehow I don't recognize any of these voices as *another*. They are bodiless. They are personless. They are a complex of ambiguous signals that ultimately reduce to either success or failure. One young man is particularly upset by our conversation and I reflect on this when it's over – reflect that I've hurt someone's feelings, made them temporarily fearful, perhaps, for their job. But it seems a very unreal thing, and like waking from a vivid dream my understanding of it seems to recede quickly.

And when Angela asks me what happened about my paranoia, about the police spying on me (she doesn't specifically mention the device on my car, though my story was very specific), I tell her she was right – that it had all just been a prank. I don't say how or what the prank could possibly have been, but she smiles and says, "That's good."

Another sleepless night. I went for a walk. The cold air helps, as does being amongst other people, or at least outside with other people, where if nothing else propriety holds you up.

In my distracted state I nearly blundered right into two men who were squatting by my car. I stopped unnaturally mid-stride, almost cartoonishly.

The streetlight hung directly above them and only the cartop and the tops of their heads and shoulders were lit. One of the men cast the other in shadow as he stood up and looked around. I had the presence of mind to retreat behind the pillar of my neighbour's front gate. I don't know that I feared them, but I powerfully feared them spotting me, as deadly as a child's game. So I didn't dare even peep at them from my cover, and instead tried to listen. They weren't there long – I gathered they were trying to find something underneath my car. For a moment I thought I'd misinterpreted their presence – I wanted perhaps to have misunderstood them, that one of them had dropped something, it happened to fall next to my car or under it, etc. One of them sounded frustrated, though they spoke quietly, and it was their quiet, urgent voices that made it clear they weren't merely looking for their personal effects.

I hoped they weren't planting another device – I wasn't ready for that. Let them look and see it is missing, it has fallen from where they placed it; let them understand the termination of its transmissions – but don't let them set another.

I waited for them to walk away, silent except for their rapid footfalls. Then I waited a lot longer. I noticed my hair was wet, my glasses specked with rain, the pavement already slick. Apparently, it had been raining for some time. I tensed at the sound of their returning footsteps – but it wasn't them, instead a drunk with his more sober friend, the friend silently enduring a rendition of a pop song. They passed me and I didn't try to seem less strange, standing by the pillar of my neighbour's front gate. The drunk continued into the next verse.

I brought Angela up on her bad advice. She took it in unusually good humour, as if bad advice had been her aim.

I told her about taking Amy to the restaurant. I pointed out that it had been one of her insidious quasi-suggestions, brought out in me through her increasingly pointed questions: *What do you imagine your reconciliation with Amy would look like? Who would be there? Would you be there?* (At one point I was sure she was suggesting my dream reconciliation would happen post-mortem, and I realized this was the most feasible scenario: that Amy would finally look past all my errors after I'd been laid to rest or blasted to ashes, whichever I finally opt for in my will.)

I believe for most of the evening Amy thought I was going to announce I had a terminal illness. She didn't trust my motives for suggesting we eat out. It wasn't a fancy restaurant, just a local Italian. To be honest, I hadn't been there in years. It had changed a little, especially the menu, and the prices. But by now money seems a nonsense, so I only glanced at the prices out of curiosity, like checking what the temperature is in Paris.

Amy said, "This is nice," in the spirit, I believe, of having a go.

She asked me if I went to Eastbourne that time and I smiled and said I had, that the trip had cleared my head a bit. The somewhat overbearing waiter commented on Amy's looks and guessed I was her father, and commented on the stark difference in our appearance, so as (I suppose) to offend both parties, and whereas before I would have smiled and nodded and perhaps laughed nervously, instead I just stared at him to see, in his face, whether he would understand his error. And I believe he did, after a moment's silence (which Amy tried to fill, though with difficulty, since I was staring quite fixedly at that point), but he didn't relent so much as harden his resolve and take a dislike to my staring, and say, "Hey, you shouldn't take it so seriously, I'm only joking," and I smiled at him and told him he had a good sense of humour, which I believe he took as I intended it, rather than accepting the superficial meaning, and so I discovered in him a keen social sensitivity that was completely at odds with his manner otherwise.

When he'd gone away, Amy asked, "What was that about?" and I said something like,

"Nothing. I've no tolerance for people, these days. An old woman asked me for my seat on the bus the other day, in a way that I didn't particularly like, and I told her the standing would do her good."

"That's horrible," Amy said, in a slightly scandalized way.

A man about my age thought that as well, I said. He told me I was incredibly selfish and unpleasant, and he gave up his seat for the old biddy, and the bus collectively glared at me in righteous indignation. And do you know what I said?

I said: "Not one of you will make me stand, though. Will you?"

And I also said, "Because you're all pathetic."

"Especially you," I said to the old knight of the realm who'd shaken his head at me, who was now standing near me. I was half-inclined to fight him, to see who had the greater prowess.

(I was half-inclined to invite the old biddy to fight, and utterly destroy her – though this I omitted in my retelling.)

Amy was understandably perturbed by my tale.

"Why?" she asked.

This is what I told Angela: I no longer possess patience. Patience for me, now, is the interval between my apprehension of someone's wrongdoing and my coming to a resolution in how to deal with it. In which case, sometimes I have a great deal of patience, being that people's wrongs can be subtle and multifaceted.

But to Amy I replied, "I'd just had a bad day," which may also have been true.

Obviously, this wasn't the best beginning for our dinner. So I tried my best at smiling ruefully, and then was actually rueful, and I told her I hoped she might restore my liking of people.

I think our mains had arrived before we'd faltered into a real conversation. Or at least Amy was talking.

You never used to hate people, she said.

Didn't I? I asked.

She shook her head. Not like this, like you seem to, now, anyway.

I don't hate people, I said. I was enjoying Amy telling me what I was like, had been like.

But you used to care. A lot, she said.

Well, you have to, to be a teacher. To be a good one, which I hope I was.

Even with Granddad, she said. Sorry, she said. I shouldn't bring it up again, but it scares me. It's like you don't care, any more. About anyone.

Of course I care, I said.

I was finding the act of eating a kind of disgrace, though I kept putting the food in my mouth as if to get through it, and then swallowing quickly in whatever pause Amy left. I was fending off her silence, or just filling it, but for some stupid reason I kept eating, methodically and unconvincingly, as if the food went from the interior of my mouth straight down a chute into the ground beneath me, and I had no sense of what a real person ate like.

She started telling a story that I didn't remember – apparently, we'd both been out one night, on the high street. She was perhaps ten or eleven years old at the time. She didn't remember why, but we were looking for something, a gift for her mother, or something like that. We came across a shop that was familiar to us, though had changed management recently.

She said that she distinctly remembered the brightness of the place, after coming in from the street, an over-brightness. The items they stocked were somewhat disparate – stationery, cheap toys, wrapping paper, hole punches, a small selection of children's books, even some music tapes. She said that I'd kept encouraging her to look at things in the shop, to want to buy things, kept offering to buy her anything that she took even the slightest fancy to.

"I thought you'd gone crazy," she said. But she began to feel the air of desperation in that shop – the feeling of observing someone's professional failure. I began to remember the story she was telling, or felt as if I did. "I started to feel bad for them," she said. She realized, then, the manner in which I cared about people.

"How you love people, in your way," she said. "Or used to," she said.

She lapsed into silence, while I was most of the way through my pasta. I suddenly felt full, but pushed on.

I still care, I said, after I'd swallowed. I think, I said.

She said that she'd never really felt that feeling, of how I cared about people, towards herself.

At first I didn't understand, but had the sense to halt myself from going back to my pasta again.

It always seemed that I was in a different category, in a way, she said.

Of course you were, I said. You were my daughter.

A strange slip, that past tense, though she ignored it.

She was very sad, and I wanted to reach to her and touch her, but felt the falseness of such a gesture, even though it was true.

Amy, I said.

At this point the overbearing waiter came over to us to enquire how the food was. Amy tried to smile him away, I just shooed him away.

Amy, I said again, what's wrong?

She shook her head, said nothing was wrong.

Why are you sad? I said.

I don't know, she said, quietly. I always felt you loved other people more than me, she said, and tried to laugh at the notion, and couldn't.

Even now you won't say. Or can't, she said.

Can't? I said.

Don't you?

Don't I what? I said, well knowing what.

I don't think you ever told me you loved me.

Of course I did, I said.

When?

I must've, all the time, I said.

She looked very sad. Again I wanted to touch her, and didn't.

I must've said it a thousand times, I said.

She shook her head.

I'm sure I did.

She looked down abjectly at her plate. I struggled for what I wanted to say.

Then she said, quietly: Do you love me, then, Dad?

And I struggled for what I wanted to say again.

Of course, I said.

She snorted disdainfully, shaking her head, and I was angry with myself, with my incapacity.

I do –

Still shaking her head, she lifted her gaze from her sad plate and stared at me.

I love the part of you that's her, I said.

Silence.

Laughs.

Half.

Shakes head again.

More than half

              I think I said.

I don't go shooting with Paul any more. That last time we went, afterwards we drove back in awkward silence, and for once it was Paul trying to get me to speak and me not saying very much. And then when we got back to his home it was a curt farewell. He didn't even mention the housing application. He looked back once at me and he knew it was over and I think he was glad it was, and he pulled his collar up against the cold and walked in his wide, cowboy, prosthetic gait into the estate, and so I watched him go back to his parents' flat, watched him fumble for the fob more than usual.

I did sit awhile in the car, in the car park, and I missed him already and regretted not saying much to him, and I wanted to go after him and apologize and explain everything, not just everything I was planning and why, but really everything, about Amy and the letter, and how when I looked at him I thought *What have they done to you?* or *You're a ruin*, and sometimes other similar thoughts.

I looked around in case anyone was watching me. I peered up at a CCTV camera mounted at the entrance to the estate. And then I started the engine and pulled out of the car park.

And part of the reason it had to be the last time, and maybe part of the reason Paul was glad, was because I was a lot better than him by then. Because even when I can't shoot live rounds I do the drills – target acquisition, reloading, unjamming, readying, etc., etc. And plus, because I spend time maintaining the weapons, stripping and cleaning and oiling them, I have a kinship with them which he hasn't. But mainly because I have all my limbs and he hardly has one.

We both knew even that first time when the P226 jammed because of an ammunition failure (the gun itself never fails) – and I had to rack the slide to dispense the faulty cartridge – that our time shooting together was doomed. Every magazine I loaded for him, though at the time we both thought it a fine thing, a bond between us – and it *was* a bond between us, and even so at the same time it was a growing rift – every magazine I loaded was one he couldn't – and I believe he had a count of every magazine I loaded for him, in his head, and the total grew towards some unspoken maximum threshold, and then when I was finally a lot better than him, a lot more capable on every front in handling the weapons, it seemed the threshold was breached and there was nothing more for it.

There was another thing, though, about Paul and I, that last time. It wasn't just because I was a lot better than him at shooting. Maybe that was some small part of it. A Contributing Factor.

One of Angela's lessons: you can't lie to yourself, but sometimes you can believe your own lies.

So the reason it was the last time we went shooting – the real reason – was because we were nearly discovered. Someone nearly found us.

So Paul, finally, put his foot down. We'd arrived back at the car, after aborting our shooting and hastily gathering our things. We'd heard the sound of approaching quad bikes – in a lull between the thunder of our shots. Paul was swearing more than usual as we gathered everything up – as the sound of the engines grew. We snaked our way through the woods, away from their noise. I had the gun bag slung over my shoulder and was carrying the targets loose under my arms. Paul was loping behind me, swearing at the branches that swung into his face. He fell over a few times and we had to stop to get him upright – but by then the sound of the quad bikes was fading into the distance. So we walked the last ten minutes, and when we reached the car Paul said, once he'd caught his breath: "Tell me now."

I turned and made to put the things down by the car.

"What this is all about," he said.

I nodded. "You'll judge me negatively," I said.

He looked at me strangely.

"We're both in deep shit if anyone finds us," he said.

I tilted my head in mute challenge.

"Not that I give a shit." He went to the car and leaned his good elbow on its roof. The car was specked with fine drizzle, so I guessed his position wasn't very comfortable and there was some meaning to the pose. "But what the fuck is going on with you?"

I opened the boot and put our bags in, then laid the target plates on top. "In the car," I said.

"No. Now!"

I opened my door. "We should really move," I said. "Please, Paul." I got in and unlocked his side.

As he struggled into his seat, I asked him to give me a minute to compose myself. He gave me rather more. I think he knew there was no going back now, that I had to tell him, and he was happy to wait. I suppose it was several miles before I glanced up from the road and said: "Well, it's about ███████."

You have to imagine, the feeling of actually saying the name out loud. To Paul, of all people. After saying it so many times just in my head, or to Angela (which is nearly the same thing). You have to imagine how it felt in relation to everything – to what had just happened – most of all in relation to the guns and cartridges and magazines stowed in the boot. For the first time, we were driving with loaded guns in the back and I was saying ████████'s name to Paul.

It felt very real, as they say. I tried to concentrate on the road in front of us, in case we might fly off it.

And when Paul queried, "████████?" it again seemed like everything had been ratcheted up.

"I don't expect you to agree," I said. "But I've spent a long time thinking about it. Working it out."

"You're going to kill him?" he said. He sounded surprised, somehow.

"Yes," I said.

"Really?"

"Yes."

He seemed amused. "You're really going to try?"

I didn't respond.

"Fuck." He was silent awhile. We both looked at the road ahead. "When?" he said. "How?"

"You won't tell anyone, will you?" I said. He looked at me like I was simple. "I mean Amy, really. You won't tell her?"

He shook his head, blew an exhausted puff of air.

"You won't tell her, then?" I said.

It was only when we'd reached his estate that we spoke again. After I'd cut the engine, we both hesitated, knowing the issue wasn't quite settled. As if it ever could be.

"I can help you," he said.

I didn't quite understand him. "You've been a tremendous help," I said. "I'm very grateful to you."

"Do it, I mean. I can help."

Was I surprised? Part of me must have expected it.

I shook my head, pointed towards the boot with my thumb.

"The council are finally relenting. They've said they should be able to put you up in your own place quite soon. In a matter of weeks, in fact – it was going to be months – "

"I don't care about that, I want to help you."

Yes, I was hurt.

"Paul, I've put quite some time into – "

"Yeah, I know, I'm grateful obviously, but – "

"Grateful is right," I said. "When someone puts a lot of effort into something, it's wrong of you to dismiss it out of hand."

"Look, I'm sorry but – "

"Sorry is right," I said. "Sorry is fucking right."

He was stunned. Was I speaking to a pupil then? I don't think so. For the first time, perhaps.

"And no, you can't help."

I don't know whether he was angry or upset.

"Look at you," I said. "You're a mess."

Sheepishly, he said, "I know, I drink too much."

"I'm not talking about your drinking," I said. "You're a mess. Physically. How can you help me? You can barely *hold a fucking door open for me*. So, please, take up your new home, and don't talk any more about helping."

"You're just like everyone else," he said. I didn't know what he meant, I only resented his phrasing, as if it was something repeated from somewhere. "You're a user," he said.

I nodded. I looked him in the eye, maybe for the first time properly since his injuries – or maybe it just felt that way. His good eye seemed to be flicking between both of mine, as if he was checking which was the better to see me through.

"You've helped me a lot," I said, "and I've helped you, I hope almost as much."

He shook his head, breaking off our gaze, blew another hot puff of air. "A fucking user." He opened the passenger side door and made to get out.

"You should be more grateful," I said.

He stopped, looked at me again as if I were very simple. "Should I," he said.

I got out on my side, and watched him struggle a little more than usual getting his legs through the door, getting them planted firmly on the ground (was he drunker than I realized?). I went to open the boot. Paul's estate was deserted, but even if it hadn't been I don't think I would have cared about the guns spilling from their bag. Caught underneath the bag – and gathering a pool of loose nine-millimetre cartridges where they'd spilt – was a yellow ring binder with all the notes for Paul getting his new flat. I picked it up, tilting it to let the cartridges roll off on to the floor of the boot. I weighed it in my hand briefly, before closing the boot again.

He knew what I held in my hand, and I suppose he was a little embarrassed because he wanted it – he still needed me to explain it, highlight the relevant names and numbers, outline the procedure. And for myself I was a little embarrassed, too, and nervous in case he'd open it too soon and discover the letter inside, so I kept it firmly in my grasp, trying to judge the moment to give it – even though there was no chance of him opening it here, with his one good arm.

He looked at me sullenly, waiting, and I loathed him a little, then. I should have been gracious and just handed the thing over, explaining that if he had any questions all he needed was the name and number on the first page.

I said, "You know there's barely a day I don't think about you."

If he thought I was warming up to declaring my love for him, he didn't really show it. Though I suppose I was, in a way.

"My wife, and you," I said. "Those are my two biggest regrets."

Was it the slightest frown on his face? Hard to get a good reading in the orange streetlight.

"I'm OK," he said. I was very touched by that. It surprised me.

"I hope so," I said. I handed the ring binder to him. "But I don't think it's true," I said.

He had a dejected look, as if he agreed.

There was a shout from a walkway high up on one of the estate's buildings, which caught our attention, and then some yelling back and forth which we tried to ignore.

"Well," he said, loud enough over the distant noise, "I'm sorry I didn't work out for you." He turned and gestured like a wave with the ring binder in his good hand, then appeared to change his mind, paused, half-turned. The yelling stopped.

"There was nothing you could've done," he said. "If that matters." He looked at me enquiringly.

"That's kind of you to say," I said.

He looked at a loss for words – as if there was something he was about to say, but couldn't quite formulate – and he nodded and turned and walked away, not waving with the ring binder this time. I watched him all the way into the estate – watched him grapple the ring binder to his chest while he sought for the fob in a pocket, then watched him shoulder the door open, watched him disappear into the fluorescent lobby. I suppose I knew it was the last time we'd speak, and so I was very sad when the door swung closed, and I struggled awhile, even after I'd fumbled my way back into the car and into the driving seat.

Good and Bad describe outcomes, while Right and Wrong describe decisions.

That is, a Right decision can lead to a Bad outcome (for instance: prolonging someone's suffering by saving their life). And *vice versa* (killing a mass murderer for their shoes). This is one of the vectors by which we encounter so-called *moral grey areas*.

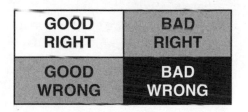

GOOD RIGHT	BAD RIGHT
GOOD WRONG	BAD WRONG

It is a truism that difficult decisions abide in those circumstances in which we must determine between, and traverse, Bad/Right and Good/Wrong.

But the greater difficulty lies in interpreting *moral complexity*.

Moral complexity describes how a given decision doesn't exist independently but adds to, subtracts from, multiplies or mutates other decisions – both past and future – in often unpredictable ways. It describes how individual (simple) moral nodes are chained together to form a (complex) moral network, so that a spree of Wrong/Bad decisions may ultimately yield a Good/Right outcome. And *vice versa*. (Though truly there can be no *ultimate* or terminating node(s) ((that is, every node is both a consequence of, and gives rise to, other nodes, though we may establish boundary nodes for the consideration of a particular moral event)).)

Further, these node chains can better be described as a *continuum*, so that the boundaries between nodes (and therefore decisions) are better understood as fluid, permeable and even possibly *asynchronous*. That is, though judgements in the present can never effect past decisions, there can be a degree of *moral latency* in which decisions are made in reference to a former or future circumstance and not the present circumstance at all (for instance, when *honouring someone's wishes*, or else when *setting an example*).

Therefore, it can be said that we exist in a state of *moral flux*.

Today I discussed my retirement quite frankly with Angela. I think she was gratified by it – that she is glad of having *opened me up*, as it were. I regretted using the word *heartbroken*, but have come to think that perhaps sentiment can be honest, sometimes (though I won't admit this to Angela, possibly ever, given it would do her no good and she by far needs to place less trust in the feelings in her gut).

So maybe I was "heartbroken" when I returned from my short leave of absence. (Even now I wrap the controversial word in quotation marks, though I quote myself.)

I came back to work from a two-week break, and the two-week break was caused by a faltering in my spirits. My wife noticed a few days before I did; she was the one to suggest a *break* from the school for me (signally not a holiday). I was experiencing some kind of primal funk or malaise or miasma – whatever it was, I'd lost my edge. I was deliberating on matters I'd usually resolve decisively, now and then I was trailing off instead of terminating a sentence. Things – decisions, judgements, occurrences in general – had become less clear to me – and, worst of all, the boys were less keen in their regard of me.

(I'm unqualified to say whether any of this was true, except in my experience of it.)

My spiritual crisis – or whatever it was – occurred towards the end of the Spring Term. So after discussing it with my deputy (who had nothing to do with what followed, I'm sure), I arranged a two-week leave of absence immediately following the Easter holiday, in order to gather my spirits, I suppose, or rest my soul – or whatever you do when the injury you're recovering from is not strictly identifiable.

I discussed with Angela an incident that happened just a few days before the end of term, when I was at the gates after the school day had finished. Perhaps because of the looming holiday – or because of my looming spiritual crisis? or the volatile combination of both? – the boys were in increasingly unruly spirits, and I saw some of them playing rather boisterously at the bus stop outside the school gates. A handful of them were fighting, seemingly all against all – playfully, I suppose, at first, but of course it got out of hand.

As I was crossing the road to interrupt them, I saw that the scuffle had taken a nasty turn and that four of them had rounded on one. That wasn't too bad, usually – often the more who piled in, the less effective their violence. But the character of this exchange turned drastically, because the outnumbered one took, rather ingeniously, to wielding his bag. It so happens that some boys, by whatever combination of timetable and weighty subjects, come to carry an immensity on their backs. And this boy, now unallied, had managed to swing his cannon-ball-like bag off his back and at the heads of his enemies. By this point the few members of the general public hardy enough to catch the bus at this hour and at this bus stop retreated yet further from the melee with worried looks. The attackers took umbrage with having been beaten back, and one of their skirmishers managed to dodge wide around his deadly radius and jump in behind him. Which was well enough, as far as I could see, except that he began to strangle the boy with the strap of his bag.

I was among them in a few quick strides and able to free the victim's neck without any real harm coming to him – he suffered more, I believe, in his red-faced fall to his knees on the concrete – and I soon had the strangler in my usually reliable grasp. The others ran and I was content with this outcome. Except that the strangler, in a further demonstration of cunning, pushed his body closer to mine, so that I felt the need to step back and plant my feet wider. And as I shifted my stance backwards he burst violently away and out of my grip, nearly tripping over his victim as he did so.

This shouldn't have posed much of a problem. He had barely any start on me, and on my best days I've closed ground at much greater distances. But for some reason – perhaps I was startled by the strangler's move – I hesitated a moment, before giving chase. What it was, I think, was that we were in the street – not in the school grounds or on the heath. In retrospect, I should have either acted more quickly or not at all; I recognized most of the boys involved in the *fracas*, so a wiser action may have been simply to wait for them to return to the school, to stake out their form groups one by one. But, even so, there's always virtue in apprehending them swiftly – it is a victory that resounds for days after in the schoolyard. Similarly, to give chase and be outrun by them – that is a defeat that can bolster a boy's legend, and diminish mine. And there was also, of course, the probability of the boy truanting until the Easter break, requiring further energies to finally track him down when school resumed.

By the time I had reached full stride in pursuit of the skirmisher, I had a strong sense that I wouldn't catch him. It wasn't his speed exactly, but his strangely surging pace, which made the distance between us waver erratically, and his odd, hunched little run, which I struggled to imagine getting a firm grip on. In any case, as I got close to him, he cut inside between two parked cars and began running along the road. I shouted his name sternly, then, partly to demonstrate I knew who he was, partly out of desperation to pull him back on to the kerb. I suspect that part of his game was to push the risk factor, a test of nerve. And my nerve amounted to this: shouldn't I just stop? He'd won – he was willing to put himself at outrageous risk. And by chasing him, wasn't I as well? I slowed my pace, but kept jogging along the pavement, a gesture intended to inform him we could happily resume the chase on safer ground. But he kept up his sprint and – spotting the slightest pause in traffic – he darted across the road, and was away.

I went, finally, to see my father again in the hospital.

There was something abject in the sequence of it: my wife, then my father, though they were separated by years and miles. Looking at him lying there only dimly conscious, it was as if I could see his life force fluttering, like the flame of a low candle. I felt very strongly, looking at him, that I needed him to keep going, for no good reason except my own selfishness.

I apologized to him for my shortcomings. As a son, and as a husband and father; shortcomings he'd bridged himself, at a heavy toll. I apologized for not taking the blows, for dodging them, for letting them fall on him instead, which wasn't fair. I told him that I hadn't been quite right, ever since she went. Which obviously he already knew. Most of it or all of it he already knew. That was the sad part – the need to speak in summary, to recap and underline. To review.

I'm sorry about a lot of things, but I think at least I did right by you when Mum left, I said to him. Then when Mum died, I should've done my bit again, which I don't suppose I did, and I'm sorry for that as well. It was stupid, really. I viewed your separation too literally. I didn't think about how you must've felt. I decided it didn't mean much to me, and presumed likewise for you. I was angry with her. I presumed you were as well. I was angry with her on your behalf. More than was necessary, I'm sure. I should've accounted for your feelings better.

Then I thanked him, for the whole lot. I thanked him for being my father. I told him that fathers could be a lot worse than him, and sons a lot better than me. I could have followed your example, I told him, but I never really did, in the end. And that was my mistake.

Thank you for helping Amy, as well.

I told him it was a shame he couldn't speak, and possibly not even hear, by now. It was a shame he couldn't make sense of what I was telling him. And that I couldn't remember the last thing he'd said to me, though I understood that was a base kind of sentimentality.

So I came back to the school after the Easter holiday, and after an additional two-week absence (gathering my strength, etc.). And I believe my strength was gathered well enough and that I was, more or less, renewed by the time I walked again through the school gates and took up my post outside the school that morning. Were the boys surprised by my return? I was stern with them, with the ones in improper uniform. Perhaps I imagined it, but it seemed to me that standards had slipped already, that, in some small, testing way, the boys were beginning to take the piss, as it were. Probably it was just the hangover of the holiday, but it didn't strike me that way. How many ties did I insist on being adjusted, that morning? And one poor Year Seven got caught in my sights, whom I was very short with, though it transpired he didn't have the first idea how to tie the sorry thing that was hanging around his neck.

But when I returned to my office after morning registration had begun, one of the receptionists told me the chair of governors was here to speak to me, and was already waiting inside, and unlike all my other encounters with the wretched fools (the governors, I mean) this time I felt an honest dread. Perhaps I already sensed what was to come – sensed what I'd already ceded in my short spell away. So in the end I hardly put up a fight. I went in and managed no courtesy towards him, which usually I could (usually I offended his type with my courtesy at first, then offended them with my discourtesy – if they lasted that long).

"Why are you here?" I said, or something like that, as if I

wanted it over with. And he said, "I'm here on the behalf of the governors, and the teachers," delivered as if unwrapping it slowly.

I didn't want to sit down, but did anyway.

"Jim, is it?" I said, well knowing his name.

Jim – the absolute worst of them (hence their chairman, I supposed). Instead of my usual steel I was equipped now only with pointless mean thoughts (I had the strong urge to call him a *turd of a man*, for instance).

"Am I to understand you've finally found the means to be rid of me, Jim?"

I think he was at least unprepared for that.

"If that's how you want to see it," he said.

I leaned forward on my elbows and said, "How's it to be, then?"

He leaned back, as if my breath was rotten.

"The teachers have asked the governors to appoint a new headmaster in your place."

I nodded, scratched my head.

"Do you want to know why?" Jim asked me.

I smiled at him, like at a boy asking another stupid question – smiled at the possibility of him learning, yet.

"Jim!" I said. "There's no need for you to tell me why."

He frowned and thought me trying to mock him, probably, and shook his head, as if all the terrible things he'd heard about me were true (most of the terrible things he'd heard probably originating from his own mouth).

"You're not even curious why the teachers have lost patience with you, are you?" A glow of sunlight came through the blinds, striping Jim's features.

"How long have you been a governor?" I asked, as I stood

up, then I stopped him with a raised finger and said, "I think I need a cup of tea, don't you?"

"Coffee, thanks," he said.

"I wasn't offering coffee, Jim."

"I don't drink tea," he said.

I had the impulse then to ask him what variety of cunt that made him, but instead I said, "You don't have to drink it," and by then I was by the door and had opened it and was calling to the receptionist if she wouldn't mind making two cups of tea, two sugars for me (she'd know that meant bad news) and none for the chair of governors.

"Has it been ten years, perhaps?" I asked, closing the door behind me.

He had to turn in his seat to face me. "Eight years," he said.

I nodded, ambled as if in wonder back to my seat. "Eight – long – years," I said. "And yet I remember it like yesterday, when you joined the governing board." I smiled at him. "Do you?"

"Not quite so clear as that, maybe."

"I remember," I said. "I remember you were very keen on discussing the school's *vision*. Do you remember that?"

He shook his head.

I nodded. "Yes, you were absolutely adamant that we sort out the school's *vision*. Our ethos, our values, that sort of thing, I think you meant?"

"That's what a vision is, yes," he said.

"Ah. Is it? I don't think so," I said. "A vision tends to happen to crazy people. Or religious types. Prophets have visions."

"Here you go again, so disdainful of everything you disagree with."

"If I wasn't why would I disagree? If I didn't think it was the stupidest kind of nonsense what cause would I have to demean and belittle you for it? Do you remember that? Of course you do, Jim. I hectored you for it. I told you our vision – I was very deliberate about it – under me, the school's vision was this: To Teach Children. Let it be written on a banner above the gates. Boys, specifically – well, that would be our ethos. And so our vision and our ethos could be expressed like so: To Teach Boys. I was so angry with you, then, Jim. I was close to hating you."

He was eye-rolling me.

"I suppose that's no surprise to you. No doubt all sorts of people hate you. But I despised you for your mind, in particular. For being dull, and for being near me. For infecting my day with your dull thoughts. Eight years, Jim, you've been squandering my time with your dull thoughts."

I shook my head.

He said, "That's quite enough, Michael. I'm not here to be insulted by you."

The receptionist caught the last of his sentence as she opened the door, bearing a tray with three mugs of tea, and she gave me a funny look to indicate she understood the awkwardness of her timing, and then she set the tray down and too playfully – to break the mood perhaps – tried to work out whose mug was whose ("Mine's Mr Lazy, it's ironic obviously"). Jim told her it was fine, he didn't drink tea anyway, he didn't know why I had wasted her time asking for tea for him when he didn't drink it. The receptionist left without a word, without even another funny look to help me out.

"Come, then," I said. "Say what it is you want to say."

"I don't take any pleasure in this, Michael," he said.

I did a kind of fast-forward gesture with my left hand.

"I'm sorry you can't be more professional about it. But anyway, the teachers have been growing more and more concerned about your – " he sought the word, in the bare pantry of his vocabulary " – teaching style, about your approach to discipline, and especially your focus on what many people consider outmoded models of learning."

I leaned back in my chair, took a slurping sip of my scalding tea.

"I'm sorry to say that your staff no longer have confidence in your ability to lead the school."

"Don't be sorry, Jim," I said. "You've wanted this since the start."

"I want what's best for the school," he said.

"And what's that?" I said.

He shook his head. "To have a headmaster the kids actually like, not just fear.

"And the governors, too, would like to be more involved in how the school's run. You've sidelined us, and it's not good for the school or the community."

I shrugged, capped my ready responses – there was no point in describing to him his folly.

"We all know what you think of the board of governors," he said. "But it's just your arrogance, that's the root of all the school's problems – your arrogance."

I nodded. "*My* arrogance?" I let slip.

He arched his eyebrows – I sensed he wanted me to fight back. "Yes," he said. "We do an important job, a very important job, and all you do is sneer at us."

"I suppose I have been arrogant, in my way," I conceded.

He was surprised – but profoundly gratified, too, I think. He nodded.

"You have been," he said. "Like the way you've spoken to me this morning, with no cause at all. Absolutely unnecessary." As if I might apologize for that.

I nodded. "You know, it's so difficult sometimes. It's like – " I raised my gaze slightly above him, so he could understand the depth of my thoughts – "it's like I'm a giant, surrounded by these tiny people. Like Gulliver in Lilliput."

I returned my gaze to him. His expression was blank, as if reverted to factory settings.

"It's hard sometimes to even bother stooping all the way down to hear what those tiny people have to say, and then – do you know what they ask me? They ask me what the school's vision is. And each time it happens, my arrogance grows. Until I suppose I feel, quite wrongly, that I'm the only one who has any brain at all, that I'm the only one who isn't utterly demented or simple or..." I trailed off.

"Or whatever you are, Jim," I said.

He stood up, angry. "Enough!" he shouted, arms slightly raised as if ready for combat. I observed him. I think in that moment I experienced my first curiosity about Jim. How does a man like that get angry? Do they even possess dignity or is it just something they've heard of?

"I'm sorry you can't be more professional about it, Michael," he said.

"You've already said that," I said. "Have you run out of phrases again? Do the one about vision, Jim, for old times' sake."

He'd turned around, was speaking to the door he was walking

towards. "We'd like your notice by next Monday, though earlier would be courteous of you." He turned back with a withering look, before opening the door.

Paul rang me on my mobile. I was exercising at the time, and I put down my weights to stare at my phone. This was the first time he'd ever rung me, in my life (to my recollection).

I looked at his name pulsing on my phone and my instinct was that it was bad. I actually thought it was the police. I was a coward, and let it ring. I thought perhaps I was waiting to catch my breath before answering. And it rang and rang, and I caught my breath and I should have answered him. Out of courtesy, if nothing else, to a friend. I owed him an answer. But as far as I was concerned it was the police, and as soon as I accepted the call they'd swoop upon me, perhaps shoot me with the hollow-points. Then my phone went dark and I was left contemplating the police operator I was sure was on the other side – whether they'd redial, from whatever terminal they were operating in Scotland Yard.

I braced myself for that second call, which never came.

Dear Angela,

<u>This isn't a so-called Self-Expression.</u>

I don't know how many times I've started this letter to you. But I have a good feeling this will be the last go.

Firstly, I'd like to thank you for all your help. I know I haven't been the best – client? patient? Whatever, I know our discussions have been trying at times.

I'd like you to know that I've come to admire you a great deal.

I think you were right to wind down our appointments. The specialist you referred me to was very young, very kind, quite handsome – do you know him well? I hope you do. Maybe I'm being sentimental (maybe with good reason), but I imagined you and him together, and you made a nice pair in my mind. I spoke warmly of you, though I doubt the opinions of an old fart like me really matter to him. If you haven't already, you should consider courting him. I feel you two would get along (though maybe you're already *an item*, as they say? If so, I'm glad).

I must apologize to you for what I'm about to do. I think you might take it one of two ways – either very badly, with lots of guilt, or else with levity. In the old days I would have leant towards the latter. These days, I'm more concerned about you. You know, you're the last kind of person I'd ever have spoken with, spent so much time with. You've been invaluable.

So I want to assure you that you're essentially blameless in this. And I want, as far as possible, for you to be able to understand what I'm about to do. I believe I owe you that much. Or else I'm too attached to you and want at least one other soul to have some kind of idea about this decision I've made. In any case, I'm sending you all of those Self-Expressions I wrote, or at least all the ones I still have. They may be a bit out of order.

I believe I've come to a sound decision. I believe that very strongly. That decision is this: tomorrow I will try my best to kill ███████. My best, by now, is very good, and I believe my chances are excellent. But I want to firstly confirm – as you must suspect – that I resisted such a decision for a very long time, and that I had to overcome my nature, and that, even though I fully believe in this decision and this line of action, I approach the undertaking with a great deal of fear and perhaps some sadness. This is what I've written, in one of my notes:

> I won't die a good man. My silly life's aspiration, or a big one. But maybe someone won't judge me so wrong. Maybe after all Angela will forgive me. She might understand it perfectly, in the end. She might say, in that appointment we'll never have, that though it was wrong, it was right, too, and perhaps more right than wrong, in some respects. I hope so.

So, Angela, goodbye. I'm sorry to burden you further, but, if you can, please make sure Amy's OK. I think she'll like you. I think you'll be able to help her.

Frank,

I know your first instinct by now will be to hand this to the police, but please take a moment to read this letter and consider the offer I'm making you. I don't expect you to understand why, but I need you to publish some documents I'll be sending you.

I'm going to kill ███████████. The documents I'm sending will explain why. If I'm successful, the documents could generate a great deal of interest, and perhaps even prove lucrative for you.

With that said, I've enclosed with this letter the technical diagram of the distributed system I've devised to:

1) Facilitate your receipt of the necessary documents.
2) Encourage your cooperation with the task of publication.
3) Discourage your non-compliance with the task of publication.

The technical diagram should contain enough information to get you started. All you need to know to begin with is that:

1) You'll receive some documents in hard copy and the final text by email.
2) When you confirm receipt of all documents (via an online portal), you'll receive access to my bitcoin wallet (worth £1,952.23 at the time of writing).

3) If you fail to distribute the text within six months a written statement will be submitted to the police outlining the manner in which you are accessory to the (manifold) crimes I will have committed by the time you read this, including pictures of us both planning the outrage at the DSEI.

Along with the technical diagram I've enclosed some blog posts with tips on how you might approach the matter of publication, along with the contact details for a handful of journalists. I leave the details up to you.

Note that the first documents I'm sending will include a provisional ending. I may not live to write the final act, but in the case that I do, I will supply the *de facto* ending to be substituted into the text. You'll be given full instructions on how to make the substitution when the time comes.

One final, important request: this letter must be included in the compiled documents at publication (the technical diagram and other materials should be excluded). The letter should be inserted after page 370, where it will make the most sense and provide the most pleasure to the reader.

Dear Boys,

I think I've been writing this for you. In the end, you're the ones who know me best.

It's important you don't mistake my actions for those of a madman. Or a hypocrite. I hope you'll agree I spent years doing right for you, and perhaps I continue to do so.

I hope you'll take the time to read what I've written (heaven knows you've listened to me long enough over the years). It's up to you to judge, to weigh my reasons with my actions, and see if they tally.

There will be a crowd who proscribe all violence and condemn me by default: I've described the folly of this position. As you all know, a world without violence is a fantasy. The only ones who can judge me are those who understand the seam of necessary violence that joins us, as necessary as love and cooperation. Sometimes a fist is necessary. We can wield violence, to protect or prosecute.

So this is my account to you. I'm no more demented or crazy now than I was when you knew me. I'm responsible for every word I've written, and for all the bad I'll do, and for all the blood I'll shed.

When I wake crunched into the back seat of the car it takes me a while to work out where I am. As soon as I do, I feel depleted and regretful, regretful of a bad night's sleep when today is so important. I'm very cold.

I'm near the forest, on a little road near where Paul and I did our drills. It feels a long time ago. A tractor passes while I write a letter to Angela on one of the laptops.

I get out of the car, a little unsteady on my feet. There's a distant manure smell. The air's damp, the ground's damp, but it's bright, even though it's early. I check on the lockbox in the car's boot, just a quick glance at the weapons there, the MP5 and the SIG, three magazines of 9mm rounds for each, and the Spectra vest and some webbing. A single fragmentation grenade. I thought I'd included a flashbang in the lockbox, but it turns out I haven't.

The police, I imagine, by now, are ransacking my home. I wonder how quickly some left paperwork will send them to Elcock Crest's HQ in Park Royal, and all the good things I've amassed there. The FN SLP for one (I feel for it, as for a lost friend), but also the Five-seveN, the M249 and the MP7, the FN P90 and two G36s, one equipped with a 40mm under-barrel grenade-launcher. Then there is, of course, the cache of HE grenades and flashbangs, and a few breaching charges. There are NV goggles and two sets of body armour, one of ceramic plating (far too heavy for my needs). I wonder if they've found the sole white phosphorous grenade in my possession, the one

I never in the end attached to the tripwire, partly out of pragmatism, partly because I decided that anything that melted a person's skin was too sinister for my purposes. I wonder how soon they'll draw the line between Philip Swiles and myself.

They have it all, now, except for my slim provisions – the MP5, the SIG, the lightweight body armour. I send a thought out to my lost arsenal, then I close the boot of the car and spend a few moments contemplating the horizon, where the sun is now fully up. My last day, possibly, which I try not to think about.

Yesterday Paul rang me again. I was at the laptops in the front room and reached to answer it, but flinched when I saw the name.

I watched his name pulsing on my phone again, and again my instinct was that it was bad. I felt perhaps the police had begun toying with me. I had a sinking feeling, watching it ring, until it stopped.

It felt like a long time passed, and I was trying to fool myself that I might return to my work, rather than be fixed by fear for the night (and maybe beyond). But then the phone blinked and indicated Paul had left a voicemail message.

Foolishly, I still thought it could be a police officer – still dimly thought they might grab me through the walls as soon as I played the message.

"Mike," he said, unnaturally (he never said my name in any form). "I wanted to speak to you, but maybe this is better." He paused, and I didn't need to hear the rest of his message to know my instinct had been right – that it was bad. I've listened to his message many times since, but that first time I only half-listened, only listened enough to confirm that I should be vacating my home, that I should leave very quickly and go somewhere secret. There was something rehearsed about his tone, as if he was repeating something.

"I wanted to talk to you about what you're doing. I've been thinking about it a lot and – and I wanted to tell you to stop."

He paused here, as if the script was uncertain. I was quickly packing a few changes of clothes, one-handed, pushing the phone to my ear with the other hand.

"I thought you were right. At first. That's why I wanted to help. To do it with you, maybe. But I've been thinking about it." There was a wave of static on the line – an outward breath? "I've come to my senses. What you're thinking, what you're doing is madness. It's madness. That's what I realized. And over the years – you've taught me a lot, and – and I don't think you'd want me to just, stand idly by." (*Stand idly by* – had I used that phrase when delivering some dreary moral lecture?)

"You taught me to do what I think's right. I still want to help you. But not like that." There was another pause. I wondered whether he was drunk, to have reached this level of sentiment.

"I can't let you do this," he declared. "To yourself. And Amy. There's still time to stop." I was shaking my head, perhaps because I knew what was coming next. I began to slowly shut down the laptops in front of me, one by one, in a kind of sad trance. It felt permanent, turning them off, like euthanasia.

"I'm going to phone the police after I hang up. I'm going to tell them about the guns. I know I'll probably be in trouble, too. I don't want to do it. You know I'm not a grass. But I'm going to ring them. And I hope they stop you. For your sake. OK."

Some cheery voice asked me to press 3 to listen again, and I chucked the phone into the holdall and ran out of the house. When I crossed the road to the Underground station I looked back quickly in case anyone was following, in case they'd give chase, in case they might give chase through the barriers and down the escalators and on to the platform and on to the train, possibly with the hollow-points. But no one followed. And then I was in my car at Park Royal, wondering whether to call on Paul one last time, but thought clearly I shouldn't, then I wondered whether to stay the night in the car right there, and I thought that a terrible idea, too, so I drove out to this spot where I am now, near where we used to do our drills, near the forest, because there were still roughly forty hours before ████████ would be on the train with his client, in the secret meeting, in the private carriage, on the Underground.

I have the MP5 and the P226 in the holdall. I'm wearing the body armour, underneath my jacket.

I ride the trains in a variety of directions, swapping lines here and there. I pass some hours this way. They will reconstruct every step, I know. They will gather the CCTV footage of my erratic last journey. They will try to gather my meaning in the stops I make, in the lines I swap to here and there. They will map out every footstep and wonder at the lines I draw across the city, and ask themselves what secret language it is. They will ponder every pause and upward glance, every hesitation under the glowing LED displays. By then they will have most likely analysed the source code of my programs, they will describe the manner in which their systems were compromised. They will have ransacked the family home, taken apart the old piano, and even tried to decrypt the manuscripts, her songs and mine, they will reflect upon a change of time signature, tell themselves what it represents, possibly. "A fairly accomplished musician, by the end," perhaps they'll say, in the extended documentary, the exhaustively researched documentary, and they'll read out a written statement from Amy's lawyer, perhaps cast an unknown as her in the reconstructions. They will recount the failure of their surveillance methods, every lapse in judgement, every missed opportunity. Greying authority figures will describe the character of their regret, the difficulty in tackling *lone wolf terrorists*. They will take apart the biographical details in an effort to identify the causes, perhaps ineptly.

I hope they aren't too hard on Angela. It will ruin her. I hope she forgives me.

Above all, I know, they will play again and again, over and over, the dark blurry footage of me, after the last south-bound train on the Northern Line has departed, as I disappear into the darkness of the tunnels on foot, of myself merging with the black, the footage thick with pixels, reproduced, as it is, desperately enlarged, and played, often, frame by frame. And they will discuss, perhaps at length, this question, dramatically posed to the viewer as I imagine it in the extended documentary version: why did he disable the CCTV relay to the station office and the Service Control Centre, but not stop the recordings themselves? And they will conclude that he wanted to be filmed, perhaps – or at least the other plausible explanation is too detailed, too esoteric, too contingent upon the dated systems architecture of the Underground's communications network, its thorny and troubled integration with Thales's Automatic Train Control systems, and the design of their fail-safes, though some may uncover a clue in the source code of my programs, which is quite heavily annotated (and they will conclude these annotations were yet more remarks to an intended audience, the audience of the extended documentary or the audience of the general public at large, and not simply kindly reminders to my bewildered and forgetful future selves). They will wonder how I spent my night, in those tunnels. They will posit the likely explanations, perhaps that I stood vigilant, watchful, until the appointed hour, or else conducted some other preparations.

I slept, fitfully. I briefly tried to imagine the news item I'd inspire on the BBC World Service, imagined the grim satisfaction of the newsreader when they utter "London, England", instead of one of the usual hot locations where death abounds.

I thought about the last time I saw Amy. I thought of what she said to me, about her breaking heart, now that Granddad had died.

She said: Please, Dad. *Please.* It was the quality of those *pleases* that nearly destroyed everything I intended to do.

Please, she said. *Please* go see Mum.

This is her main complaint, that I don't see her mother. She believes I'm cruel, for abandoning her. But I've told her – how many times?

Her mother is dead. My wife is dead.

Amy cries bitterly when I say this. I've said it before. It was, in the end, the source of our bitterest fight – the hospital visits, my slow-dawning refusal to go to the hospital, to have anything to do with it at all. Of course, it was completely selfish of me. Of course, I should have acted like a reasonable person, especially for my daughter, who was suffering as much as me or more – and even for my dear old dad, whom it would have helped if I'd been more kept-together, less completely shattered by the whole thing. I've no doubt I could have spared his health, if I'd done my bit more ably.

We went to the hospital every day in the beginning. Her condition was very bad. In the beginning I went as my duty to her, though I was racked with fear to see her on the brink of her death. I was nearly insensible with fear.

But slowly I found it harder to go there, to sit by her bedside and wait for her to die or live, to wring my hands and stare at the floor, the clock, the beds, the bedside curtains, the transiting nurses, anywhere except her damaged body.

First, we fought about: "Why aren't you visiting Mum?"

Amy thought I owed it to her mother to be by her side. I saw her point. I felt it, powerfully, too. Of course, I hated my weakness. But more than that I hated the fear of being by that bedside, the elemental grief of her not-getting-up, of her not-speaking-to-me and not-touching-me or doing anything that she should rightly be doing.

One day I refused to go any more. I waited until Amy and my father left the house – after much urgent discussion and rising bitterness, until finally my father in his wisdom stood between us, allowed me my recess, and then I went to the bathroom and locked the door to cry until I was nearly sick.

My father, I saw, was fearful, too – for Amy, that she'd somehow lose both her mother and her father. Had lost already, was his fear.

It was the worst torture, I thought, to see my wife unconscious in that bed, fearing what I believed was the worst. But it was worse than that, by far, when she woke, finally. When she blurted non-words at me. When she couldn't close her mouth – when she hectored me with her spastic vocalizations. And I begged her in silence to stop, and to be who she really was, and I insisted in the brunt face of her brain damage that she would recover, over time – she would relearn who she was, and we would become husband and wife again, even as the nurse's mothering tone seemed to condemn her forever. I said to that nurse, Please don't talk to her like that, and she looked at me with pity, and retreated a distance. I told myself she would recover. And she didn't. I spoke to her as my wife. I reminded her of how we used to be. I spoke to her about Amy, asked if she remembered this or that, how she used to play the piano? And she might groan and grunt back at me, and it defeated me every time. I began to imagine my wife sitting just behind her, that she was deep inside the husk of her damaged body, and I spoke beyond her grunts and groans and her snarling, dribbling rictus to the person I was sure was beyond. I begged her to recover herself. And she didn't.

I dedicated myself to her, for some few months. I fed her, clothed her, washed her, did my utmost to nourish a miraculous recovery that would never occur. I told myself she was getting better, that I saw signs of improvement, in the smallest movement in her eyes, that she looked more alert when she didn't, since there were absolutely no outward signs of any improvement to her condition whatever. I invented the signs of recovery, I told Amy about them, hopefully, invited her to collude with me in the fabrication, and she couldn't bring herself to, but stayed silent, falsely upbeat, tried to speak to her mother like the old days, only sometimes raising her pitch as if to a child, and catching herself and stopping.

I made a shrine to my wife, with her bodily remnants. I mourned her every day, but always with the false hope of her return, so didn't mourn her at all but prayed she'd return. Sometimes I broke down in front of her and while I was wallowing in my tears I tried to discern if there was any difference in her. There was none, of course. She was utterly insensible. She was alive, in that she reacted to stimuli, to light and sound, she could just about eat and defecate, her body functioned. But the person I loved was dead.

When did I give her up? I couldn't give her up while looking at her, while seeing her awful gurning face, and sitting just behind her was her perfectly intact old self, grave and serene. I saw her so vividly, there. And I said to her, eventually, "You're dead, aren't you? And she rolled her head forward, as if to acknowledge it. But the sitter behind her nodded sad-eyed at me. You're not there, are you? I asked her, and she rolled her head back round, and then looked at God knows what. And then the sitter was gone. And I was left all alone with the mind-less body. Once I went on my knees and hugged her around her neck like a child and asked her was she dead or not? Eventually, I resolved she was. Eventually. Eventually, I understood I was tending to a de-brained thing, like a fallen limb, like a severed piece of her, and calling it her and having conversations with this severed piece, even though the rest of her was dead.

Amy understood when I moved her mother into a care home, even helped get funding from a charity. It's too much for one person, she said. They'll be able to give her the support she needs, she said. None of it mattered by then. I'd resolved finally that she was long dead. I mourned her, dawningly. This stump that was left – what did it matter what happened to it? Some-times I wished she'd been in a coma, brain intact, even never to awake, but I could know she was dreaming as her old self, and I could reach her, dimly, there, and imagine when I slept that we shared that space, that I was the one who left her by waking, and returned to her when I slept, and I could be glad for her to sleep peacefully forever, and I'd talk to her forever, and go to sleep next to her and dream with her. But it was all fantasy.

I thought of that thing, in the dark of the tunnels. I thought of the remains of my wife. I thought about how Amy and my father visited often – before my father's health declined. They visited that shrine of gurning flesh, as if it was her, and

I began to pity them, though we never talked about it, except Amy might try to, and I'd stop her, by leaving the room or changing the subject or telling her not to talk about it. I put my holster on.

And then there is that moment I could never tell Angela. When I hit Amy, for the second time in both our lives. It was, perhaps, immediately after the conversation where she understood I was putting her mother in a home, and she was sympathetic and encouraging and understanding.

She said, *They'll give her the care she needs* or *They can give her the care she needs.* She said it somewhat in her mother's direction – because her mother was in the room, slouched over in her wheelchair. I'd given up, by then, tending to her posture, correcting her skewed stance. I was sitting negligently next to her, scarcely looking in her direction.

Maybe I wanted to free Amy, in the way I'd been freed – freed from thinking my wife was alive, from begging and wishing her to come back. But I think it was anger, mainly. I didn't want her to contradict me, perhaps – I didn't want her to act as if her mother was alive, while I knew she was dead, because that was a kind of madness, I realized.

So I said to Amy, "Your mother is dead," and she was scared at first, uncomprehending, and then she was outraged, and this was the part that sickened me – that she felt I shouldn't say such things, especially *in front of her.* "Don't talk like that," she said.

"I've come to realize it," I said.

It cost Amy to admit that her mother was *different* now, but she insisted she was still her mother. "She still loves us," she said.

"*How?*" I said. "How on earth can she?" And I suppose it was at that moment I turned to my dead wife and said, "Do you still love us?" Certainly, there was no love in my voice. Amy told me to stop, she shouted and burst into tears.

"It hurts," I said to her. "But it's best to realize it."

And Amy said, "Stop it."

"She's not *alive*, Amy," I said.

And she said, "Stop talking about her like that!"

And it was then, I suppose, that I turned again to my dead wife, and laid my left hand on her head, and pushed it, neither softly nor roughly, but like an object.

"She's gone," I said, quietly, so that I'm not sure Amy even heard me, she was crying quite fiercely by then and bellowed at me not to touch her, and my hand softened its grip and I felt my dead wife's hair, even stroked it momentarily, before I realized what I was doing, and before I became disgusted at myself and angry at myself, and before I pushed her head away, in hate, perhaps, then, and Amy launched herself at me and struck uselessly at me and I rose out of my chair and slapped her hard across the face and she paused – we both paused – and she forgave me by raining more blows on me, and I didn't stop her then from her attack, knowing that her blows were a concession to me, and that her retaliation was a kind of forgiveness, an evening of the score, and I only pushed her away from me when she knocked my glasses from my head and I tasted blood in my mouth.

I think, in that pitch-darkness, about my daughter, and am filled with regret. I think of the letter I wrote her, delivered into a postbox near her house as a kind of time-delay. She'll receive it tomorrow, perhaps. My futile attempt to explain myself. I don't remember all of it, but I talked of our shared love for her mother. I struggled with a particular sentence: *We both love her very much.* My every instinct was to speak of the past, and it surprised me, the cost of speaking of my wife in the present tense. It upset me a great deal, seemed to open the old wound, which is so fresh already anyway. I struggled with the idea of loving my wife still, daily. "I know we disagree and have fought bitterly with regard to her current state," I proceeded, pompously, trying to stand upright, trying to plot a steady course.

I tried to explain to my daughter how much I miss her mother. That I miss her with every sense: the heat of her body against me, the touch of her, the simple animal joy of holding hands. The sight and smell of her, of course, and the sound of her humming in the other room, the sound of her sighing at the television news, and of course her laughter so much. But I miss even the spaces she left, the emptiness of the house when she was just-gone, when she was not-yet-returned, instead of this other emptiness where she is always-gone, where she is never-to-return. I miss the sound of the key in the lock, and the pause between the door opening and her voice – the tidal lift in the mattress when she got out of bed, the dip in the mattress when she leapt into bed – I miss the detritus of her every day, the mugs of cold tea and the discarded manuscripts and the idle stabs of a piano key in a moment of frustration.

I tried to explain to my daughter that there is the person, and there is the imprint they make on the universe. But none of it exists any more.

And I think of that last argument, our last words together, the part I never told Angela or anyone else, not even Amy (because, why?). Obviously, I have no sense of proportion when

I try to revisit that morning in my mind, the whole memory has become distorted, everything too-significant, so that it's barely a real memory at all now, just a collection of vivid regrets. But I remember enough of the real parts – that we argued about her songs. Because slowly she'd taken to writing her own songs, as I'd so often encouraged her to, and every song of hers brought me such joy. She kept a slim manuscript of her own songs. And I asked her to see the manuscript, and looked at her black markings on each stave and marvelled at them, though I had no idea what they meant back then. If her mood was right she'd play me a song. I'd try to make the black marks and the song correspond in my head, though it was useless trying. And I told her what part, what detail, was my favourite bit, because I knew my general flattery, though heartfelt, was lost on her when it came to her music. And I said that she must record these songs and she laughed it off. How many times? She laughed it off or just smiled and shook her head or by the end just barely smiled and shook her head. And then one time I treacherously enlisted Amy. I told Amy about her mother's songs, which she already knew about, but then I showed her the manuscript and got her mother to play, and then I asked Amy shouldn't her mother record these songs? And, of course, she agreed. And then one time I remember Amy actually played one of her mother's songs, which amazed me, which struck me dumb. And always – if I pushed – my wife would tell me, They're not good enough. Technically, she said. Technically weak. Pretty enough, was her highest estimation of the best of them. They're still doodles. I disagreed. Amy disagreed, and she was a trained musician, too, wasn't she? My father disagreed, said how good they sounded. So then one day I took her manuscript to the computer and scanned each page. I was so slow, it took me half the day. I printed out the copies and sent them to a few people I'd researched with a note explaining they were by my wife and did they think them any good? And then nothing and I would have forgotten about it, except I thought about it every day. And finally a letter came, saying what I already knew. Asking if she'd be interested in meeting informally. And I was so pleased by the news I showed the letter to my wife without even thinking. Undeniable proof as far as I was concerned. And she was angry with me, of course, for doing such a thing, for going behind her back, for taking something so private and touting it. "How many people did you send them to? I probably know some of them." It was a professional embarrassment, she said, as well as a personal betrayal. That word was too much. And so we argued. She had a meeting with a client, she was delivering another arrangement, she'd already been made late by our argument. And I said, "Please don't leave." And she said she was going to be late, and so she had to. And she left. And when your train comes in I experience a wild surge of nerves. You must understand, that this is the apex of my whole life, when your train comes in. I check my weapons by torchlight. I check my magazines. I check my solitary fragmentation grenade. I think about my flashbangs back in Park Royal, now in police custody. I think again about the shotgun, like a happy memory. It will outlive me, that gun – no matter how long I last, it will outlive me. It will be my monument. It is as much as I could have wished for, that gun. And I experience a surge of affection for the guns in my possession, the MP5 and the P226. I feel blessed to wield them, to have known them. I am honoured by them. By now, I can only hope my programs are effective. I pray to them, that they work without fault or exception. I check the surveillance feeds on my phone, cycle through the many carriage cameras, but the delay is unbearable. I can hear my wild heart in the long pause between each feed. Empty carriage after empty carriage, one angle after the other, so that I almost laugh at the thought there's no one on it. Then I see the driver's cabin, and I'm stricken and desperate and sad, but the next camera shows them all, and I don't even take the time to wonder at the fault in my program, that its feed allocation should be so senseless. I breathe. I breathe. I count them. I increase the volume, but there's no sound. I forget how many I counted. I tell myself it's fine. I increase the volume more, because I think I can hear something, but the sound I can hear is coming from inside the train. The warlord is speaking loudly. Then he laughs loudly. And I watch him laugh. There is a noticeable delay between the sound of his laughter and the image of him laughing. I didn't test the program under low bandwidth, and that's fine as well, except I pray it doesn't fall apart in my hands.

I count them, paying attention: four private security personnel. I'm not sure which is whose, perhaps he and the warlord have two each today. And there's another, a police officer in plain clothes, and there's the photographer taking pictures of the two of them together, the warlord and he, so that there are – eight. Eight. Eight. Five combatants, two non-combatants, and ██████.

Eight. I accord them each their share of rounds:

Forty-four between both weapons before reloading, divided by eight.

Five rounds each, remainder four.

Thirty-one rounds with the MP5. Conservatively, I accord them six each, allowing for a missed shot pairing. Five targets, remainder three.

Thirteen rounds with the P226. Four rounds each, remainder one. By the forty-fourth round, all targets should be down.

I set off down the tunnel with the MP5 readied, and the P226 holstered. They will replay this footage of me walking in the tunnels, where the cameras finally pick me up again, and they will wonder at that interval of night ever after. I can see the back of the train, stalled in the tunnel, its light spilling out against the tunnel walls. I open the back door of the train and I step up into the empty carriage. They're towards the front of the train, the second carriage. I traverse the four carriages between us quickly, each pair of doors like an airlock, bearing a sign that reads DANGER OF DEATH. Perhaps they can hear my progress, perhaps they think it the noise of an Underground worker coming to explain the hold-up – except too quick-footed by far. In each carriage a dirty scattergram of shoemarks colours the floor in front of the seats, stark in the emptiness. The warlord's bellowing laugh can be felt as much as heard. I quieten my steps, but there's a security guard looking at me through the door to the second carriage. I hasten towards him, raise my hand STOP, meaningfully. He is reaching for his sidearm so I close as much distance as I can before drawing the MP5 and firing two double taps just below his neck. The sound of the bullets snapping through glass and flesh is louder than the shots. I have to run light-footed now. I enter the second carriage a moment after the body hits the floor. There is an uncomprehending shout. Some are drawing their weapons – one has drawn already and must be my first target. Broadly speaking, I hit the left row of them first. There is – even in this pitch silence – really very little sound from my shots, except for the clack of the quick-falling hammer and the patter of ejected cartridges against the carriage wall, and the potch of cracking glass and the thud of flesh being struck, the breathy grunt of those as they're hit. One shot pings sonorously against a blue pole, like a bell, chips the paint. It's a matter of fluke that it is the warlord who's seated on the left side – that he and ████ are seated opposite each other, so that in this configuration there is really very little care I need to take in acquiring my targets on the left side, and it is a fairly clean sweep through them and they have almost no idea what is happening except that death is happening, and it's when I move forward and begin to acquire the targets on the right side that they understand the nature of events, and some of them rise from their seats and while I'm shooting, carefully, now, so as to spare ████ (though with some little regret I do hit the photographer twice in the face and in his camera which bursts), I notice in the hazy perimeter of my sight that in fact the policeman is struck brutally by a shot from behind him, either carelessness or ineptitude strikes him in the back and he falls loudly to the floor and I panic that they'll do the same to ████ in their fear. Compared to mine their shots are loud flat percussions in the enclosed space, the air seems to bend and compress with their gunfire. There is, by now, a great deal of blood around them, on the floor and walls of the carriage, even on the ceiling, and one of the men slips as he moves crouching forward, and I hit him in his flank, and there is a great splash of flesh that erupts behind, splattering one of the glass partitions and obscuring my sight of ████. I feel the first impact of a bullet against my

armour, I sense I have taken a hit to my left leg. I have to drop
the MP5 and draw the P226, and now it is my shots that bellow
and crash and make the air pulse around me. And I manage,
somehow, to even hit the man who is deliriously behind ███,
right up at the back of the carriage against the door to the next.
I take a moment to let things settle. I shoot the plainclothes
officer, who is lying prone, in the top of his head. ███ doesn't
move from his seated position, except he is leaning back, away
from me. I shoot the bodies around me, one by one. I reload
and shoot the others, in their heads and upper bodies. The
mess is rather gruesome, even for me. I am fully aware, now,
that I've been shot, that my leg is bleeding, that my body
armour is undefeated, but my left leg is bleeding quite heavily.
I don't feel any ill effects yet. I feel alert, sprung, ready. I holster
the P226, after loading a fresh magazine. Go for a gun, I say, if
you want. He stares at me. I nod for him to pick one up, any of
them. They are all Glock variants, I notice, and I laugh to
myself. Most of them are compacts, except for the plainclothes's, so I gesture to that one, to the policeman's Glock 19,
since he stands a better chance with it than the compacts, and
I tell him, Try that one, and he stares at me. I am beginning to
feel the ill effects of my wound, or wounds, as they must be. I
notice there is blood on my face, trickling down my neck. There
is actually a hole in my cheek. Some of my teeth are missing,
and I realize my speech is slurred and perhaps he hasn't heard
me, so I point at the policeman's gun again and slur again, Try
that one, and he stares at me. I must blink, and do, repeatedly,
and I realize I am beginning to teeter, and I anger at myself
and tell myself this is what I prepared for, but even so I fear
despite my preparations I'll fail, I'll succumb to bloodlessness,

and perhaps it is my bloodlessness that makes me yell at him, *Get it*, and he stares at me, and I feel myself slipping, and I fall to one knee, and slip forward on the viscera, my own viscera as well as theirs, and I see that he has darted forward, finally, seeing his chance, and picked up the weapon, and I barely even curse him, barely even realize I need to go for my P226 now, and he has the gun pointing at me, finally, as I'd suggested he do, and I feel very stupid for a moment, but then I realize I have pointed the P226 at him and shot him twice without realizing it, because, at the last, my body took action from its assorted muscle memory, so that I felt inept in its presence, and it took me a great deal to realize that ▮▮▮▮ had fallen back to the seats and was being very still. And I tell myself, again, This is what you bloody prepared for. *Bloody*. I laugh mutely at my own pun, at my own bloody innards that seem to be pouring out. I stand up, say, Concentrate, to myself, mostly. *Concentrate!* I slosh my way forward to ▮▮▮▮, skating through the spilt matter, stumbling on a shoulder. I fall forward and sit next to ▮▮▮▮'s body. Concentrate! I say. I raise my left hand to his neck. I begin to sober, at the touch of his warm neck. I've hit him in a tight grouping in the chest, his shirtfront abloom with blood. Worthy shots. He looks old and waxy, highly reflective, his hair like steel wool. I keep my left hand to his neck. I wait, try to concentrate on the sensations in my fingers, though it seems all my senses are retracting, tunnelling or dimming. I say, You're a snake. My mind clears. I get unsteadily to my feet, still with my left hand to his neck. *You're a snake*, I say. He's still holding the gun in his right hand. Open your eyes, I say, still with my hand on his neck, and this time I point the gun at his head, at his glossy dome. Open your eyes snake, I say, and he does. He's still holding the gun in his right hand but I think nothing of it. I holster the P226. I lean forward, over him, steady myself on his shoulder. I don't lean too close because I don't want to get blood on him, on his jacket or collar. He stares at me and doesn't move. I fix the knot of his tie, align it smartly with the opening of his collar. I pat the tie down and tap him lightly on the shoulder without really meaning to. Then I stand up straight and draw the P226 and shoot him in the head, and his head snaps back and his eyes widen and he jerks as if to get up and I actually think he is going to shoot me and I watch to see it happen, to marvel at him shooting me, but instead he seizes in a strange posture, and then jerks again as if to rise again, and I shoot him once more, in the head again, and he ducks down with his arms over his head, swings from side to side in a strange dance-like motion and I stand back until he's done and sinks to the floor.

Acknowledgements

Thanks to my mum and dad for reading to me (along with everything else). My father will never know how right he was about "the soup chapter", and for that I should probably be grateful.

I'd like to thank Simon Harwood and Carole Kenny for teaching me; it all started with McEwan and Larkin, perhaps. And my gratitude to Michael Wheale for the impression he made. Thank you Jon Mee and Tiffany Stern for tutoring me, and special homage must be paid to Catherine Clark for tolerating my solo tutorials on Chaucer. A thank you to Susan Jones also for teaching me about Conrad.

I'm compelled to give thanks to the friends I made while studying for my Creative Writing qualification: Daniel Bennett, Ruth Gilligan and Lars Kavli. And thanks to Trezza Azzopardi, Amit Chaudhuri and Andrew Cowan for their readership while I was at UEA.

Thanks to Masayuki Watanabe, Mariko Tokioka and Masatomo Nakano for giving me time to write.

Gracious thanks to Kevin Tang for the treasury tags and corporate ink, and Oli Rahman for reading. Thanks likewise to Flo Nicoll for taking the time. A firm embrace is owed Alex Spyropoulous for his consultation on Greek names.

I'd like to thank Roseannah Murphy for introducing me to JG Ballard and BS Johnson. And my fondest thanks to Kandiah Sothinathan for believing it would happen, and his wise counsel vis the handbag book.

Large, glowing thanks to my agent Andrew Gordon for sticking with me through thin. And then to James Roxburgh for his by turns sensitive and outrageous editorship. Thanks, too, to Ian Pindar and Poppy Mostyn-Owen for advising and tolerating me for long periods.

Finally, the greatest thanks of all to Hayley Sothinathan, who knows why (or should). None of it would have happened without her.